TERI WOODS PUBLISHING
PRESENTS

CIRCLE
OF
SINS

Published by Teri Woods Publishing

Circle of Sins by Nurit Folkes

For information on how individual consumers can place orders, please write to Teri Woods Publishing, P.O. Box 20069, New York, NY 10001-0005.

For orders other than individual consumers, Teri Woods Publishing grants a discount on the purchase of twenty or more copies of a single title order for special markets or premium use.

For orders purchased through the P.O. Box, Teri Woods Publishing offers a 25% discount off the sale price for orders being shipped to prisons, including, but not limited to, federal, state, and county.

Published by Teri Woods Publishing

**TERI WOODS PUBLISHING
PRESENTS**

CIRCLE
OF
SINS

Published by Teri Woods Publishing

Note:
Sale of this book without a front cover may be unauthorized. If this book is purchased without a cover it may be reported to the publisher as "unsold or destroyed." Neither the author nor the publisher may receive payment for the sale of this book.

Published by:
TERI WOODS PUBLISHING
P.O. Box 20069
New York, NY 10001-0005
www.teriwoodspublishing.com

ISBN:
Copyright:
Library of Congress Catalog Card No:

CIRCLE OF SINS CREDITS
Story by Nurit Folkes
Written by Nurit Folkes
Edited by Nurit Folkes
Text formation by Teri Woods

Printed in Canada

Dedication Page

To the loyal fans of my work. I appreciate you like you wouldn't believe. You stay true to me. You respect my labor of love and appreciate my perseverance. So I push forth despite all the BS. I vow to continue to give my all with every line in every book.

Life is a *GIFT* not a given, so open it.

Appreciation

I want, no, I need to THANK GOD for every single blessing, every righted misstep, every accomplishment, every revelation, every joyous occasion, every dismal experience that has added to my character, every and anything that has brought me through to this point in my life. Because only you know how insane it's been. Only you could deliver me from the evils of NYC. Thank you so much, God. I'm so glad we're tighter than Beyonce's lace front weave.

I want to thank ALL my readers for travelling on this sinful journey with me throughout the years. We've come a long way, sweeties. And although the SINS trilogy has come to an end, our bond has not severed. There will be more adventures, unique voyages and I'm hoping that you will all stay on this ride with me regardless of the bumps along the way. I do this for you. Always will.

God bless this world. We certainly need it.

Chapter I
Rehashing the Past

৯৯৬

The drive to Morganville, New Jersey was short but undeniably, sweet. The vehicle's effortless purring was overpowered by cackling, airy giggles and humorous yammering. Andre could only watch the backs of the heads of the two attractive people seated in front of him. Their movements conjured visions of bobble heads and he smiled to himself. He then turned his attention to the adorable bundle of joy cooing in the inverted infant car seat, facing the Corinthian leather seats of Shawn's immaculate, freshly scented, Escalade.

Natalia's plans to fly off to the Virgin Islands after she assumed Shawn hated her guts were thwarted —to her and Andre's delight. Thankfully her assumptions were inaccurate since she was sitting next to her husband gazing into his slanted brown eyes, wondering what in the world did she do to deserve his dedication. She had sinned against this man in the worst way, yet he found it in his heart to forgive her.

Shawn had since moved back to New York in hopes to change his life for good this time. Although he didn't plan on staying in New York long and contracted private builders to start construction in New Jersey on a complex architectural structure that would blow the one he built in Atlanta out of the water. When he pulled up in front of the 23 acres of excavated property, Natalia's eyes widened as a subtle gasp escaped her slightly parted lips.

"Daddy, is all that ours?" she asked, still gazing out the window at the struggling green grass bombarded with brown weeds dominating its vastness spreading out for miles under a pastel blue sky.

"Not really all ours," he took a daunting breath before filling her in, "I've got some other investors going in with me and we're not just building residences this time. We're going all out. We're building a mall and not just any mall. This is going to be one of the tallest, biggest malls in the East!"

Natalia turned to catch the enthusiastic grin plastered on the bottom half of her husband's handsome face and it reminded her why she'd fallen so hard for him. The splendid combination of one part tenacity, two parts ambition drenched with tons of confidence made up the enigma she affectionately dubbed, 'Daddy'.

She admired him as he appeared entrenched in his own thoughts of grandeur and sighed, "God how I love you." He palmed the side of her delicate face and moved in slowly to kiss her..."WAAAH!" Baby Everton ruined the moment with an alarming wail. This siren-like noise jarred poor Andre out of his serene dream world where his man, Adonis bathed him in a creamy bath of silky milk.

"What in the hell?" Andre shot up from his cramped position and tended to his Godchild.

"What's wrong with mommy's baby? Are you after mommy's boobies again?" Natalia, cooed in her baby's direction as Andre freed Everton from his car seat shackles. After pulling him out of the seat, Andre swaddled him tightly then passed him to his lactating mother. Shawn's eyes followed the bundle to its final destination right under Natalia's melons.

Everton eagerly latched onto his mother's supple taupe nipple after she popped it out of her tank top and nursing bra.

"See? That ain't fair man," Shawn playfully palmed the infant's curly haired noggin and chuckled, "You know those nips used to be mine, lil' man?" he sighed, the kind of sigh

2

that if it were translatable would mean: *What if this little motherfucker ain't even mine?*

Shawn still struggled with the whole paternity issue. After all the infidelity between them, he was surprised to find that he really still loved his wife despite the fact that she had sex with his best friend, his brother and secretly he suspected unknown men whom he fought desperately against grilling her about. He definitely wasn't a Saint and he kept that in mind every time second thoughts about making up with her plagued him. Subconsciously, he feared her being the cause of him murdering his best friend would ruin their future happiness some day. This secret he planned to take to his grave for sure.

"Damn, save some for me," Shawn joked as he watched Everton's tiny pursed lips devour Natalia's nipple in one motion. His tiny mouth puckered and retracted with precision. Natalia looked up at Shawn and smiled mischievously as thoughts of him suckling on her gorged breasts enticed her. But in the back of her mind she knew it would be a little while longer before they'd be able to do the nasty. She had a lot of healing to do— mentally as well as physically. She was still dealing with the backlash from all of the idiotic decisions she'd made thus far. She wished she had done things differently after finding out about Shawn's extracurricular activities with countless women including her once believed to be best friend, Talea. As the name popped into her head she regretted what she set into motion like robbing Talea of her beauty by hiring a thug to slash it away. Now Talea would never model or act ever again with her newly carved up face. This secret she would carry to her grave.

It never ceased to amaze Shawn how wonderful his wife was with Everton. She was a devoted, doting mother who managed to clean house, cook dinner and tend to him at night whereas Shawn tried desperately to carryout his secret agenda—getting Natalia pregnant. This time he'd know for sure if the baby was his. Regrettably, Everton was Natalia's baby and still his maybe.

Tonight she looked ripe in her booty shorts and tight t-shirt. Milk does the body good, well breast milk that is. Since Natalia breast fed Everton her stomach was flat again, curves formed in the right places and her already bodacious boobs were even fuller. Shawn watched as she leaned over Everton's crib, attentively, adoringly. Her back arched, ass poked out and he wanted to spank her in more ways than one. He inched up behind her, palmed her plumpness and whispered, "Daddy's home."

"Shhhh," she simpered and led him out of the newly furnished nursery in their upscale duplex rental. Shawn hated staying there but Natalia convinced him it made more sense for now rather than live out of hotels until their new home in New Jersey was fully complete.

"You are so naughty," she grinned, knowingly. She had been ready for some of Shawn's hot sticky pounding ever since she conked out on him the night before. Their passion had returned with a vengeance. It was as it used to be back when they made love for the first time. Shawn's stamina was back once he cut out all the drinking. They were serious about making the marriage work now and forever. She pulled him to her, slid her arms around his neck and they kissed like there was no baby, like they were the last two people on earth. In between Natalia's legs were on fire, oozing readiness and Shawn's loins were ablaze, his tool handy, preparing for a momentous eruption.

Shawn grabbed her buttocks and lifted her from the parquet floor. She clamped her toned legs around him as their kiss approached crescendo. He carried her out to the spiral staircase, pressed her curved back up against its supporting beam. He groped her feverishly as they panted loudly until he couldn't wait to be inside her. Shawn lowered her legs until her feet touched the floor. He slowly undressed her enjoying the view with each revealing tug. His eyes remained glued to her supple mounds of female fat for a brief moment then he tossed her clothing. When she stood before him in her birthday suit he all but tore off his shirt then hastily unbuckled his jeans and let them drop to the floor. Natalia knelt before him and was just about to give him the blow job of the century when her cell phone rang, the vibration forcing the glass coffee table to tremble. She was distracted for a bit but decided against answering it. She tugged and pulled until his boxer briefs were off and she was face to face with his sexy, thick magic stick. She massaged it up and down then in and out of her warm mouth as Shawn adored her from his imagined celestial view. Again the moment was interrupted by her phone. He was ready to throw the phone out the window now. He calmly excused himself from her taut mouth's powerful suction and picked up the cell phone, putting the call on speaker phone for his wife to answer it.

"Hello?" Natalia called out as she approached Shawn about to take the phone from his hand.

"Hello gorgeous," Seth, chimed. Seth's timing was the worst and Natalia could've died at that moment from fear of her husband misconstruing the call.

"Seth? Wh-why are you calling me?"

"Well, I'm in New York and I was wondering if I can take you out tonight."

"What? I haven't spoken to you in ages! And what the hell...you know I'm—"

"You gon' take me too motherfucker?" Shawn growled.

"What? Who is that?"

"Don't worry about it nigga. Just tell me if you're gonna take me out too when you take my wife out."

"Uh, well, I didn't mean—I apologize," Seth stumbled and hung up abruptly.

"Who the fuck is that bitch ass nigga?" Shawn asked, while getting dressed.

"He's—"

"He's another nigga that fucked my wife, right?" Shawn spat and stormed out of the room. Natalia ran after him and grabbed a hold of his arm. Shawn snatched his arm

5

away from her, slamming the bedroom door in her face. Natalia slammed the side of her body into the door forcing it into Shawn's body. Shawn threw open the door and grabbed her by her shoulders, his stare cold. Natalia nervously and softly uttered, "I'm sorry. I was only trying to open the door..." Shawn could see her fear and realized that she was actually afraid of him. He wasn't going to harm his wife but he was going to get to the bottom of the story behind the strange man calling her now, after all the promises they'd made to one another.

"B.G. you know I will never hurt you again. Don't act like you're afraid of me cuz that shit bothers me. You know I won't hurt you don't you?" he asked, releasing his grip on her shoulders and backing away. She seemed to be relieved now and she walked over to him, slipped her small hands around his waist and laid her head on his well developed chest.

"Yes, daddy, I know." Shawn gently pushed her away, looked deep into her eyes and asked, "Who is Seth?" The look of panic that flashed across her face said it all. Shawn now had an inclining of what he was about to hear. It was something he'd come to dread. Finding out that his once perfect wife was not all she was cracked up to be. The naive, conservative woman who seemed to have it all together was actually a perfectly disguised disaster. His hand swooped over his face and rested at his chin for a brief moment before dropping to his side. Natalia's eyes saddened and she began almost in a whisper, "I met him before I met you and when..."

"I can't hear you. Speak up," Shawn commanded. Natalia took a deep breath and added little volume to her tone, "Wh-when we um, were going through our problems."

Shawn let out an exasperated sigh and walked over to the bed and slowly lowered himself onto the edge of it.

"And?" he inquired, and leaned forward with his elbows resting on his knees. He couldn't even look at her. He didn't really want to hear any more yet his mind raced and all kinds of questions gnawed at him, he felt inclined to get the rest of the story. Natalia came over, knelt down in front of him taking his hands into hers she said, "You have to understand something," she paused to choose her words carefully, "I wasn't just out there. I've never been involved with different men like that before. I mean, somehow it was as if I could do the things that I've always thought were wrong. I was always doing the right thing and regarding myself so highly that I barely dated before Mark. I only had two sexual partners before Mark and I guess I felt cheated of the many experiences I've missed. I was always being the good girl yet people were hurting me constantly... like Tracy and Mark having sex. I mean there they were having sex behind my back and he got her pregnant. My husband got my best friend pregnant! Then there was all of you're cheating!"

"So I'm the reason you became a ho?"

Natalia dropped his hands and stood up, "That's uncalled for. So is this how it's going to be? You're never gonna let me live it down or forget?"

"How can I, B.G.? Everton might not be my son. How do you expect me to feel now especially since I'm finding out that there's another nigga that could be his father?!? This shit is crazy!"he jumped up and got dressed then left the condo in a huff.

Natalia didn't go after him this time. He called her out of her name for the last time. She truly felt that she wasn't a ho. She knew in her heart that she was not built like that. Admittedly, revenge and curiosity fueled her sexual trysts with three different men. But she accepted responsibility for her misjudgment of choosing her husband's best friend and his only brother as sex partners. Now that she'd made such huge mistakes she realized that there was no turning back. Shawn would either be stronger than most men and deal with it or end what she wanted most in life right now, their marriage.

Shawn caught the elevator down as he cursed himself

7

for allowing Natalia to convince him to rent the most expensive apartment available. It was their home away from their brand new house on a secluded hill top property in New Jersey practically overlooking his proposed mall site. The apartment was amidst Manhattan's elite but was a major inconvenience for Shawn since he wasn't used to being surrounded by so many blue bloods. His bourgeoisie neighbors always made it a point to remind him of how unwelcomed his "kind" was in their presence. Although, his wife reveled in the duplex apartment's expansive opulence he was unimpressed. They both had money now and although Shawn's net worth couldn't put a dent in Natalia's, he could keep up with the Jones' and afford to take care of his high maintenance princess. He bought a bevy of expensive trinkets to make up for their past tribulations including his extramarital dalliances which caused Natalia so much grief. They were starting anew and Shawn was serious about the changes they both agreed on making and accepting. But now he wondered if he would ever be able to get past *the past,* especially now when it was resurfacing with a vengeance.

Would he forever be reminded that his wife had turned into a whore no matter how brief? He kept imagining her with Maleek. He fought visions of his brother pumping into her and was thankful he didn't know what this new guy Seth looked like. He believed that she wasn't still seeing Seth but it was just too much for his pride never mind his ego. He sat in his car seething over everything. Then as if a swarm of calm encircled him, he realized the one constant that made his forgiveness take precedence over all the cons concerning Natalia. He *really* loved his wife. No ifs ands or maybes, there was no way he could fight it, she had his heart in a choke hold. He believed that he was mature enough, strong enough to withstand their issues. He believed that their love had beat the odds already so why not this?

He got out of his S.U.V., went back upstairs to his wife and they hashed and re-hashed until there was a mutual understanding between them. After making up verbally their bodies made up, incessantly. He made love to her like only he could in order to convince himself that he was still the alpha male and to mark his territory so that his wife would never forget who it belonged to.

‎৯৵৶

"It is unfortunate that we have to tell you this Mrs. Bryant but the term life insurance policy you're husband purchased lapsed," an insurance representative informed Maleek's widow.

"And? What the hell does that mean to me?" Faye angrily spat into the phone.

"Well, the two million dollar policy lapsed in the first year so we cannot disburse funds on that policy but the first-to-die permanent policy was paid up and we will be able to get the $250,000 dollar check out to you pending our internal to authorities' investigation comparative."

"So you're saying the main policy we paid up for a year doesn't exist? So what happened to all the money paid into it?"

"Mr. Bryant defaulted on the policy when he failed to make the monthly premiums even during the allotted grace period. It's not a universal policy which accrues cash value so it was simply canceled once it lapsed. This is all standard ma'am."

"So when will I get the check from the other policy?"

"It can range anywhere from 10 days to 3 months."

"Three months? What the hell...? I waited almost a year to hear this shit? I was told I would receive a check a month ago. Now I'm being told 3 months? I had to pay out of my pocket for my husband's funeral. As if I don't have enough to deal with now I find out I'm only collecting on one policy nearly a year later?!? That's crazy! Just send the damn check as soon as possible!" Faye sucked her teeth and threw the phone down. She began sobbing and Fayette ran over to her bereaved mother and tried feeding her the half eaten chocolate chip cookie she'd been nibbling on for the past five minutes. Faye tried desperately to crack a smile as she obliged her daughter's kindness. Her teeth barely chipped an edge of the chocolate confection. She kissed Fayette's wrinkled brow and said, "Thank you baby."

"Your sthelcom, why you kwying thmommy?" her adorable lisp, was music to Faye's ear at that moment, soothing her, pulling her away from the morbid thoughts of her deceased husband.

"It's okay, baby, mommy's going to be okay." Faye lied. The emptiness in her heart plagued her from dusk till dawn. Maleek was really gone. She still hadn't accepted it and unconsciously awaited his homecoming. The Dora the Explorer theme song sounded from Fayette's bedroom so she abandoned her mother for her daily Dora fix.

Alone, standing next to a vacuum cleaner, Faye unraveled its cord as she embarked on her cleaning ritual. She was stuck in her usual routine and often tried to pretend that her husband's death was a nightmare she could wake up from. Since her sons were with her sister at the mall at Peach Tree Center she knew they weren't coming home anytime soon. She relished the quiet whilst her rambunctious boys were away. Fayette was no problem and was quite independent just like her mother. Faye schlepped around the house cleaning relentlessly until she passed the door to Maleek's den. She palmed the door and felt a rush of emotions swell in her chest. She hadn't been in the den since the last of Maleek's personal belongings like clothes, electronic gadgets and papers were packed into boxes and neatly stacked away. But today, a force of some kind beckoned her to the room. Today, she would go through his things, salvage momentos for the children but discard the rest. Her hand trembled as she turned the knob to enter. She could've sworn an icy breeze blew past her as the door eased open. *Oh, it's just the AC on full blast in here, she nervously assured herself.*

The first box she opened was full of his prized

basketball jerseys. She knew that her sons wouldn't want to part with these treasures. She re-taped the box and moved onto the next box, she rummaged through DVDs, computer software even a barrage of cell phone accessories. She grabbed a bunch of the DVD cases and one fell from her hand, hit the side of the box and aptly landed in her lap. She reached for it and noticed two yellow post-its were stuck to it. The top post-it had her name written in Maleek's handwriting as clear as day. Faye's heart nearly jumped from her chest. Each breath became shallower as she inhaled and she realized that she had to calm down to keep from passing out. Eerily enough, she flipped over the DVD and read the title, "Fahrenheit 911" and she shook her head in amazement. She lifted the post-it with her name and read the one beneath it: *MY WARRIOR PRINCESS, IN CASE OF AN EMERGENCY, TEXT THIS MESSAGE, MB119 TO PB'S CELL.*

Faye exhaled and placed her hand over the words. Her husband was communicating with her after his death and it didn't frighten her, it saddened her. It was then that she realized her husband would've wanted her to exude strength, handle her biz and get on with life. She remembered how he always referred to her as his next in command. He believed in her as she in him. Now he saw to it that she could get the much needed help she needed ever since their legal money in the bank accounts had dwindled considerably. She knew what to do and wasted no time. She sent a text to Shawn's cell with the special coded message and awaited his reply.

⇦⇦⇨

Shawn's smartphone cranked out a snippet of a Southern Fried snap rap song as he snapped it right off its case hook. He scrolled up on the screen to read the text. The room fell silent; the Earth stood still, his heartbeat echoed in his ears like the bass line of 90's house music. It took him a minute to realize that the only way this message zipped into his inbox was through Faye. He knew exactly what was

11

expected of him. The memory documenting the origin of this code and his dead best friend rewound and played in his head. They were joking around in Maleek's Escalade EXT and Maleek popped in the Fahrenheit 911 DVD. They watched and had a meaningful discussion about America's inept president George Bush and his corrupt family's dealings with kin to the most hated man of America, Osama Bin Laden. Maleek created the code out of necessity. He told Shawn that in the event that either of them ever got in a jam that their code would be their initials and 911 backwards which would signal that they needed financial assistance. It was a red alert translating to money inconspicuously finding its way to their respective wives in case they were indisposed. Shawn stared down at the text on the screen and wondered what it meant now that his right hand man was dead.

"Daddy what's wrong? You look like you've seen a ghost?" Natalia waltzed into the room wrapped in a plush rose colored towel with speckles of water reflecting the early sunlight peeking in their window. Shawn shifted his focus to his half naked wife. The thought of ravaging her right then and there with the unsettling text message wrestled in his thoughts for a bit before sex tapped out rendering the 'ghost message' priority number one.

"B.G., I may have to go away for a hot minute," he started to leave in search of privacy to call Faye.

"Why?" Natalia followed behind him.

"Lemme go handle something right quick and we'll talk about it when I get back okay?"

"Okay," she barely smiled as he kissed her forehead then hurried out the door.

Shawn's Escalade seemed to wink at him as he approached the gleaming heap of metal. He pressed down on his car starter remote and his ears along with passing patrons' ears were immediately overwhelmed by the blasting bass line blaring from his state of the art sub woofers.

"Shit, forgot to turn that off," he cursed himself

reaching for his remote in the armrest caddy and turned off the elaborate system. He looked down at his cell, tapped a couple of keys with his thick thumbs and started his car. He could hear the drawn out ringing in his Bluetooth headset until Faye's brash voice interrupted with, "Hello?"

Shawn was lost in the source, enveloped by menacing scenarios. What if this was a visit from the grave? He remembered Maleek's pleas for his life, how he begged for him to let him live for Faye and the kids before he let off the fatal shot that ripped through his frontal lobe.

"I said, hello!"

"Oh, sorry about that Faye, it's Shawn. How are you?" Faye's face lit up and it was as if Shawn's voice took her to an alternate universe where her husband was still alive and joking with her like he used to when she'd answer his phone then he'd say, "Give me the phone and stop yapping!"

She looked around and moved all the piles of papers and compact discs from the camel brown leather sectional and flopped down into the oversized throw pillows adorning it.

"Shawn! It's so good to hear your voice. It's been too long. I'm sorry about the last time we spoke. I could barely keep it together then. Sorry I didn't return your calls either. I was just trying to hold it down, you know, for the kids and all." Shawn had attempted on many occasions before selling off his house in Atlanta and moving back to the North East to be of help to Faye but she was too distraught to accept it. Once while talking to Shawn on the phone she grilled him for leads on her husband's murderer and when he couldn't offer any useful information she slammed down the phone on him, frustrated. Shawn continued to call out of guilt but Faye never answered so he gave up and left Atlanta without saying goodbye or attending his best friend's funeral.

Faye ran a mental marathon even before Maleek's murder since her mother passed only a month earlier and she took on the responsibility of burying her mother because she was the oldest sibling. Then she was burdened with

13

planning Maleek's funeral and shipping mementos off to his mother in her native country of Montserrat. She dealt with all of this and the strain of having a multitude of bills to contend with thanks to their lavish lifestyle. Without the insurance money coming in she'd only have the measly fifty-seven grand in their bank account. That money basically belonged to all of the creditors that came out of the woodwork almost immediately after Maleek died. They made sure to have the children's college funds set up safely in educational IRAs which she avowed never to touch because her kids were going to college even if she had to sell her ass to get them there!

"Faye, don't apologize...I know what you went—been going through. I'm just sorry for everything..." Shawn realized that his over empathizing was too much of a giveaway so he reeled his emotions in and asked, "So that was you texting me, right?"

"Yes...um, Shawn, I'm kind of struggling financially right now. I went through Mal's things and there was a DVD with a note and it's weird but it told me to call you in case of a financial emergency."

"Yea, I figured that part out. So how much and when?" he asked a bit relieved.

"Well, I wanted to just pay off Fayette and MJ's school tuition for the year, pay up the salon's mortgage for like a year then we got some other bills I want to just pay them and get it over with, you know? So, like two hundred would get me back up to speed until I can get the second salon up and running."

"I can swing that. So how do you want to do this? In increments or straight up in a duffle bag?" he asked.

Faye, giggled and quickly blurted, "I'll take the duffle bag, Alex!" They both laughed hysterically then after composing himself, Shawn said, "Alright then, I'll set up and fly out there next Wednesday. I'll meet you at the house okay?"

"Yes and thank you so much Shawn. You're such a

good friend. The kids will be so happy to see you. We love you, you know that right?"

"Yea Faye, I know and I love y'all right back. I'll call you Tuesday to remind you." After getting off the phone with Faye, Shawn felt a dull pain creeping up into his temples resting its laurels at his cranium. He knew it was only guilt consuming him. How could he ever look at his Godchildren again knowing he was the reason that they were fatherless?

ॐॐ

Faye's doorbell rang repeatedly and if it weren't for the fact that she was trapped behind mounds of cardboard boxes she'd have saved her ears the trauma they received from the piercing chimes.

"I'M COMING DAMMIT!" she screamed at the top of her lungs, pissed. She finally knocked down a tower of empty boxes with her swinging elbows as if she were King Kong himself maneuvering through the Big Apple. She stomped her pudgy feet to the front door and flung it open without caring to ask whom it was beforehand. When she recognized the visitor she threw her arms around the tall man's neck standing in the doorway. She squeezed with all her might while he cradled her upper body as if she were too delicate to squeeze back. She looked up into his attractive brown face and gushed, "We missed you. Where have you been? Your cousins have been asking for you." The man barely smiled as she backed away from him to allow him to step inside the house. He seemed troubled and Faye didn't like the fact that he wasn't his usual comedic self.

"Malcolm, what's wrong?" she asked worried. Her deceased husband's cousin looked almost exactly like him except that he was darker, a bit more slender and shorter. He bowed his head as if it were too heavy, sighed and spoke softly, "Faye...I don't know how to tell you this shit..." Faye gripped his forearm.

"What is it Malcolm?" she admired the swirling

15

patterns of his cornrows as his bowed head began to rise. His eyes bore into hers with a sympathetic stare as he broke the shocking news he himself just heard, "I just found out who killed Maleek," he became visibly angry and began pacing, wringing his hands, occasionally pounding his right fist into his left hand. He shook his head, gritted his teeth and exclaimed, "PB did that shit, he killed my cousin, yo...I'm gonna kill that motherfucker!" Faye's jaw dropped, her heart hurt—literally as if it were in a vise grip. She felt her knees buckle and she collapsed to the floor.

"No...that's not true. It can't be...Shawn loved Mal, they were like brothers, she murmured as Malcolm helped her to her feet. He guided her limp body to the sofa in the family room. He kicked one of the kid's toys out his way as he paced.

"Faye, I swear to you he will pay for this shit."

"But it can't be Shawn..."

"That's his real name? Shawn?"

"Yes."

"That's good to know. It's a wrap for that nigga!"

"But Shawn wouldn't...why would he kill Maleek? Why?" Now Malcolm was conflicted. Should he give her the real answer or make up one that excluded the fact that her husband cheated on her with Shawn's wife? Should he ruin the picture perfect vision of his cousin for Faye in order to preserve his memory? He decided against lying since he knew that she would find out about Maleek's bad deeds eventually. Besides, the news was out on the streets so rather than have her hear it from one of the blabber mouths at her salon he wanted to ease her into the reality of Maleek's betrayal.

"Listen, what I'm about to tell you shouldn't take away from the kind of man that my cousin was. He took good care of y'all. He was a good father..."

"What the hell are you talking about?" Faye's eyes were emblazoned with disappointment fused with confusion. Realizing there was no real way to cushion the blow that the

16

truth would hit her with, Malcolm went on with giving her the bad news, straight, no chaser.

"Maleek was fucking Natalia." Her eyes widened to the size of golf balls.

"NO, NO, NOOO!" she shouted. She slumped off the sofa onto the floor and began tearing at her hair, yanking at her weave tracks as she moaned like a wounded animal. Her body shuddered with each howling sob. This was all too much information for her to handle. Malcolm hadn't a clue how to console her. He approached her cautiously for fear that she'd lash out at him but she curled up on the floor and cried her eyes out instead.

"I'm so sorry, Faye...," he knelt beside her and gently rubbed her back as she bawled and trembled.

"How could he do that to me?" she muttered.

"Sometimes men can't fight temptation," Malcolm offered. Faye ignored his feeble attempt to persuade her that Maleek was somewhat a victim and then it hit her. Natalia was smiling in her face the whole time she was stabbing her in the back.

"Oooh, that backstabbing, phony, BITCH!"

"I should've known that bitch was no damn good when Maleek paid me to slash some other bitch's face for her." Now Faye was really confused. The world had flipped on it's axis in the matter of minutes and the unsuspecting turn of events just kept coming. She crawled over to the sofa, pulled herself up and slouched over bracing her elbows with her knees, "You did what?" she asked, very interested in what she was about to hear.

"Maleek hired me to mess up that model bitch Talea's face and her car over in Marietta."

"Talea! Oh, my God, Malcolm... she tried to kill herself behind that. I can't believe it...you did that?"

"Yea, I feel fucked up about it now."

"Why did Natalia want to hurt Talea?"

"Cuz she was fucking PB!"

"What the...? What's with all of this fucking around?

17

Everybody was fucking but me! So while I was struggling with taking care of my dying mother, being stressed the fuck out of my damn mind, this motherfucker was sticking his dick in my friend's pussy?!? I can't believe this shit!" Faye sprang up from the sofa as if she popped right out of a toaster and paced back and forth.

"I'm saying Faye you knew that nigga wasn't trying to fuck up what y'all had so I know that she must've thrown the pussy at him. Mal wasn't trying to catch no heat from you over another bitch."

Faye ignored Malcolm's bullshit excuse for her dead, cheating husband and came out of left field with, "I want those lying, phony motherfuckers to hurt just like me and my babies. Will you help me?"

"Whatever you need I got you. How do you want to handle this?"

"First things first, that murdering bastard P.B. is supposed to bring me some money so we need to set his ass up. I want to be there, for him to see me before y'all fuck his ass up. He sat up there and cried to me like he really gave a fuck about Mal, me and the kids! I should shoot this nigga dick off!"

"Damn, y'all women don't play," Malcolm chuckled and shook his head then said, "But I can arrange that. Now, what about his bitch?"

"Oh, that bitch is mine. I'll take care of her ass. You just make sure that they don't kill PB. I have plans for his ass. They're gonna suffer."

Chapter II
After the Storm
೧೧

Shawn boarded a plane for Atlanta with his brother's long time friend and right hand man, Big Stew. Big Stew was fresh out of Brooklyn House detention center only serving 48 hours thanks to Tymeek's faithful old lawyer and ironically enough, lady justice herself. The charges were trumped up anyway even though marijuana paraphernalia was found in his brand new Range Rover. Call it plain ol' envy but the overworked yet underpaid Caucasian officers weren't about to let this stereotypical moment escape their grasps. The shimmer of the luxury vehicle was enough to light the entire block and just the mere thought of a young black man being able to afford such a prize had them foaming at the mouth as they accosted Big Stew, unnecessarily using excessive force by smashing his burly body onto the asphalt—repeatedly.

Big Stew refused to resist arrest because he knew the consequences and he would rather allow the NYPD to punk him now and chance an acquittal than fight now and pay for it later with an unnecessary stint in prison. He was too strong not to harm at least one of the officers so he willingly allowed them to wrestle him to the ground otherwise they would have never subdued his Hulk-ish form. But he got the last laugh when the judge ruled in his favor noting that finding the remains of burnt blunt papers in a car with 3 passengers hardly qualified for an arrest much less one that ended with the suspect getting hurt in the process. Big

19

Stew's case against the city was pending and although he knew he'd probably end up with peanuts or perhaps nothing at all, the satisfaction of besting the corrupt legal system for once made it all worth while.

Big Stew was eager to fatten up his pockets quickly and go legit just like Shawn had managed to do. He even contemplated permanently moving to Austria and working with Tymeek who had long since deserted Amsterdam and Svelanka, his longtime subservient white woman, for Austria's greener pastures and even friendlier white women. But Big Stew remembered how much he missed America when living in Amsterdam with Tymeek and he couldn't deal with being abroad. He was a New Yorker—for life.

"So you want me to just wait outside?" Big Stew asked Shawn as they pulled up in front of the iron gated community in Atlanta that Shawn built. "Naw, man you can come in with me. I'm gonna spend a hot minute in there cause I gotta catch up with Faye and my God kids."

"Damn niggah I ain't feel like sittin' up in nobody's house. We need to keep it moving. I got some shit to take care of, ya feel me?"

"Aiight, son, it'll be quick. Just come inside right quick."

"Damn, man." Big Stew muttered before conceding and trailing behind Shawn up to the house. Shawn rang the doorbell and waited.

The doorbell rang and Faye panicked when she peeked outside the guest room window. She stumbled to her room and rummaged through her purse to find her cell phone. She tapped the buttons until she found Malcolm's phone number and called him.

"Malcolm, Shawn's outside ringing the bell! He never said he was coming today. He was supposed to get in tomorrow."

"Shit!" Malcolm wracked his brain trying to figure a way around scrapping their original plan to ambush Shawn. Then he figured it all out and told her, "I know what we're gonna do now. I need you to pretend nobody's home and don't make any noise. If he don't call you to find out where you're at then wait a while, call him and go in the bathroom or something and cover the phone while you tell him that you're on your way back home but you won't make it in till late so tell him to meet you over by Big Mal's old club tonight around 11."

"The club? Won't he be suspicious? He knows I don't like to go there since I sold it so why'd I want to meet him there?"

"Look, I'm trying to get him somewhere familiar since we can't do what we was gonna do by getting y'all at the gas station. At least the club has no connection to you anymore."

"You think him showing up a day early and here at the house instead of waiting for me to pick him up at the airport like we planned is because he thinks something is up?"

"Nah, I doubt it but to be safe just do like I told you. I'll take care of the rest."

Shawn dabbed at his nose with a soft terry cloth rag and stuffed it in his back pocket. He wrapped his knuckles against the unique whirly designs in the lustrous oak doors and blew hard from aggravation.

"What the fuck? She don't work in the salon anymore, so where the fuck she at?"

"Yo, Braniac did you even tell her we was getting in a day early?"

"No, but she should still be here. She told me that she's always home."

"Shoulda, woulda, coulda, muhfuckah. Now we standing here like a couple of dummies."

"Fuck you, you fat motherfucker," Shawn shot back and they both burst out laughing. Just then a hip hop ring tone gradually emitted from Shawn's cell.

"Yea?"

"Hi, daddy we miss you," Natalia's delicately airy voice was music to his ears even with Everton's wailing in the back

21

ground. She put the receiver to Everton's tiny ear so that he could hear Shawn's voice.

"Awww, hey, baby girl, what's my little man doing?" Everton began to coo as Natalia placed the phone back to her ear.

"Helllooo?"

"Sorry, daddy, I'm here," Natalia said.

"I said what's my little man doing?"

"Smiling because he knows that's his daddy on the phone."

Riiight, he doesn't know who his damn daddy is. The negative thought ran through his mind even though he didn't invite it.

"Oh, yea? Well kiss him for me. I miss y'all too. Daddy will be home soon."

"So is everything okay with the meeting?" Natalia quizzed. She had no clue that her husband was in Atlanta to give her dead ex-lover's wife a bag full of cash. He wasn't about to explain why he felt obligated to Faye and he knew it would raise more than questions. He hated having to lie after vowing to change but he knew it was his only option. He couldn't tell her that he was the reason Faye ended up a widow.

"Well we're kind of early so I have to go to a hotel. In fact I have to call and make sure we're at the right location." Shawn lied. He couldn't bear conversing with his wife when he was forced to lie to her.

"Okay, call me as soon as you're done. I love you sooo much, MUAH!"

"I love you too baby girl." After ending the mushy call he noticed Big Stew's smirk. "What's so funny?" Shawn inquired. "Nothing man...I'm just amazed by y'all. Y'all are some crazy ass people. Y'all belong together." Big Stew chuckled.

"Yea, that's my baby for life," Shawn said smiling briefly. He seemed contemplative as he thumbed the keypad then paused and looked up to drive his point home, "Me and her...we some fucked up individuals but at the end of the day it's all love. We're built for this shit," he laughed while he finished dialing Faye's cell phone.

"Faye, where you at?" Shawn asked after hearing her voice on the other end.

"I'm on my way back to Atlanta now."

"What? You left and you knew I was coming?"

"It was an emergency. And you weren't supposed to be there until tomorrow anyway. But I'll make it back by tonight. In fact I need you to meet me at Mal's old club around eleven."

"What? Why?"

"Oh, one of my top clients is having her birthday party there and I have to do her make-up and hair."

"Faye, I really wasn't trying to be here long."

"I understand but I really can't tell this client no. She expects me there. So you'll be there?"

"Yea."

"So you got that for me?" she asked sweetly.

"Of course you know I have to take care of you and the fam."

"Thank you so much for this."

"No problem," Shawn answered and hung up. Big Stew threw up his hands, "So we stuck out here for another day?"

"Don't worry about it. As soon as I hit her off we'll just catch a red eye home."

It was the hardest thing for Faye to fake gratitude to Shawn knowing that he murdered her husband. The whole time spent listening to his voice angered her. *How could he live with himself?* She asked herself after hanging up with him. She slowly moved about the house as to give him time to leave from her property. When she saw that he'd driven off she quickly dialed her friend's house. This call would be another task. She couldn't begin to figure out an explanation for the heinousness of what Natalia caused. The fragility of her friend's voice made her second guess her decision to spill the beans. Then she knew that this news was what her friend needed for ascension from the bellows of her private hell.

"Hello?" Faye asked.

"Faye?" the cracking voice raised an octave with interest.

"Yes, Talea it's me. Girl, are you still asleep?" Talea coughed and replied, "No, Faye, I'm awake this time. I'm sorry that I fell asleep on you the other night when you came to visit." Talea seemed to perk up a bit more.

"It's okay. I need to talk to you but I don't want to do it on the phone so I'm headed over to your house okay?"

"Okay, see you soon."

Talea hadn't completely recovered from the fateful day that her face was sliced and diced at the hands of an unknown, cruel assailant. Even with all the plastic surgery she underwent, her once beautiful face was still far from what it used to be. She looked a helluva lot better than she did while in the hospital under suicide watch. She regretted trying to dig into her radial artery in her wrist with pieces of her sisters' broken compact mirror. It was strange as the sharpness sliced into her skin and she felt nothing. Her body was numb. But after the doctor treated her wounds and the morphine wore off, she was left with tangible agony until she received several intravenous morphine fixes.

Talea placed her phone down and wondered if she should at least straighten up for company. She looked around her living room and thought how clean it looked considering she hadn't cleaned for over a week. Ever since the incident she mostly lay in bed or surfed the internet for new cosmetic surgical procedures that could restore her looks. She was lucky to have listened to her agent who advised her to get an insurance policy on her face and body since they were her only source of income. It was suggested after she was caught red handed with a lover who was married and his wife literally tried to take Talea's head off, leaving claw marks all around her neck. So after joining the Screen Actor's Guild and securing a lucrative endorsement deal with a cosmetic company Talea was sitting on a nice chunk of change but had already cut into it with seven plastic surgeries. Her boutique still made its money and her clothing line seemed to fly off the racks even more now that she was a local celebrity due to her highly publicized attack.

She darted around the house tidying up any little thing out of place. When that was done she wanted to make sure that she didn't look like Freddy Krueger's scratching post for her visit with her friend who still had the attractive face God gave her. Faye was very pretty and it never bothered Talea before because although Faye was pretty Talea believed herself to be even more beautiful. It wasn't conceit that kept her on a high horse; she was told about her beauty time and time again and she was actually paid for it. But now with stitches keeping her once creamy skin attached in order to accommodate the structure of her eyes, nose and lips she knew that Faye had the advantage. She stared in the mirror at her disfigured face. The only thing she could think to do was plaster her face with make-up to make up for the hideous scars pilfering her self esteem.

Faye showed up at Talea's house with a brand new un-beweavable hair-do, her make up beat to perfection and her still hot-to-trot post children body in a sexy pair of jeans that held all the junk in her trunk in its rightful place. Talea opened the door and she seemed taken aback by her friend's appearance. It was a combination of envy and surprise. Even though Talea knew that Faye cleaned up nicely, Faye always worked or traveled so much that she rarely donned dressy, high fashion apparel. She rocked designer sweat suits, yoga and workout gear and hardly wore a full face of make-up. Luckily Faye was a natural beauty so weighing her features down with pounds of make up was unnecessary.

"Girl, you look great!" Talea complimented, hoping

that her jealousy wasn't revealed in her facial expressions as her mouth expanded into a forced grin. She wondered if Faye showed up at her house dressed to kill and all beautified to rub it in her shredded face.

"Hi sweetie," Faye leaned in and hugged Talea. Talea barely hugged her back still caught up in her envious mode. She looked behind Faye then asked," Where's your entourage?"

"My entourage?"

"The kids, silly," Talea giggled and led Faye into the house.

"Oh, they're with May for the weekend. So how've you been mama?" *How the hell you think I've been bitch?!? I've got over two hundred damn stitches in my face!* Talea strained as she attempted to hide her annoyance with Faye's flagrantly redundant question and answered, "I'm hanging in there." She walked away from Faye and headed toward the kitchen. Faye caught on to the air of attitude and decided that if she cut to the chase and gave Talea the news that she'd come to tell her in the first place she'd make Talea's day if not her whole damn year.

"Talea I've got something to tell you that is so crazy... so important."

Talea's interest was piqued and she whipped her head around, neglecting her cup of coffee.

"What is it?"

"I know about you and Shawn—"

"Me and Shawn? What about us? There's nothing between us."

"Talea," Faye said with a stern, condescending glare which all but spelled out the disappointing skepticism she felt at the moment. She put her hand on her hip and continued with disapproval weighing in on her words, "I know you fucked Shawn okay so let's not bullshit each other. Throughout our friendship I've heard a lot of shit about you, Talea but I never let it sway me one way or another and I think you know that." She seemed to pause to offer Talea a moment to rebut yet Talea seemed to be stuck on pause.

"I still love you girl. We all have our demons and none of us are exempt from making stupid mistakes. But this one time Talea, this one time cost you your face." Now Talea stirred as if God himself hit the fast forward button.

"What? What are you saying to me Faye?" she responded defensively, swiveling her neck with each word, her hands swatting the air as if she were killing flies. Faye sighed and readied herself to divulge the whole sordid tale to Talea. She leaned back onto the dishwasher before taking another breath and saying, "You were set up. Natalia knew about you and Shawn and put out a contract on you. And you won't believe it—"

Faye was about to fill Talea in on what Natalia had set into motion but a flood of emotions pummeled her all at once and she began tearing up, sobbing and failing miserably at sucking it all up. Talea reached out to her, palming her shoulder, "Awww, Faye, don't—"

"It's just so crazy you know? Natalia did that to you and she's the reason my Maleek is dead." Talea slapped her chest with her hand as she stumbled backwards, grasping the edge of the granite counter top behind her. Astounded she exclaimed, "Oh, my God!" Talea was contrite learning that she was indeed the leading domino knocking the rest down causing the rippling effect of madness in all of their lives. She couldn't begin to find the words that would ease the pain her friend felt at that moment.

Faye didn't expect any consoling words so she continued with her tirade, "That spiteful ass bitch! Can you believe it? She made Shawn kill my Mal!"

"What in the world? Shawn killed Maleek?" Talea asked, still in disbelief. Having said it out loud brought back the ton of anger that already weighed heavy on Faye's heart and it showed in her face as she spoke, "Yes! That phony bitch fucked my husband and Shawn found out so he killed him!" her mouth trembled as she recounted the horrible secret that left her a widow.

The entire time Talea couldn't help but think of how she not only caused her own bleak outcome but that of her friend. It was at that moment, a truckload of empathy bathed in remorse made Talea want to make it all up to Faye. She reached for her friend and they hugged each other and cried. Faye cried for the man she lost, the father her children would never play with again, the end of the life she was promised when she said; I do to Maleek six years ago. Talea cried knowing that the life she lived and loved was really over, and anger resonated inside her as she accepted that Natalia took that life away from her. Natalia made her a monster.

After the *blubber fest* ended the two women had come to realize that they maintained one common goal—ridding the world of Natalia Foles.

Chapter III
Chaos ensues
ॐ∞ॐ

Shawn and Big Stew visited some of Shawn's old hang out spots when he ruled the ecstasy trade in Atlanta and although he was barred from ever selling ecstasy again in Atlanta, there was nothing to stop him from visiting or having a good time. He saw some of his old workers who had apparently moved up in the ranks which Shawn gathered from their lavish vehicles adorned with crystal studded rims and the amount of bling twinkling from their ears, necks and wrists.

He wasn't looking forward to showing up at Maleek's old club since he only partially believed that his secret about Maleek's murder was safe. Even after covering his tracks and Mr. X's help with disposing of the body, he felt that somehow, some way, he may have slipped up and someone knew what he'd done.

When eleven o'clock approached, Shawn said his goodbyes to all his old buddies and he and Big Stew raced over to Maleek's old club now called "Hotlantaz Own." The new owner clearly had a thing for chandeliers because everywhere Shawn looked there were crystal chandeliers dangling from the ceiling. The bright prisms of light reflecting from them made aesthetically pleasing designs on the walls. Shawn knew that his virtuosity would be tested tonight in more ways than one but he was prepared. He was no longer a lush one step away from a twelve step program. He'd grown into the man he knew that he was meant to be. He felt wiser and definitely more settled. He actually enjoyed being married even though the paternity of his "son" plagued him on a regular basis. He tried not to harp on Everton's paternity but with his dead best friend and his own brother being possible fathers it was hard for him not to agonize over it.

Big Stew on the other hand invited temptation to hang out with him even though technically he wasn't single. But his bevy of women all knew their place. He took care of each of them in his own way so none of them gave him any grief about his comings and goings; and *coming* is what he thought he made them do best. He was psyched to be in Atlanta, a place where the women were considered juicy as peaches and as soft as the fruit's fuzzy skin. He was on the prowl inside the club trying to find Stewie's fourth angel. He thought he'd found one ripe for the plucking at the bar so he cock blocked a man who so generously bought her a hurricane. The poor sucker was in mid-sentence, conversing as she swished the grenadine, rum and pineapple juice around on her tongue then swallowed, Big Stew slid in between them. The man did nothing. Big Stew paid the young lady a compliment that would usually get a lesser man either slapped or a splash of liquor in his face.

"I'ma taste you tonight and I know I'm gonna get Diabetes with that sweet ass." Big Stew said with an air of confidence.

"What?" the girl asked a bit flustered yet intrigued. She already noted Stew's size, his cute face and the New York accent cinched it. Stew knew he was definitely a front runner.

"You heard me, shorty. Don't play like you didn't cuz it's not cute. So let's go over to that table so you can give me all the info I need to make a meal outta you."

"You're crazy," she giggled nervously and shook her head. Stew looked at her with serious intensity and as if he hypnotized her with one glance, she followed him to a table. Now he monopolized her time while the clown he practically stole her from was stuck at the bar with his bruised ego.

30

Shawn ignored all the chicks lusting after him as he perused the club in search of Faye. He was bothered by the fact that Faye would be so late. It was well past the eleven o'clock appointment they set and he was ready to get back to his new illegal free life with his wife and child. Just as he revealed his phone's contact list to call Faye someone touched his arm, tugged on it.

"Shawn!" Faye grinned and hugged Shawn with all her might. Shawn was a bit surprised at how good Faye looked tonight but even more so about the way she greeted him. Then he remembered that she still thought of him as a good guy because she didn't know what he'd done.

"Damn Faye look at you."

"What?" She asked, coquettishly grinning.

"You look good, girl. I see you taking your vitamins, huh?" he chuckled.

"Mmm hmn, vitamins. It's called laziness," they both laughed and she continued, "Now that I don't have to stand on my feet for over ten hours a day, I feel healthier than ever!"

"That's good. So are you done or you still have to sew a horse's tail in somebody's head?" he laughed.

"No, crazy I'm finished so we can leave if you want."

"Oh, aiight. Let me get Stew."

"Who? I thought you came alone."

"Naw, I'ma tell him we leaving." Shawn went to track down Big Stew and found him right before he was leaving the club. Big Stew told Shawn that he was about to embark on a sex odyssey and needed the vehicle that Shawn borrowed from one of his former workers. Shawn agreed took the bag of money and told Stew to meet him at Faye's house.

Shawn met back up with Faye and told her his dilemma of having no vehicle.

"I can take you in my car," she offered, happy that her plan wasn't foiled.

Faye occasionally glanced over at her handsome

31

passenger wondering why it had to come to this. Shawn is too sexy to waste on death, she thought to herself. After breaking for the red traffic light her eyes gravitated towards the mound of denim in his lap. She fixated on it a moment too long, the light switched to green and a honk from the car behind her snapped her out of her trance.

"So how are the kids handling...well you know?" Shawn verbally stumbled.

"They're being strong you know. Just like their daddy," she responded sweetly, wondering if he could feel the awkwardness between them. Then she sighed and said, "Shawn you really loved him didn't you? I swear y'all were like brothers."

"No doubt, Mal was my brother. You don't know how sorry I am that he's gone, Faye. He was my nigga for real. You have no idea how fucked up I am behind this," his eyes met with hers, confirming what she'd suspected all along since learning of Shawn's criminal act. He was filled with contrition and he was hurting too.

"I know." She watched as remorse clung to his range of expressions. Part of her felt as though she had no right to judge him or sentence him to meet his maker but what of how he judged and sentenced her husband? Yes, he was wrong for what he'd done but she kept asking herself if two wrongs made a right? Now she was forced with a conflict of interest.

"I swear Faye, if there was a way to bring him back...," Shawn said, his voice cracking. He seemed to be fighting back tears. Faye's eyes watered as her body relented to sympathy for the man who murdered her husband. Shawn was for real and she could tell he felt what she was feeling. What was this other feeling creeping up on her-compassion?

Faye pulled into her garage. She fiddled with the house door lingering until she could make sure that her derriere was in plain view for Shawn to admire. She made an extra effort to sway her curvy hips as they went into the house. Shawn placed the bag of money on the floor.

"Do you want something to drink?" Faye asked as she closed the door behind him, watching his tall perfectly sculpted frame.

"Yea, thanks. You have orange juice?"

"I think so. I'll be right back." She flicked on the light in the hallway and made an extra effort to jiggle her bountiful buttocks on her way into the kitchen. Something happened on the ride to her house. She wanted to exact revenge somehow on her dead cheating husband and on her snake of a friend, Natalia by doing what she once dreamt of. Sampling the thick dick Talea had bragged so much about.

Shawn went into the familiar game room that he helped Maleek fill with classic arcade games, fish tanks and even a marble pool table. Memories of Maleek laughing and them just being men in that room hit him hard. All the guilt he kept trying to suppress while in Faye's presence was taking its toll. Faye strolled into the game room and passed Shawn a glass of cold orange juice. He gulped it down like a starved cast member from Survivor. Faye watched his Adam's apple as it bounced up and down with each gulp. Her emotions were jumbled as she watched this magnificent specimen of a man. Ever since Shawn had entered their lives Faye had a small crush on him. But she was a dedicated wife and never overstepped her bounds with any of her husband's associates. Hormones raged inside her as the mini fantasies that played in her mind when she first met Shawn projected re-runs. She wanted to hate him but she couldn't. She was so alone, missing her husband, missing sex. Even before Maleek's death she'd been gone so much that intimacy for them had become slim to none. She was sexually frustrated and deprived of affection for too long.

"I'll be right back," Faye smiled, bashfully after being caught staring.

"Well here," he picked up the black duffle bag from the floor and handed it to her.

"I just want you to count it in front of me so I can be sure you got it all."

"Okay, I will in a minute. I'll be right back," she scampered off.

"Faye, I'm tryna catch the red eye back to New York tonight so can you hurry up?" he called out to her.

"Well, I'll pee as fast as I can then," she chortled on her way upstairs.

In a matter of minutes Faye shrieked causing Shawn to become alarmed.

"Faye? What happened?" he shouted as he ran out of the game room to the bottom of the stairs.

"I'm upstairs. Hurry Shawn!" she shouted. Shawn ran upstairs and followed the sound of Faye's voice as she continued calling out to him. He followed it straight to the master bedroom where he stepped inside to find a shocking sight...

"What the fuck—?"

"What's wrong? You don't want this pussy?" she rubbed her long fingers between her thick thighs. She lifted her legs in the air to give him a better view of her plump vagina lips. Shawn was flabbergasted so much so that he couldn't respond. Faye sprang off the big bed and knelt before him. She began unbuckling his belt, squeezing his limpness through the crotch of his jeans. Faye was attractive but Shawn couldn't fathom having sex with his dead best friend's wife—especially knowing that he was the reason she was a widow.

"Faye! Stop that shit. What's wrong with you?" he grabbed at her slender wrists, flinging them away from his crotch.

"Nothing is wrong with me. I want you to fuck me."

Shawn looked down at her lips as they puckered together and she tried in vain to free his still flaccid penis from its cotton prison.

He shocked the shit out of her when he shoved her face away from his precious family jewels and stumbled back

34

discombobulated.

"Put your clothes back on," he sneered, seemingly disgusted as he buckled his belt and backed away. Shawn turned and began to leave the room and something inside of Faye snapped. Popping up from her knees, she pounced on him all the while screaming, "Oh, I'm not good enough for you to fuck? Mal fucked your wife so why don't you fuck his and get your revenge Shawn?" Tears replaced the anger in her eyes as she pounded her frail hands on his powerful chest then latched on to the soft material of his shirt.

"I mean you should've just done that in the first place instead of killing him!" she blurted out. Shame consumed him to the point where he could no longer bear to look at her. He gently pried her off of him. She stood there fuming in the nude having completed her tirade. It hit Shawn like a ton of bricks. She knew what he'd done. He killed her husband, his best friend. What she couldn't have known was how remorseful he was. How he wished he could rewind time and bring back the man he once referred to as his brother from another mother. "Faye...I didn't mean to do it."

"Oh, really Shawn? I can't call it. You shot him in the fuckin' head!" she shouted then realized that she was still naked and snatched her clothes from the floor and began dressing in a huff.

"You don't know what went down. I saw him fucking my wife like a beast! Bet you ain't know that he fucked her right here in your own house did you? Right there in that bed!" Shawn pointed toward the direction of the master bed. Faye's eyes widened and tears filled them.

"W-what?" she stammered.

"That's right. I watched them right outside that window. I was hurt behind that shit, Faye. My best friend fucked my wife right next door to me and in the very house that *I* built for the nigga."

"But he didn't have to die Shawn...my babies needed him." Shawn pulled her into his arms, trying to console her.

"Faye, I wasn't in my right mind that night. I drank

35

until I couldn't even see straight. I mean I even had an accident and everything because I was twisted. But I swear... I wish I could bring him back for you and the kids." Faye whimpered in his strong arms.

"I miss him so much," she wailed.

"I know... I know, I'm so sorry, Faye." Shawn gripped her even tighter as he felt waves of compassion envelop him. He wanted to be invisible at that moment because he knew that there was no turning back from what he'd done. And now that Faye knew what he'd done he was sure that his next stop was prison.

"I know there's nothing I can say to ease your pain but—"

"You better go, Shawn. Go before it's too late," Faye cut him off before he could finish his sentence.

Shawn wasn't one to beg but somehow he was preparing himself to do the ultimate and ask the widow of his victim to be lenient. Although, he was filled with contrition at this very moment he had no intentions of spending the rest of his life in jail nor did he plan on allowing her to put him there if she wasn't willing to forgive and even pretend to forget when the police came snooping.

"Why? Did you call the police already?"

"No, worse! Just trust me. Don't wait for your friend. Go out the other end of the cul-de-sac on foot and have him meet you further down the road and go as fast as you can."

Shawn's eyes narrowed as he realized why Faye warned him, "You have a hit out on me?"

"Malcolm does. He's the one who told me everything. Shawn I hate you for what you did but I don't want you to die...I don't feel right about any of this." Shawn couldn't believe the compassion and forgiveness he'd found in Faye's eyes at that moment. Here was an easy out for him but somehow he felt wrong but that didn't stop him from heeding her advice and running like the wind. In his mind the coward that runs today lives to retaliate.

He called and called Big Stew's cell phone and of all the times for Big Stew to ignore a phone call, this should not have been one of them. Big Stew was preoccupied with expelling sperm all over the buttocks of the girl he'd met in the club. He refused to hold it in just to address Shawn's interruption. Shawn was up shit's creek without a paddle because although he made it out of the gated community without detection, Malcolm had already shaken the truth out of Faye and was hot on his trail and in a vehicle no less. Shawn skulked outside the towering quarry stone barrier wall of the complex. Malcolm and his accomplices pulled up in a tricked out S.U.V. alongside him and jumped out. Shawn ran as fast as he could but a wooden bat thrown at the back of his head knocked him down to the pavement. As he struggled to get back up, the four men descended upon him, dragged him to the massive vehicle and stuffed him in the back seat. They held him down despite him being unconscious. Malcolm drove with a mean determination towards the outskirts of Buck Head. He ordered his lackeys to pull Shawn out of the car and take him deeper into the woods past the thick of the trees. He handed them each a wooden bat. The two men took turns bashing the bats into Shawn's head, chest and body. Even though he blocked some of them, he was still hit with a barrage of painstaking blows. Malcolm told them to stop and to hold down Shawn's arms.   Malcolm knelt down next to Shawn and began punching him in his face repeatedly. Shawn kept turning his head away from the punches, enabling his face to escape the brunt of the hits. This angered Malcolm and he kept on wildly throwing punches.

When he attempted to open both of his eyes Shawn realized that one of them was swollen shut. Before he could use his one good eye to focus clearly enough on the faces glaring down at him, he could feel the brush of wind that precedes an object moving with force. Crack! The piece of wood splintered as it broke in two on Shawn's elbow. He instinctively wrestled an arm free from one of the men, raising it to shield his face. Even in his beaten daze his reflexes were still keen. Shawn began flailing his fist, swinging with so much force that he heard his bones snap, crackle and pop like Rice Crispies cereal. There was an enormous amount of pain shooting throughout his entire body from their vicious beating.

"Hold his fuckin' ass down!" Malcolm spat and steadied his hand as he aimed his gun at Shawn's left knee cap, "Yea, you ain't so pretty now, huh, nigga? You killed my cousin but I'ma leave you alive but without a life. How about that, muhfucka?"

"Fuck you bitch ass nigga! Suck my pretty dick!" Shawn spat , blood spewing from his swollen lips. He scoffed at Malcolm's threat and even laughed maniacally to further infuriate him.

"Fuck me, nigga? No fuck you cuz you're the muhfuckah who's gonna be a real bitch when I'm done with yo' ass tonight!" Malcolm shot back through clenched teeth and squeezed off two shots. Luckily his sideways *"gangsta"* positioning of the gun sent the bullets off course and they ended up burrowing into a patch of dirt near Shawn's leg, leaving his knee cap in tact. Shawn laughed at his own expense and in spite of his dilemma, was actually mocking Malcolm who was now pissed off to the tenth power.

Malcolm was about to bend down and press the barrel of his gun onto Shawn's knee ensuring a bull's eye on his target when Big Stew emerged from the misty darkness and whacked him in the side of his head with his abnormally large fist. Malcolm dropped his gun and staggered a few steps sideways before collapsing. Malcolm's crew couldn't react fast enough because Big Stew's experienced, steady aim disabled both of them for good. One of the men stood up to rush him but a bullet ripped straight through his stomach and exited through his back, he keeled over. The other man was tripped by Shawn as he attempted to help Malcolm up.

As the man stumbled to his feet again, Shawn had already grabbed Malcolm's gun from the floor and let off a barrage of bullets that peeled into his bird chest.

"Fuck!" he gurgled on his way down to the ground. Big Stew kicked Malcolm in his side just as his hand snaked through the dirt in search of his gun. He grunted and curled up in the fetal position. Big Stew didn't feel like exerting anymore of his energy since he'd already given the pretty young thing from the club most of his strength so he tapped Malcolm's jaw with the barrel of the gun and said, "Open up!" Fear swallowed Malcolm as Big Stew tried to force the barrel of his gun past his tightly pursed lips.

"That's aiight, son, I can just shoot you right here," Big Stew chuckled as he slid the opening of the barrel up the middle of Malcolm's face until it was right between his eyes. Just then Shawn mumbled, "Don't... kill him... yet," releasing an exasperated sigh.

"What?" Big Stew asked annoyed. Shawn had a hard time speaking much less having to do it loudly and with each word he gasped as his lips burned and pain flashed throughout his chest and ribs, "I ...need... answers."

"Today's your lucky day, nigga. You get to breathe a little longer," Big Stew kicked Malcolm in the stomach with his giant feet.

"Damn P.B. you got knocked the fuck out!" Big Stew shouted, laughing hysterically, as he hovered over Shawn's body sprawled out on the ground. He assessed the damage to Shawn's face, "Damn, son! Won't be calling you P.B. for a minute," he chuckled and said, "Gonna hafta call you Don Knots for all those lumps on your head!"

Shawn tolerated the excruciating pain flaring through him like lightning to sit up and look directly at his comedic savior. Big Stew's silhouette appeared illuminated for a split second then he ruined it with a loud thunderous, belly laugh similar to that of Santa Claus. Shawn couldn't help but join in. Although his laugh was understated his gratitude came through loud and clear in the appreciative look he gave Big

Stew with his one good eye.

"How did you find out that Shawn killed Maleek?" Big Stew slapped Malcolm's face with his chunky sausage fingers spread wide to keep him from passing out. Malcolm was busy trying to ignore the pain in his side from where Big Stew's size fourteen boots connected with his rib cage. He was positive that his ribs were cracked. He tried to form a sentence but now the stinging sensation from Big Stew's hand was causing him to see spots.

"Talk bitch!" Big Stew shouted as he grew impatient, he glanced down at the receipt in his hand with the questions that Shawn managed to scribble with the pen he gave him since talking had become unbearable. After gingerly rubbing his sore cheek, Malcolm leaked all the answers necessary. It was the Federal Bureau of Investigations stirring up trouble, throwing salt into old wounds and trying to create new ones. Undercover agents attempted to weed out Mr. X by trying to get to his biggest money makers. Since Maleek was Mr. X's top man there was no doubt that when he turned up dead, the FEDS tried to pin it on Mr. X who had no choice but to give up the real culprit in order to get the FEDS off his back. But he also knew that without the actual evidence, Shawn would relatively be untouchable. Fortunately for Shawn he buried that evidence in a watery grave and it would not be found. But not only was Maleek's death highlighted but now Niro, the soldier turned general's murder was under microscopic scrutiny and once again it was rumored that Shawn did it. Now that the news was out on who killed Maleek and Niro the word got around, infiltrating privileged circles. Now it was apparent that Malcolm wasn't the only one who knew and that made Shawn very nervous.

The information spilling from Malcolm's lips made Shawn even more uncomfortable than his physical condition. Big Stew had asked all the questions that were on the slip of paper and now looked to Shawn for the O.K. to permanently rid them of Malcolm the menace. When Shawn figured out why Big Stew was staring at him he gave him the go ahead with a weak nod. Big Stew grabbed Malcolm's long braids, yanking his head up from the patchy grass and said, "Open up, bitch. Trust me this shit is for your own good. You won't even know what hit ya." At this point Malcolm realized that his death was inevitable so he complied with Big Stew's request and opened his mouth. Big Stew jammed the gun in Malcolm's mouth and pulled the trigger, watching as the back of his head fray outwards from the force of the shot. He dropped Malcolm's bloody head onto the dirt then effortlessly scooped up Shawn and carried him to the vehicle.

"How did you know where to find me?" Shawn strained to speak. He was too pained to raise his voice.

"I went to that broad's house and she told me everything, even how to get over here," Big Stew answered and laid him in the back seat then asked, "Hospital or Airport?"

"Airport," Shawn mumbled. He was a trooper plus he knew that he started a war and was on enemy soil. He had to get out of Atlanta and back to New York. Every time he tried to escape the grips of his past criminal existence he was ultimately thrust back in. Now he'd have to watch his back all over again. The stakes were high this time around and he knew at some point he'd have to up the anti.

Chapter IV
Reliving the Past
ॐ

Natalia was hunched over Shawn's bedside as he reached up and pinched her cheek, "Why are you pouting baby girl?"

"Look at you," she sucked her teeth, "I can't believe they did this to you. I can't wait until the cops find them and lock them up and they spend the rest of their lives getting ass fucked!"

"Damn, girl you're vicious," Shawn laughed trying to add levity to liven up his wife's mood. Again, he lied to her. He didn't want her knowing what he'd done to Maleek so he couldn't keep her up to speed with all that really happened in Atlanta or even about the potential danger they were in. He didn't think she could handle knowing that she had caused him to commit murder which left a trail of violence. So he told her that he was mugged on his way to the airport by a gang.

"Where's my little man?"

"With the Mary Poppins of all nannies."

"Who?"

"Well, since I was diagnosed with post partum depression after junior was born...," she paused to suck up the tears that wanted to form then continued, "My doctor insisted that I acquire an au pair. So he helped me find Gabriella. She's very sweet and extremely helpful."

"B.G., you're not sick again with that are you?"

"No, why?"

"Well, I'm just saying, I know how you were with Junior when I was on the scene and you were very hands on. No nanny."

"I know and I still am. I'm just doing everything right this time."

"I understand."

"Enough about me, how are you feeling?"

"I'm good."

"You don't look so good," she cracked half a smile.

"You got jokes?" he chuckled, obviously pained by his swollen lips. The swelling of his eye went down and the welts on his forehead left light traces of scabbing as they healed. His bruises were still evident and he had slight contusions on the top and sides of his head, hairline fractures in his skull, hands, elbow and ribs so Lenox Hill hospital was keeping him overnight for observation especially since they suspected that he was hemorrhaging internally from the severe beating because he didn't go straight to the hospital afterwards. But all in all he was healing quite nicely as the physician had put it, "You're doing pretty good considering that you've been beaten within an inch of your life!"

"Baby girl I'm gonna be okay. And don't worry they are gonna get what's coming to them." Her delicate fingers fluttered gingerly all over his still handsome, yet lumpy, scabby face and said, "They were just jealous of how sexy you are," she said, inching closer to his face. She placed a slow, sensual kiss on his puffy lips.

"Don't start what you can't finish," he said in his seductive velvety baritone.

"Oh, daddy I can start it and I can definitely finish it," her eyes revealed the naughty thoughts filling her head.

"Oh, really, well then, Max needs a kiss too," Shawn grinned mischievously while sliding his hand down to his growing bulge and grabbing it through his hospital gown.

"Your wish is my command, master."

Natalia rushed to lock the door of the private hospital

43

room which she made sure they assigned to her husband since he *was* a wealthy self-paying patient. She climbed onto the hospital bed and softly kissed his tender mouth, slipping him a little bit of her tongue at a time. Then she slid herself down his body hospital gown-hidden anaconda, gently coaxing it out from under the material with her tongue. As his penis rose to the occasion, she devoured it. She went to town on it as if it were her last meal.

Feverishly she sucked and pumped him with her hands simultaneously until his load coated her tonsils, glided down her throat. Her husband's sperm didn't taste bitter as she anticipated now that he gave up drinking alcohol it was virtually tasteless. Hmmm, maybe I'll get my protein this way from now on, she giggled, leering at him. Shawn could only smirk as he was thoroughly satisfied at this moment and all but forgot that he was still after all in a hospital. He knew that his wife was horny and her silky secretions were probably oozing down her leg by now and he felt that it was his unselfish duty to clean her up.

"Come sit on daddy's face," he invited with his deep sultry voice.

"But daddy your head and your mouth are messed up... won't it hurt?"

"Sit on my face!" he demanded.

She promptly obliged by rotating her lower body into position so that her crotch hovered over his head. She carefully lowered herself onto his face. Shawn expertly and attentively tasted her until she shuddered, releasing her creamy sweetness all over his battered mouth. He lapped it up. She flopped down on her stomach beside him and exhaled with satisfaction. As she lay there content, she thought how lucky she was to be with this man. This man that had put her through hell then pulled her from it. Shawn smoothed his palms over her bronze legs. He turned to find her feet right by his head so he kissed the bottom of them. Adoring her pretty feet, at that moment he felt a sense of tranquility come over him. His eyes diverted to the I.V. in his arm connected to a bag hanging from an iron pole reminding him that he was in a hospital. The unfortunate events that landed him there jolted him from his Utopia and he realized what he had to do. He had to keep her safe from his past that seemed to be catching up with him once again.

"Baby girl, I'm gonna start teaching you how to shoot a gun."

"Why daddy?"

"You might need to protect yourself."

"Oh, okay. Hmmm, I think I'm going to like having all that power in my hands. Pulling the trigger and blowing holes through niggaz' heads!"

"Listen to you!" he laughed loud, "Damn my baby's violent!" he laughed again, palmed her ass and squeezed, "Ready for round two?" Natalia sprang up with a wide, cheesy grin and said, "Bang, bang, bang!" pumping her groin, humping the air with each bang.

છ≫ઉ

Shawn took Natalia to the edge of the woods where construction stalled on the rest of the extensive property that he and his investors purchased. He pensively paced from the three cinder blocks he set up prior to driving back to get his wife from the main road. He drew a line in the dirt once he reached a certain distance. He ran back over to the ATV, helped Natalia out then lined up three glass bottles on three separate cinder blocks.   He gently guided his wife 20 feet away from the intended targets.

"Hold out both your hands," he tentatively instructed. She did as she was told and he placed a Glock 9 mm and a .45 GAP cartridge in her hands. He reached into his pants pocket and pulled out six hollow point bullets and said, "Lemme show you how to load the cartridge first." He pressed a bullet into the bottom of the cartridge right above the springy mechanism with his thumb.

45

"Now you do it," he prompted. Natalia did as she was told but nervousness made her fingers tremble to the point where she ended up dropping the cartridge and bullets. They both knelt down to retrieve the weapon and its parts. As they rose, Natalia spoke apologetically, "I-I'm sorry, daddy. I don't know if this is such a good idea. I can't kill another human being." The worried, horrified look upon her face was piteous and Shawn knew he'd have to push his wife to her limits. If he didn't she stood a slight chance of getting them both killed with her fear and apprehensiveness. He stayed on her to learn how to load the cartridge, to pop it into the gun, how to aim and shoot until she finally got it right.

"Because you're a girl and weaker," he sneered. Natalia rolled her eyes and sighed while he continued,

"You're gonna hafta hold your wrist like this so the kickback don't break your wrist, heh, heh," he demonstrated by firmly grabbing his own right wrist while holding the gun pointed straight ahead at the glass bottles.

"Pay attention baby girl," he called out before pulling the trigger. One of the glasses atop the cinder block exploded, hurling shards of glass everywhere. Shawn appeared to be a sharpshooter and it not only impressed his wife but turned her on to see him finagle the gun with such finesse, control and preciseness. Shawn turned to see the glazed, dreamy expression on her face and walked over to her, "What's wrong?"

"Nothing, I'm just watching and learning." Shawn kept at it until his wife was able to shoot better than he expected. Her aim was still a bit off but she had grasped the important parts of the lesson, putting his mind at ease.

For the following days Shawn took her out and trained her even more hoping to instill a sense of diligence. He wanted firing a gun to become second nature to her. She would be prepared, his Bonnie and he, her Clyde. They would have to be on their P's and Q's. He had finally got his family back, finally resigned himself to be the man that he knew his woman needed and a father figure to little Everton.

He wanted to just live his life but his past caught up to him, forcing his back to the wall, now he had to come out swinging.

❧

"Shut the fuck up bitch and stand over in that corner!" the robber waved his gun to direct the young woman. The frightened woman backed up into the corner and crouched down, trembling with fear. His accomplices made haste in tying up the other workers in the popular 24 hour Laundromat that belonged to Shawn Wilson. It was the third business that Shawn still owned in New York that was robbed and trashed in the same night. The men had bandannas tied around the lower halves of their faces when they barged into the Laundromat through the back entrance. They made sure that almost every washing machine and dryer's glass window was smashed in from their heavy aluminum bats. They went as far as to steal all of the detergents and cleaning products. They took their time drilling into each coin box on each machine, relieving them of its silver treasure of quarters. It was one o'clock in the morning and they were smart enough before breaking in to cut the wires to the fuse box causing a brown out inside the Laundromat. Armed with flashlights they overpowered the three unsuspecting workers easily and locked the front entrance. The lookouts in their respective getaway vehicles blasted music to cover up the suspicious noises coming from inside the Laundromat. Until now, no one was really hurt in any of the robberies.

The petite young woman hovering in the corner's face was hot from the bright light of a huge flashlight aimed at her by one of the men. He seemed to be enjoying her discomfort. As she turned her head away from the light he'd follow her face with it and snicker. He lowered the light onto her bosom and watched as they rose and fell with each heave of fear. She knew that he couldn't tell that she'd already wiggled her slender wrists and tiny hands free from the cord behind her back. She carefully eased her right hand towards her waist to tug at her cell phone. When it fell to the tiled floor she panicked thinking there'd be no way to get it without him knowing what she was up to. But as his attention was divided between the commotion surrounding them and her perky breasts she maneuvered her body in a manner that allowed her to get the phone in the proper position where she could feel the buttons and could remember exactly how the key pad was situated on the cell. She dialed 911 and slid the phone in her back pocket.

The man returned the beam of light from the flashlight back in her face.

"Fuck you fidgeting for?" She didn't answer, only squinted at him in disgust. This offended him. To be a real prick, he flicked his boney finger across her clothed nipple and smiled to himself. He enjoyed watching her flinch with his every movement. He took the liberty of palming her breast through her t-shirt, enjoying her uneasiness, fear even the lone tear sliding down her cheek. She closed her eyes tight to avoid seeing his malicious grin. She kept sniffling to keep from crying.

"Yo, get over here and bust that box open on that side," the tallest of the thieves commanded.

"Shit, I'm coming." He looked at her regretfully as if he would miss torturing her. She looked away from him as he smirked, as if he knew something that she didn't then joined the other men in their quest for coins. Now she felt it was her chance to get out of there.

Although it was dark, she pretty much knew that she was not too far from the back exit. The trick would be getting to it without falling or being noticed. This would be a task but she believed the men would kill her and her co-workers once they retrieved every last quarter. She felt that her life would end had she not made the choice which forced her to her feet. Looking out first to make sure the men were still occupied, she crept towards the back exit while palming the walls, soda machines and washers along the way.

"What the fuck? Yo, get that bitch!" the tall intruder shouted as soon as he detected her movements and flashed light on her. The girl panicked and began to run. One of the men lifted a gun up with his stubby hands and let off two rounds. The girl yelped and fell to the floor.

"You ain't have to shoot her, nigga," said the one who had become smitten with her. He walked over to her limp body and shook his head solemnly, "Tsk, tsk. What a waste," he mumbled apathetically.

"Come on nigga get the casings and let's get up outta here." He did as he was told and they all vanished into the darkness.

৯৺৻

The ambulances and cop cars surrounding his laundromat was not a welcomed sight. Shawn received disturbing news two o'clock in the morning when a police officer and an employee called to give him the bad news about his businesses being robbed. When he heard the news about his cousin, Tasha's death he nearly threw the phone clear across the room. This can't be happening, he thought. Not his baby cousin who begged to work in the laundromat and started that very same night. He pulled into the parking lot and just stared at what was the catalyst of his legitimacy. Now it only brought a disturbing vision of his lovely cousin's lifeless body to mind. An officer approached him as he stepped out of his S.U.V.

"Are you the owner?"

"Yes."

"I need you to I.D. an employee." Shawn instantly knew they needed him to confirm Tasha's identity and it hurt like hell that he'd have to call one of his most favorite people on the planet, his aunt Freda and inform her that her only daughter was dead. Shawn's pained sigh let the officer know

49

the emotional turmoil he was experiencing at the moment and said, "I understand... take a few minutes then join us inside," he placed his hand on Shawn's shoulder. Shawn glared at the unwelcomed touch and walked away from the officer towards his Laundromat. Inside he saw the devastation the perpetrators caused. There were thick pieces of glass and twisted, holey metal boxes everywhere. The door to the office dangled from its hinges. Shawn` felt a sharp pang of hurt when he spotted the smeared blood on the tiled floor. His eyes followed its trail to his petite barely legal cousin's body. She was sprawled out on the floor face down. Anger swallowed him at that moment and he couldn't maintain his composure any longer, "Those motherfuckers!"

"Calm down, sir." An officer tried to offer comfort but Shawn ignored him, knelt at his cousin's lifeless body's side and took her small hand into his.

"Tasha, baby, I'm so sorry..."

"We have to allow the coroner to do his job Mr. Wilson so can you verify the identity please."

Shawn scowled at the detective before he finally complied, "Her name is...was Tasha Thompson."

Shawn checked the entire Laundromat and realized that although it was salvageable he did not want it anymore. All of his products and profits were gone. Insurance would cover most of the costs of all three of his businesses being burglarized but all he could focus on was the ninety grand the thieves got away with. Whoever targeted him was going to be on the receiving end of immense pain. Shawn made all the necessary arrangements with his contacts in the streets in order to find out who was behind the robbery spree.

꿍

Shawn wanted desperately to call his wife who had no idea of what happened since she was on a flight coming back into New York with her best friend Andre. Natalia had taken one year old Everton to Jamaica to meet family and acquaint him with his Jamaican heritage. Now as Shawn drove to his aunt's house he called knowing he'd get her voicemail. When he heard her sweet voice he decided against leaving a message. He didn't want her to find out about it that way. Then he thought of his wonderful aunt and the man he called uncle even though they never married. How they were getting married in two more days and Tasha was to be the maid of honor at her parent's wedding—a wedding that was long overdue. Of all times for such a bleak turn of events to take place. Shawn's eyes glossed over as he pictured his cousin dressed to the nines and standing beside her mother at the altar. He pulled into their driveway and fought back tears before dragging himself to the front door.

"Hey man," Clarence opened the door and hugged his soon to be nephew in- law. Shawn walked in the house but lingered in the hallway as if he were stalling.

"Come in man. What's wrong with you? You look like you've seen a ghost or something," he chuckled and patted Shawn's back.

"Uncle Cee, I don't know how to tell you this... where's Aunt Free?"

"She's in the kitchen cooking up a storm as usual," Clarence practically had to push Shawn to get him to move so he had to ask, "What's going on Stretch?" Shawn entered the kitchen listlessly and when his aunt Freda saw him she jumped up with joy and rushed to hug him.

"My handsome baby! Oh, sweetie what's this scar doing on your face?" she trickled her fingers lightly over the line of raised scabs under Shawn's left eyebrow.

"What happened to your adorable chinky eyes? It's a little swollen over here. Now wait...you busted your lip too and look at this," she said touching a black and blue mark on Shawn's creamy light skinned cheek.

"You were in a fight sweetie? Some jealous ugly boy tried to take away those good looks your momma and daddy gave ya?" she giggled. Shawn was at a loss for words, unprepared for delivering the bad news to the wonderful

51

woman he'd always secretly wished was his mother.

"Stretch? What's wrong, baby?" she palmed his cheek as she looked up at him concerned, "Something happen to Ty-Ty? Can't be, I just spoke to him the other day." Shawn pulled her into his arms and held onto her, he looked over at Clarence who watched him intently waiting for the bomb to drop. He then took a deep, troubled breath before bringing their worlds crashing down.

"What is it? What happened, man?" Clarence insisted.

"They robbed Bubble Brite and shot—"

"NO! DON'T YOU SAY IT, DON'T YOU SAY IT!" Freda screamed at the top of her lungs as she wriggled free from her favorite nephews' defined arms. Clarence's knees weakened and he gripped the counter top to keep himself standing, "Oh, God, no," he murmured. He appeared to be hyperventilating. Shawn grabbed for his aunt once more and this time she gave in and held onto him tightly while she cried uncontrollably.

When Clarence's breathing became more erratic Shawn led his aunt over to the kitchen table and eased her into a chair. He searched her cupboards until he found a brown paper bag and he blew into it and narrowed the opening with two fingers then demonstrated to Clarence how to breathe using the bag in order to stop him from losing consciousness. Clarence did as Shawn instructed. Clarence began breathing normally again and he asked the inevitable,

"How bad is it?" Shawn's empathetic stare was enough to let Clarence know that his little girl was gone.

"She can't be dead! No, Shawn, No!" he broke down and began wailing from an insurmountable soul-wrenching pain. He slumped down to the floor and sobbed loudly. Freda just sat staring blankly ahead frozen like a statue. Shawn tried to hold her but she was too stiff. He didn't know how to handle their grief and called his mother and told her to get over to Freda's house right away. As he hung up the phone his aunt whispered, "My baby... my baby's gone?"

52

Shawn knelt at his aunt's feet, he wiped away the tears streaming down her face, "I'm sorry," Shawn uttered, overwhelmed with compunction. At that moment Freda realized her once auspicious offspring would never bear the grandchildren she so insistently dreamt of, never fulfill her pre-laden destiny of becoming a math professor. It was then that a bereft Freda lost consciousness and fell from her chair onto the floor.

೧೪೬

Niro's half brother, Manny, vowed to murder Shawn after the Feds put a bug in his ear about their informed leads on Niro's murderer. First he set up Shawn's two Laundromats and his recently opened soul food restaurant in Queens to be robbed. The take was ninety-thousand dollars but the money did nothing to fulfill his need for revenge, especially since he had to split it with eleven people. He learned a lot about the object of his hatred and found out that not only did Shawn have a wife but she was more than a dime piece. Manny had his heart set on not only hurting Shawn beyond recovery but he wanted Shawn to suffer the humiliation of seeing his wife violated right in front of him. Manny was sure this would be more than enough payback for his brother's death. He didn't care that his brother wasn't a Saint. He knew that if he was the one man to stamp out Shawn's ability to breathe he would be widely feared in the streets. Shawn had a stellar reputation in the streets of New York. His clout withstood even though he was out of the game. In fact many small time hustlers aspired to be like him, get out of the game free and clear despite having lived through all that he had. Shawn was a living legend having survived murder attempts, incarceration and even the Feds. He had Queens on lock with his celebrity status. This rubbed Manny the wrong way most of all. His envy clouded his judgment regarding retaliation for his brother being snuffed out. Manny found out all that he could about Shawn's movements for the day. He also put a tail on the main pawn in his plan...

Natalia was in hog heaven watching the delectable chocolate delicacies being paraded in front of her on a silver electroplated platter. There were raspberry filled truffles, chocolate fondue with ripe red, plump strawberries patiently awaiting their enamel chomping fates. The sweet temptations floated under her nose atop the palms of a doting employee of the baroque beauty spa boasting top notch clientele. She sunk her pearly whites into the richness of the milk chocolate caressing a sweet strawberry. "You look like you're doing a commercial for sucking dick or should I say licking ass," Andre laughed heartily and finished with, "Wipe that doo-doo from your lip."

"I know you don't want to go there with the amount of shit you've probably tasted from all the asses you've licked, fudge packer!" Andre playfully slapped Natalia's cheek, "Watch your mouth before I tear *you* a new asshole."

"Oooh, come on baby," Natalia giggled and jokingly hopped out of the recliner and pretended to pull her low rise jeans down.

"See? You're such a freak now," Andre cackled. He snatched up his pageboy cap from the empty recliner next to him and put it on his head and said, "I'm all dry and ready to go."

"Good because I've been dry and ready to go like twenty minutes ago and these strawberries have started something. I'm hungry now."

"So what do you feel like eating?" Andre asked as they left the spa.

"I don't care. I just want some food in my belly. Where did you want to go?"

"No where really since I'm not the one that's always so hungry lately, you Fat Bastard," he joked.

"Ha, ha."

"You know I'm kidding, lil' Miss Skinny Minnie. Well if you're leaving it up to me I've been dying to go back up into Harlem to that cute spot where we had that party for Adonis."

"Oh, yea, okay. They did have delicious food. But geesh Andy that's so far...it's okay we'll go. But you're driving."

"So aren't you glad I made you leave the baby with the nanny?"

"I am. I really needed a break."

"Girl, I just hope that you installed nanny cams all through that monstrous penthouse y'all got."

"Oddly enough the owners already have a couple installed."

"Good because nowadays you can't be too sure with all these violent nut jobs running around out there trying to molest babies and all that outlandish shit."

"Uh-oh, you've got me worried."

"My bad, Nat I take it all back. Ain't nobody gonna mess with you and your gangster husband's spawn."

"How dare you talk about your Godchild that way?" Natalia feigned offense.

"Oh, please. You know that little boy got the devil in him. And he got it honest too, look at who his parents are!" They both laughed heartily. Secretly, Natalia was worried. Worried that part of what Andre said was true. What if the sins of the father were passed through to him intravenously? The men who could be Everton's father had all sinned. Who was Everton's father? That question plagued her the most. She knew the answer to that question could possibly make or break her marriage.

Andre sped into a high priced parking lot adjacent to the restaurant. As they exited the lot a bunch of rowdy men blocked their path.

"Excuse me," Natalia uttered politely. "Damn!" some of the group exclaimed as they eyed Natalia like a pack of hungry wolves. Natalia was intimidated to a degree because of the size of the group of men idling by. She was more afraid for Andre and didn't want to get the miscreants riled up any further. One bold young man grinned at her and proceeded to invade her personal space by stepping up right in her face. Grabbing hold of her forearm he smoothly said, "Sup ma, I know that bitch niggah ain't your man," he nodded his head in Andre's direction. There was thunderous laughter amongst the men and this is when the butch buried inside Andre decided to make his appearance.

"I'm not a bitch nor am I a nigga. But maybe you can be my bitch." Andre puffed out his chest, exuding machismo at this point. Natalia was astonished by Andre's brazenness but feared for his life now.

"What the fuck you say?" the young man got into a fighting stance.

"This is not necessary. Let's go Andy," Natalia stepped in between them attempting to pull Andre away. One of the men laughed menacingly repeating, "Andy? That niggah is a fag! Yo, Splint you gon' let a fag come at you like that?" All of the other men began heckling, instigating and escalating the situation.

"Just let us leave. There's no need for this macho bullshit!" Natalia was disgusted with the men's behavior.

"Shut the fuck up bitch and move." Someone shouted from the assembled crowd. Just then Andre gently moved his best friend out of the way and within moments both men swung at each other. Andre wasn't a slouch and his fists of fury were taking a toll on his gangly opponent. When it looked like their friend was not only getting his ass beat but doing their crew a disservice with his embarrassing fighting skills, his crew attacked Andre.

Natalia looked on in horror, helpless. When it dawned on her to call the police she realized that someone beat her to it because she could hear sirens off in the distance. She screamed her head off when she saw a sea of feet pounding her best friends head. "STOP IT! PLEASE STOP!" she tried to pull the men off of Andre but was thrown to the floor. The sirens were closer now so the men scattered quickly. Natalia was never so happy to see the color navy blue when patrol cars screeched up onto the sidewalk and officers popped out. She crawled over to her best friend who struggled to breathe through his mouth. His battered face no longer resembled the handsome, well groomed man that he was. Blood saturated his twill jacket. Natalia sobbed as she tried to clean his swollen face off with napkins from her purse.

"Andy, baby it's gonna be okay," she delicately patted his lumpy head. Andre tried to reply but gurgled instead.

"Don't talk sweetie." But Andre was determined to loan levity to the moment.

"Am I still sexy?" he gasped.

"Always," she lied, knowing that if her vain best friend could see himself he would die from fright alone. He tried to chuckle but something went awry and Andre began losing his battle to breathe. His eyes rolled up then shut. Natalia became hysterical.

"NO! Andy? ANDY?!?"

"Ma'am let us get in here now so we can help him," an EMS technician said as he dropped to one knee beside Andre. Natalia moved out of their way, watching as they ripped Andre's expensive clothes to shred's in order to save his life.

Inside the hospital Andre was hooked up to all kinds of machinery and it brought back memories of her past bid in the hospital. She recalled the events in her life that would appear to be hyperbole to an outsider hearing about it. They would accuse her of fabricating it all. To her it was the threading in the eclectic quilt of her existence. Lately, she knew nothing other than drama.

There appeared to be no respite. She watched as orderlies came whizzing by wheeling in a flood of gurneys with young bloodied African-American men. A doctor stepped out of one of the operating rooms to investigate the commotion, "What now?" he asked, nonchalant.

"Multiple GSWs," one orderly offered. Natalia looked at the doctor who only sighed and headed back into the operating room.

"Please doctor can you tell me about Mr. Howard's condition."

"Are you his wife?"

"No, his best friend, I was with him."

"Oh, well he's sustained severe head trauma and he's being transferred to I.C.U. He'll need to be observed for several hours before we'll know anything definite although there are hematomas present."

"That's bleeding right? Oh, God his brain is bleeding?"

"Yes, but it doesn't necessarily mean he can't recover."

"Is he conscious?"

"No, but he's responsive and isn't in a coma yet so that's good news."

"Yet? You mean he can slip into a—"

"I'm sorry I have to tend to other patients right now. All I can tell you is that we'll have more information for you tomorrow after the specialist sees him."

Natalia was at a loss. If anything happened to Andre she would be lost. Tears welled up in her doe eyes but before they fell she sucked them back up. The thought of Andre's true love, Adonis popped into her head. She looked down at her cell phone, deliberating on how she'd actually relay the news to him. She scrolled through her cellular's address book and a nurse stepped in front of her, "Miss you cannot use cell phones here especially on this floor where machines are keeping critically injured patients alive!" she scolded.

"I'm sorry, I forgot...," Natalia glared at the back of the nurse's head as she walked off feeling accomplished. Natalia sighed in frustration and scoured her purse for change then found the payphones. She scorned the receiver as if it were immersed in dog poop. She dreaded it touching her skin for fear of the millions of germs she knew were cohabitating on its plastic surface. Her hand fished out a small bottle of hand sanitizing gel and a napkin from her purse. Then she quickly smeared a dollop of sanitizing gel directly onto the phone receiver using the napkin. Now came the hard part, figuring out how to deliver the tragic news to Adonis.

"Adonis, it's Nat, Andy is in the hospital and he may go into a coma. No, um, Andy is in the hospital but the doctors say he's not so bad off," she whispered as she practiced near the row of pay phones in a corner of the emergency room's waiting area. She looked up and noticed a couple of stares and realized how disturbed she must've seemed with all of her pacing and talking to herself. She smiled sheepishly at a nosey group of orderlies and referred back to her cell phone's screen for Adonis' number then put the payphone receiver to her ear. Her hand was unsteady as she began dialing.

Adonis did not take the news well. He was a wreck on the other end of the phone. He bawled, sniffled, yowled and screamed. Natalia begged him to stay where he was while she headed over to pick him up. Finally, he agreed to wait for her so Natalia made a dash for her car in a parking lot across the street from the hospital. As she neared her car she could clearly see there were two hoodlums loitering by the front end of her car. Intuition told her to run so she did. She didn't get too far since there happened to be a third accomplice who popped out in front of her blocking her path. "What do you want?" she asked, shaken. No words were spoken but his flying fist landed dead on which said a mouthful. Natalia's head swung from the weight of the blow. She toppled to the ground, the side of her head crashed onto the concrete. Again with the darkness, she thought as her cognizance diminished.

Chapter V
That Which Does Not Kill Us Only Makes Us Stronger

ॐॐॐ

Shawn pressed the send button on his cell again. The repetitive ringing in his ear pissed him off. He called the penthouse and got the au pair who informed him that Natalia left Everton with her and was gone all day. His wife was missing in action and this time inappropriate scenarios ran amuck in his mind. *I'ma kill this bitch if she's out there doing some dumb shit!* Fed up with being unable to hear her sweet voice he left a threatening message on Natalia's voicemail:

"Look this is the seventh time I've called and I know you're shit ain't turned off cuz it rang out so stop the bullshit and you better fuckin' call me back right now!"

He'd had enough of listening to the digital voice of her voicemail's outgoing message. He wanted his wife and he knew that she was in New York by now since the day was practically over. He realized that he'd have to call the only other person that would know her whereabouts.

"Hello?" an unfamiliar voice answered.

"Andre?" Shawn asked unsure.

"No, this is not Andre. Who is this?"

Frustrated, Shawn just hung up believing that he had

the wrong number. This time he paid close attention to what he was doing as he pressed each individual numeric button on his cell phone.

"Look, I don't have time for this okay?" the same unfamiliar male voice answered.

"I'm trying to find Andre."

"Well this is his fiancée and Andre can't come to the phone. So what is your message?"

"No disrespect, but put Andre on the phone."

"Andre can't come to the phone...he's...what is it tha you want?"

"Listen, I'm looking for my wife. She was due in JFK today at 10:35 this morning yet I haven't heard or seen her all day. They came back together and he's my wife's best friend so I just thought he'd know something."

"Oh, my goodness, Is this Shawn?"

"Yea."

"This is Adonis. Andre is in the hospital. He and Natalia were together but some thugs jumped my baby."

"What? Where's Natalia?"

"Don't fret, she was okay, they didn't attack her but she was supposed to pick me up and take me to the hospital but she never showed and I called and called her but kept getting her voicemail."

"Shit." Shawn started to really worry now, "Did she say anything about where she was or how she was going to pick you up?"

"She said that she was going to the parking lot to get her car."

"What parking lot?"

"I guess it's the only one across from Beth Israel hospital."

"Thanks," Shawn hung up and wasted no time heading to Manhattan. He drove erratic which drew suspicion from a passing squad car that followed him for five blocks before sounding their sirens signaling him to pull over. Shawn was irritated at this point and wanted to keep driving but he knew he couldn't risk being hauled away when his wife was missing. A Korean officer approached the driver's side window. Shawn tapped the controls for the window, sighing loudly as the window descended.

"License and registration," the officer commanded, peering into Shawn's S.U.V. suspiciously. Shawn complied.

"Do you know why I pulled you over?"

Because you saw a black man pushing a brand new Escalade and you're mad that you're still in a Hyundai?

"Why no officer I do not," Shawn answered, astutely. The cop's eyes narrowed into tighter slits than they already were. He thought he detected sarcasm in Shawn's answer. His presumption was correct. Shawn despised the cops and thought of New York's police as NYPD's *lamest* instead of finest. He carefully scanned the cream leather interior of Shawn's vehicle.

"Well, why did you pull me over officer?" Shawn asked.

"Remain in the vehicle sir." The officer went back to his squad car.

Moments later the officer returned with a ticket in his hand.

"What's you're hurry?" he asked, condescendingly.

"I'm late for a meeting."

"Well, this is a local street and you were driving 70 miles an hour," he handed Shawn the ticket and offered some unsolicited advice, "Just keep in mind that when you speed as you were doing you run the risk of killing innocent people."

Shawn shot the officer the look of death before putting his window back up. He looked at the time and saw that it was later than he expected. All of the advice he had just received from the cop fell on deaf ears. As soon as the opportunity arose he turned off onto a side street in hopes the cops wouldn't tail him. They didn't which gave him another opportunity to continue racing toward Manhattan.

Natalia's eyes stung as she tried to open them. The pungent odor of urine burned her nostrils. Then she felt it, warm liquid streaming down all over her face. She sputtered and turned her face away from the putrid liquid but it kept coming.

"Yea, wake up bitch!" she heard someone say off in the distance. She squinted as some of the liquid seeped into her eyes regardless of her efforts. In fact the liquid made its way into all of her orifices. Unfortunately, she could taste the bitter moist droplets sliding down her lips.

"NEXT!" she heard someone shout which was followed by thunderous laughter. She finally managed to open her eyes wide enough to see a man standing over her with his penis in his hand. It was aimed at her face and she cringed in horror as the golden trickle of piss escaped the tiny hole in the mushroom-like cap. She closed her eyes tightly, braving the burning sensations stinging her eyeballs, shuddering at the image she had just witnessed. As the liquid hit her face, she reacted as if it were acid, squirming incessantly which only amused her audience even more. She heard a distinctive voice order, "Loosen her hands."

Natalia felt her hands being yanked free from behind her. She instantly sat up and began wiping her face with her sleeves, whimpering like a wounded animal. With her eyes dried off enough where she could see again, she finally saw the faces of the sadistic and vindictive spectators.

The room was brightly lit and as she panned it she saw rows and rows of teeth. Her captors were all grinning from ear to ear. "1, 2, 3, 4, 5...," she began to count in her head of how many faces stared back at her. She finally got to the last culprit, number nine. She reeked of the horrid ammonia filled stench from old urine and the thought of what had just been done to her made her want to puke. Before she could heave, a couple of the men came over and forced her to her feet.

"Clean that bitch up." She turned in the direction of the voice and he smirked at her then said, "Yea, bitch, it ain't over. We're just getting started."

It was then that she realized the reason the room was so bright, there was a man practically shoving portable studio lights in her face while another with a digital camcorder was following her every move. She wished this was Candid Camera or some other reality show and a host would jump out and say, "We gotcha! Don't worry these people are all actors and the urine was fake!" But she knew better. She knew that people actually pissed in her face and that once again, she had become a captive, a victim. She also knew that this time there wouldn't be any romancing like with Shawn. God only knew the motives of the creepy men who found amusement in demoralizing her, a defenseless woman.

Her next stop in Bizarro world was an unsanitary bathroom where she was thrust into the rudimentary, rusted tub. She moaned when her sore body collided with the filthy rusted porcelain. The men began ripping her clothes off of her like savages. They didn't do such a great job with undressing her but they didn't care. Then as if she were a pet they turned on the shower while she huddled in one corner of the tub. The cold water made her shiver then without warning, one of the men slapped her bare thigh and said, "Mmn, I can't wait to sample this."

"Wash your ass!" the other man sneered and threw a dingy washcloth at her. It landed on her head. They left her half naked in her now tattered clothes being beaten by powerful sprays of cold water. As the bathroom door closed Natalia jumped up, snatched the washcloth from the top of her head and threw the mystery spotted material onto the floor. She finished peeling away her ripped clothes. The hot water valve had the letter H largely engraved in it which proved pretty helpful considering Natalia was too shook up to think straight. She adjusted the water's temperature, checking it with an open hand. When it heated up she closed her eyes and stuck her face in the streams of water jetting from the shower head. She opened her eyes and even though they were quite irritated she still found a bar of soap lurking on the edge of the tub. It looked as if it were part scum part filth. But she knew she had no other choice but to use it. The dried up urine all over her made her skin crawl. She dropped the bar of soap into the tub in hopes that the hot water would wash away its gray film. When the bar of soap looked decent enough to her she scrubbed her entire body down with the bar and her bare hands. She stood in the tepid water with a barrage of dismal thoughts flooding her head. Even though she couldn't feel clean enough having known what was done to her, the half-assed shower she'd taken helped alleviate the repulsion she felt earlier.

Before she could turn off the pipes the door flew open and in walked another creep. One of her hands cupped her breasts and the other darted to her pubic area. The mystery man approached her cautiously; his eyes scanned her slick wet body. Natalia was terrified as she feared his next move.

"So you're P.B.'s bitch, huh?"

Natalia didn't know if she should respond, in fact she didn't dare try. There was evident fear in her eyes and her body trembled from it along with the cold air settling over her. With a swift snatch, he yanked her hand away from her hairless mound. She lifted her knee to try and hide herself. He gripped her other arm which hid her breasts and held it away from her body. He surveyed her nudeness, his eyes stopping at her chest. He seemed to be entranced by her plump taupe nipples. Natalia began to sob as she felt incredibly violated. "A, yo, Cash!" the man hollered toward the open bathroom door. The bright spotlight appeared again and the camera guy rushed in aiming his lens at her then scoping her out with it.

"You're my star, bitch," the man said and laughed.

"Now get your ass out that tub and get on your knees."

65

"Why are you doing this?" Natalia finally felt a burst of courage.

"Bitch, did I say you could talk?" the man backhanded her causing her to slip and fall in the tub.

Her head barely missed crashing into the scummy porcelain. Everyone laughed at her.

"You know what I'ma do for you? I'll tell you why this is happening to you. Then I'll even tell you how I'ma kill you and your man." There it was. This was about Shawn. Her next thought was if she were to die who'd take care of Everton with Andy on the verge of being a vegetable? The man grabbed a hold of her arm and forced her out of the tub and bathroom into a dreary room that smelled of stale Nachos, musk and ass. The man who seemed to be in charge noticed that the cameraman and the person holding the light had followed them so he ordered them to leave until he called for them again. He sat on a sunken in mattress.

"P.B. killed my brother, Niro. Remember that name, bitch! NIRO! That's why you're gonna die," the angry man finally offered. The look of confusion on Natalia's face let him know that Natalia didn't know what he was talking about.

"Guess you don't know much about your *man*. Well now you know that he's a bitch ass nigga and he's gonna die slow for that shit. I know they call him Superman but I've got the kryptonite for that ass."

His eyes insinuated deviousness as he watched her modestly shift every so often to keep her private parts hidden.

"So you see I'ma make you a star, baby. Gonna make this movie to get him interested in meeting me. Then you can watch me make him bleed slow," he chuckled devilishly. After that news bulletin Natalia trembled and her arm shifted, exposing a goose bump riddled nipple. The more he watched her shiver the more it made his growing bulge rise.

"Come here," he ordered. Natalia knew what was on his mind and she had never been so revolted in all her life. Besides repugnance she was too scared to comply. He grew impatient waiting for her goodies so he got up from the creaking bed and grabbed a fist full of her wet hair in his hand. He put so much pressure on her head that it forced her to bend down almost to the floor.

"Get on your knees, bitch!" he demanded.

She struggled against the pressure from his fist upsetting him to the point where he flung her to the ground. Being naked was annoying the hell out of her since her body felt every blow and scrape from the old wooden floor. Another face poked into the room and said, "Yo, Manny is it time?"

"Just give me the camera," he huffed, both startled and frustrated.

"Come on man, I don't need you fucking up my shit. I paid mad money for this shit."

"Just give me the fuckin' camera!"

The man hesitantly handed him the camera then looked regretfully at Natalia's honey glazed body writhing on the floor. Watching her wet form wriggle enticed him, made him want to be a voyeur as Manny punished her. Manny saw the lust in his friend's eyes and informed him, "Don't worry you'll get your turn, nigga, damn."

It was then and only then that the man finally left. Manny walked over to a 5 drawer wooden bureau cattycorner to the door and placed the camera on an angle. He made sure that he'd be able to record anything that happened at the edge of the bed. He turned it on and went back to his awaiting victim. Natalia's body started to go numb from her skin's perpetual exposure to the room's dank coldness. He held her face in his large hands, pulling it towards his crotch, "Take it out," he demanded. Instead of doing as he told her she opened his belt and unbuttoned his jeans. At first he wanted to slap her for not following his instructions but then he liked where this was going. He believed that she had accepted her fate and welcomed the obligatory fellatio. So he put his hands on his hips and leaned back slightly, letting his head cock back slightly. When she pulled out his erect member she looked up at him and saw that his eyes were closing, anticipating ecstasy. He seemed so pleased with himself. First she massaged his scrotum, tracing each ball with her finger tips. He enjoyed her touch and sighed from the pleasure. She opened her mouth wide then sunk her canines into his two-toned pink and chocolate almost pencil thin penis' flesh with immense force. She pressed down hard onto his dick, grinding her teeth while shaking her head frantically from side to side like a predator devouring its prey. The whole time she had his balls in a vice grip and twisted them with each shake of her head. She was so angry that in her irate fit she was actually trying to rip his penis and balls right off of his body. After tasting the metallic flavor of blood she finally released him from her teeth. She spit blood at him. Not only did he squeal like a slaughtered hog but he slid off the edge of the bed, dropped to his knees and tears fell from his tightly scrunched eyes.

He keeled over onto his side, grabbing his bloody prick, hyperventilating with a flood of tears cascading down his face. To her surprise his gun had fallen from his waistband so she made haste, snatched it up and made a break for the door. She opened it to an audience. They must've thought the squeals were hers and not of their leader. She raised the gun in their direction no longer concerned with them having a clear view of her naked body. She slowly inched past the assembled group, gun still in hand.

"Excuse me, how do I get out of here?"

The stunned men could barely speak. They were in awe of her at the moment. Not just because she was nude but they wondered how this petite beauty overpowered a six foot two, two hundred and ten pound man. One of the men pointed toward the door leading to freedom and Natalia quickly exited, ran up the concrete steps leading from the hell hole.

She ended up in a back yard and it took her eyes a quick moment to adjust to the sunlight. Then she had the task of getting past a large vehicle parked at the side of the house that lead to the front of the house and the gate. Once she managed to squeeze by the vehicle and opened the gate she ran as fast as she could, gripping the gun in her hand.

"HELP ME!" she screamed while running down the gritty concrete. Dirt particles and sharp objects raked against the tender skin of the soles of her feet but it didn't slow her down one bit. The autumn chill raised all the hairs on her body to stand on end, manipulated her nipples to resemble thick pencil erasers, and irritated her clammy skin forcing an array of goose bumps to form all over her. She spotted cars in the street and ran out into the oncoming traffic waving her hands and shouting, "HELP! HELP ME, PLEASE!" She approached the first car waiting on the traffic light pleading for the elderly man inside to save her. The man sitting inside his pristine white Nissan Altima appeared to be too petrified. And as soon as the yellow traffic light dimmed he quickly maneuvered his car around her and sped off from her. Thankfully, the second car in line with a middle aged white woman inside pulled right up to Natalia's naked, blood-smeared body and she lowered her driver's side window, "Are you alright, honey?" the woman asked with trepidation.

"Please take me to a police station!"

The woman took one look at Natalia then her car and debated allowing this naked, bloody woman in her clean car. She grabbed a newspaper from her briefcase on the back seat, laid it out on the passenger seat and unlocked the door. Natalia sighed with a heap of relief as she carefully lowered her adequately sized gluteus maximus onto the course paper. She unconsciously dropped the gun on the floor of the car. Horns galore blared as pissed off drivers stuck behind the woman's sedan grew annoyed with the amount of time she spent blocking their way. The woman put her car in gear and stepped on the gas. A man swerved around her into oncoming traffic just to get from behind her. He slowed down as he neared the driver's side of the woman's car and shouted out his open window, "You dumb ass bitch!" before speeding off. The woman wasn't concerned with his road rage at the moment. She was too busy trying to figure out the deal with the strange, yet beautiful bloody woman she had let into her car.

"What's going on?" the woman probed as she stole looks at Natalia in between checking the rear view and side view mirrors. Natalia really didn't have the strength to go into the sordid details of the ignominy and fiasco that nearly claimed her life. She could barely wrap her mind around the past hours of her plagued existence. She stared out the darkly tinted window, surprised at how she could still recognize the colors of the blurred scenery whizzing by. The woman noticed that Natalia had mentally checked out of the vehicle.

Her aloof gaze out the window made it clear that she had no intention of answering questions. So the compassionate stranger accepted that Natalia must've been too traumatized for an inquisition so she backed off. After driving a few minutes she attempted to endear herself to Natalia by offering her name as well as her fresh piping hot cup of hot chocolate that she didn't get a chance to sample, sitting in the cup holder.

"I know you're probably not in the mood to talk but you should drink something hot. I just came from buying this hot chocolate at the Duncan Donuts drive thru," she said sweetly, motioning towards the cup with her hand. She saw that Natalia still refused to budge.

"I at least want to introduce myself. I'm Lucinda and you are...?" At first Natalia hadn't really paid any attention to the woman's moving lips. Then the fog lifted and she could tell that the woman was asking something.

"I'm sorry, what did you say?"

"I said, my name's Lucinda what's yours?"

"Natalia," she answered sheepishly, yet more so exhausted, defeated.

"Oh, that's pretty. Oh my stars, I'm sorry, I forgot to call the police."

"It's okay, I couldn't really tell them where to go...I don't know where I was... who that was..."

This new piece of information induced Lucinda's curiosity and she had to find out what would force a woman into the streets butt naked on such a cold day.

"I don't mean to pry but what happened to you?"

Natalia sighed, imagining respite from her dramatic life. She looked over at the kind woman's worn face, surmising that Lucinda had to be over fifty. For the first time since she'd been offered the hot chocolate she lifted it from the car's cup holder and took a sip to whet her whistle. Her parched throat was now hydrated enough for her to tell her story by reliving the hell she'd endured at the hands of the maniac seeking revenge on her husband. As her semi dry lips parted to dispense words, Lucinda's cell phone rang. It was a wake-up call for Natalia. She realized Shawn was probably worried sick about her, calling her cell phone like a madman. It would do him no good since it was in her purse which was probably lost forever now. Natalia turned to Lucinda and interrupted her call, "May I please use your phone to call my husband?"

"I'll call you back, Shay," Lucinda hurried her friend off the phone then passed her clam shell cell to Natalia. She was thoroughly interested to hear how this conversation was going to go.

"Daddy?" Natalia asked, full of emotion after hearing her husband's silk laden vocal chords utter the word, "Hello?"

"B.G.? Where are you? What the hell happened to you?"

"Daddy some men abducted me and they...they...," the thought of what Manny and his cohorts had done to her forced her to break down.

Lucinda pulled over to the side of the road and tried consoling her. Shawn was livid on the other end of the phone. He had put two and two together and instantly knew that whatever happened to his wife was caused by her

71

association with him. It pained him knowing that once again he'd brought a world of pain into her life.

"Tell me where you are, baby girl."

"I don't know...this woman, she helped me..." The woman acknowledged her cue and took the phone from Natalia's trembling hand, "Hello?"

"Where are you?" Shawn asked, impatiently.

The woman rattled off the cross streets to him, told him of his wife's lack of clothing and as usual Shawn hung up without so much as a goodbye or even a thank you. Natalia wept quietly, hunched over with her face in her hands. "Sweetie, I don't know what you've been through, but you need to know that you're safe now, Okay?" Lucinda rubbed her palm over the soft, bronzed skin protecting Natalia's vertebrae as she continued sobbing. You don't know the half, Natalia thought. She was thinking how Lucinda probably wouldn't be able to handle all of the shit she had dealt with. She was certain that Lucinda would be horrified at what she'd experienced, seen, endured.

Chapter VI
Revengeful Revelation
৵৶

Shawn was wrought with emotion as he rushed to the nearest clothing store he could find along the overly populated stretch of concrete and asphalt named Broadway. He double parked forgetting to switch on his hazard lights. At this point he did not give a damn about the greedy quota quelling-ticket issuing police officers that derived an obscene amount of pleasure from adorning New York City cars with the orange envelopes that every New Yorker detests. Shawn ran into the overpriced boutique demanded a coat, jeans, a sweater and boots all in his wife's size. He rushed the clerk throughout the entire purchase and threw more money than the whole outfit was worth at her then grabbed the bags and ran back out to his S.U.V.

Oddly enough he escaped the dreadful ticket monster's wrath. He smiled to himself as he shifted the Escalade into gear. He floored his gas pedal one too many times and nearly hit crossing pedestrians. His anger nearly consumed him to the point where he lashed out at the slow pedestrians impeding his mission. He was determined to rip apart whoever terrorized his wife. As he sped down Stanley Avenue in East New York he spotted the woman's dull grey car perched at the corner near a lamp post. He screeched into the empty spot behind it. He grabbed the bag of clothes from the passenger seat and quickly hopped out and ran toward the grey Camry. As he neared the passenger's side he could clearly see his wife flanked by a leather coat, shivering. The sight sent another bolt of anger through him. Whoever did this was sure to suffer. He pulled out the full length wool coat from the bag and tapped on the window. Natalia's longing stare as she turned to see her husband was enough to yank at his heart strings. She looked so vulnerable, so innocent and sad. The sparkle was gone from her eyes as they widened with what could only be construed as relief.

Lucinda maneuvered her arm around Natalia in order to press her forefinger down on the car door's unlock button. Shawn eagerly tugged at the handle. The door snapped ajar and he quickly helped Natalia stick her limp arms into the wool blend coat he bought. Once she was covered up, he reached into the bag for the box with the knee length boots. He took one out at a time passing them to his wife whose delicate fingers could barely palm the leather and it fell to the street.

"I'm s-sorry," she said to no one in particular and sniffled.

"It's okay, B.G.," Shawn assured her as he reached down and attempted to pass her the retrieved boot, "I have other clothes but since this coat is long we'll worry about you getting into the clothes later."

She took the boot and finally managed to get them close to her foot but her trembling hands prevented her from getting her bare feet into them successfully.

Lucinda saw that Natalia could barely function let alone be able to actually zip the boots up even if she did manage to get them on. She leaned over and gingerly eased Natalia's left foot into the boot then the other as Shawn passed it to her. She zipped up both boots.

Natalia smiled the words, thank you to Lucinda rather than speaking them. She was tired. Tired from her ordeal with yet another fine mess instigated by her husband. She felt overwhelmed from what she believed to be a case of hypothermia setting in from her exposed wet skin. It seemed that each eyelid held tons of weight and the inside of her chest burned like a fire searing her lungs.

"Thank you so much, Miss." Shawn said, with genuine appreciation written all over his face.

"You're quite welcome. She needs to be seen by a doctor. There's blood on her." The words leapt from her lips to his ear and panic flashed across his handsome face. He would definitely get his wife the best care his money could buy. And in his mind grotesque thoughts of death ran throughout. He would find who had perpetrated this despicable act and rip the very skin from their bones.

"I will get her to a hospital," he finally replied. He dug into his denim pockets and pulled out a wad of cash and gratefully leaned in the Camry to place it in Lucinda's hand.

"For all of your help and the inconvenience," he said handing her the money.

"Oh, no, please, it was no inconvenience. I just hope that she's going to be okay," smiled Lucinda genuinely happy to have been there to help save a life. She glanced down at the gun still lying on the passenger seat. "Excuse me," she said pointing at the gun. He glanced downward briefly, snatched it up, then effortlessly hoisted his wife into his arms and carried her off to his Escalade.

Lucinda watched as the Escalade drove out of sight. It wasn't until Shawn's vehicle turned off the main street and disappeared before she actually closed her mouth. She couldn't believe what had just happened. *I have to call someone, no one will believe me.* It was also then that she noticed the wad of money Shawn had tried to hand her laying on the floor. She composed herself enough to count the crisp bills balled up in her palm. She peeled off the first bill which was a twenty. She lifted another bill and another until she counted one thousand dollars in total.

"Nice," she said to her reflection in her rearview mirror, "Good guys don't finish last after all."

❧

75

Shawn smoothed Natalia's hair away from her face. She stared straight ahead and slowly inhaled then painfully exhaled. He already told himself that he wasn't going to grill her until they were sure that she was alright. So although he burned with questions, he refrained from verbalizing any of them. Inside of him anger from the thought that Natalia was raped had his blood boiling. He drove maniacally until he approached a hospital. He double parked once again but this time right in front of the hospital entrance. He ran to the passenger side, scooped up his wife cradling her in his arms, looking into her eyes he said, "It's okay, daddy's gonna get you some help." Natalia's vapid stare switched almost immediately and her hand reached up to the side of his chiseled jaw and for once since being around him she spoke.

"My hero," she said in a quiet whisper.

Shawn cracked half a smile as he rushed past all of the hospital workers; patients awaiting their turn in the triage room and doctors in green scrubs or white lab coats leisurely standing around in the emergency area. Despite the security guard hot on his trail he was determined to have his woman seen by a physician immediately. To him and now to any doctor he could ambush, his wife came first.

"Sir! Sir! Stop! Don't go back there!" the security guard yelled out to Shawn as he found an empty gurney and lay his wife on it. The security guard ran up behind him and was visibly agitated as he scolded, "Sir, I told you not to come back here. You have to wait in the waiting area."

"My wife needs a doctor right now. She was attacked."

"I understand that but there are others ahead of you that need immediate medical attention. You skipping ahead isn't fair. Now I can escort you to the waiting room or out of the building, your choice."

Shawn gave the security guard the evil eye and challenged him with, "I dare you to get me out of here. My wife needs a doctor now."

Natalia grew weary of the show down and finally said something to squash their beef,

"It's okay. Let's just go, Shawn." Not only did her giving in to the security guard's demand catch him off guard but hearing her say his name for the first time in a long time did him in.

"Baby girl, you need help and I'm going to get it for you."

Natalia gestured for her husband to come within whispering distance. The security guard sucked his teeth as he awaited the end of their stand off. Shawn leaned over to hear what his wife had to say.

"Daddy, I'll be fine. They didn't get to rape me...they only roughed me up. I just want to wash their grimy hand prints off of me and get some rest." Shawn's slanted eyes squinted with concern as he realized that he'd have to back down but he was more so relieved that his wife's prize possession had gone unscathed. He took her hand into his, caressing it gently and said,

"Whatever you want." He attempted to lift her from the gurney but Natalia discreetly stopped him.

"Wook, daddy I can walk," she giggled as she slid off the gurney. It was the first time she cracked a remote smile since her ordeal. Shawn smiled widely as he took notice of her angelic titter which returned a sparkle to her eyes.

Shawn knew that returning to 'their place in the sky' was no longer safe. He was sure that the same way they could locate his wife would be the same way they could stake out their apartment uptown. He had to switch things up a bit. He decided different hotels either daily or weekly would have to be their new M.O. So he booked a room at the W hotel and ordered some dinner to be awaiting their arrival. On the way to the hotel he asked her only one question, "B.G. I know you're probably not in the mood to answer me right now but I have to know, do you remember their faces?" She stared out the windshield at first trying to recall the images of the men who held her captive. Oddly enough, at that moment she wasn't afraid of the memories. All remembering did was infuriate her, drew out an immense desire within for revenge. She thought back to Manny's features. Every nuance of his face flooded her mind. The others were blurs, specs of brown...but Manny, the man of the hour; his image was fully in tact, down to the long puffy keloid scar that ran across the top of his chest, an obvious foiled attempt on his worthless life. One thing she felt at that particular moment while rumbling along the FDR drive was a sense of safety. She was certain that her man would avenge her.

"I remember the main guy. The one who told me that you killed his brother, er...Nee, Neelo? Um, no...er," she sat pensive, wracking her brain for the name. Then finally she shouted, "DENIRO!" Her outburst surprised him. Shawn's eyes grew as big as saucers. Here it was, yet another ghost from his past haunting him. First it was Maleek with the coded message to his sidekick via Faye and now this. Niro's ghost terrorized his wife in the form of revenge. His mind went a mile a minute as he recollected the despicable thing he'd done. The pool of urine that stunk so bad leaking from Niro as he sobbed; the weight of Niro's expired corpse slumped over his shoulder as he lugged it out to the car to dump it all had a permanent home in his memory. It was now that Shawn realized his past deeds were coming home to roost. Natalia gasped as the facts hit home. She'd been a pawn in Manny's vengeful game. A game instigated by Shawn. This revelation made her question everything.

"Daddy, did you really do what he said you did? Did you kill his brother?" she stared at him with baited breath awaiting the answer as if her very life depended upon it. Her husband was many things. An adulterer, drug dealer, even an ex-con but a murderer just couldn't be one of the many titles he held. That she couldn't and didn't want to believe regardless to what she knew he was capable of. He couldn't return his wife's gaze for he had lost respect for himself at that moment. How could he look her in her eyes knowingly withholding vital points that would help her to understand why she'd been singled out and brutally accosted? Natalia

78

instantly knew that her husbands' hesitation to further explicate could only be attributed to guilt, the kind of guilt that can cause one to implode. She had her answer even before he tried to string together a sensible sentence,

"B.G., I did...I did it because I had to. I know you're tired of hearing me apologize for ruining your life...causing you all this drama, but I really, truly am sorry, baby girl. None of this was supposed to happen. But know this, I will kill again. That dude that put his filthy fuckin' hands on you... I'm gonna rip that nigga apart."

Now Natalia questioned herself. Why in hell did hearing those disturbingly morbid words come from her husband's lips not only give her a perverse rush but a smidgeon of satisfaction?

"I want to be there. I want to spit in his face, daddy. I want you to humiliate him before killing him," she said, getting more vindictive with each thought.

"And to top it off, I want you to video tape his humiliation."

Just as he'd done to her, she was willing to have done to him. She didn't mention that there was a damning videotape of her piss swilling ordeal floating around to Shawn because she felt that he was riled up enough as it is.

Shawn slid the hotel room key into place and the lock lighted up as he pulled down its handle. He turned to his wife.

"They'll pay for everything they did to you," he smirked. A roguish glow consumed Natalia's ordinarily angelic face as she recalled the stench from the men's urine drowning her, seeping into her mouth. She unconsciously shivered and bolted to the bathroom. Shawn went in after her, "You alright?" he asked, concerned.

"I'm fine daddy, I just need to get clean."

She scrubbed her skin raw and brushed her teeth and gargled three times. She dried every spec of moisture from her body and tiptoed out of the bathroom until her stubby toes detected the plush carpet. Her feet sank into the

79

carpet's softness. She whipped off the towel from her head freeing her stringy tresses which slapped the nape of her neck then dangled midway down her back. Shawn was laid out on the plump king sized bed with his cell pressed to his ear. She knelt onto the bed and snuggled up next to his shirtless torso. He propped himself up against the pillows and continued his conversation, "So get back to me with that cuz this is some nine-eleven type shit, aiight?" Natalia deduced that the person on the other end must've agreed because as usual her man hung up without so much as a bye. He turned over onto his side, facing his wife and sweetly outlined her face's features with the back of his hand while adorning her face with delicate, apologetic pecks. She loved his display of remorse. It was better than words. With the last kiss ending on the tip of her nose.

"I've never been as sorry as I am right now for this happening to you and I know that I've been the cause of a lot of wrong in your life but you've been the cause of so much going right in mine. Like your love. I've never had that...it's crazy and all but at least we have it and it feels good."

"Oh, daddy," she gushed then pushed him over onto his back. He loved it when she attempted to be aggressive. It was cute but futile. She straddled him, leaning in to kiss his lips but he flipped her over instead regaining control. Her towel had come loose from around her so he hungrily sucked on her nipples, alternating between them, teasing each one with his tongue. She moaned in delight as she watched the tiny curls on his head as he ventured between her quivering thighs. Shawn made love to her with his salacious tongue until she drenched his face with her juices. He was so turned on that he decided to make his wife have another orgasm. He mounted her gently entering her and gyrating so that she felt every inch of him with each lingering stroke. He moved with precision, sensually slow. With each expert movement from Shawn, she felt waves of currents throughout her entire body. He steadily built the momentum until he knew she was about to reach her peak then he slowed down his pace just right until she lost her composure and begged for more which he happily obliged. Her body jerked then she screamed blissfully. Her ecstasy forced a load out of him.

"Whew!" he exclaimed after rolling off of her and exclaimed, "Damn B.G., that pussy is lethal!" he chuckled. She giggled and winked at him, "And don't you forget it." Just then his cell let out a loud PING and he picked it up to read the text message he just received. "Yea, it's coming down to the wire. I'm working on finding out where that nigga is hiding so don't worry. Judgment day is coming."

"Don't forget daddy, I want to be there for all of it. I want him to look up when you're shoving his own dick down his throat and I want him to see me and know that he's going to die because he fucked with the wrong woman! No, wait, you know what I want to do? I want to cut his shriveled up pecker off myself!"

Shawn looked at her incredulously then smiled to himself knowing he had never loved his wife as much as he did at that moment. She escaped the devil's lair and was strong enough to get past it and even plot revenge with him. His baby was gully and gorgeous. What more could he ask for?

Manny's cohorts had ran into the room where they watched helplessly as he rolled around on the floor, clutching his mangled man meat, releasing gut wrenching gurgles.

"You aiight son?" one of the men with a humongous nose, asked as he inched closer to Manny. The others all glared at him, eschewing his idiotic question. Two men ran over to him trying to help him to his feet. Manny was non-responsive and practically fought their attempts. The pain was too severe for him to comprehend their assistance.

"Man, we gotta get you off the floor...stop the bleeding or something." One of the men grabbed a thick cotton hooded sweatshirt from the filthy mattress and gingerly dropped it over Manny's bloody hands.

"Use that to press on it."

Manny adhered to the advice and wrapped most of the thick material around his penis. He let out a guttural growl as his friends lifted him from the floor.

"We gotta get you to the hospital. What if that shit falls off?" One of the men quizzed with a slight smirk. Manny quickly shook his head. He refused to go to the hospital because he assumed that Natalia had the police scouring the streets for him. He had to make a snap decision. Various scenarios ran through his head when he had to accept that his plan had unraveled. First order of business was to take drastic measures to elude the cops. Against his better judgment he practically whispered orders for his lackeys to set the dilapidated bi-level home they used to call the "clubhouse" which served as a part time drug lab and hide out ablaze. He cursed himself for bringing Natalia there since he originally planned not to. He'd thought of motels but knew that the noise would elicit too much attention, nosey motel patrons would have him in Central booking by now. He was sure that if Natalia remembered anything about where he held her or what he said to her and repeated them to her husband, Shawn was going to hunt him down like a dog. This was all bothersome to say the least because Manny was well aware of Shawn's capacity for revenge. He'd heard time and time again from his own brother who apparently was in awe of Shawn's ability to survive multiple gun shot wounds from various beefs. Not only did he survive the murder attempts but he managed to come back stronger, better even faster like the six million dollar man. Manny was shook and rightfully so. His plan was to lead Shawn to him but he would've had Natalia for leverage. Without her he felt like a sitting duck. Once the pain subsided Manny voiced his requirements a bit louder, "Get me to Wanda's house." He seemed pained with each utterance. His friends helped him out to an idling S.U.V.

Luckily for Manny his ex-girlfriend, the mother of his

only son fell short of becoming a registered nurse. But she succeeded at becoming a Family Nurse Practitioner. It took some convincing from his friends before she agreed to allow him to come into her house. After Manny filled her in with half truths she patched him up all while sputtering accusations of him being a sick reprobate. She yapped his ear off insinuating that he had done something awful to have the tip of his penis damn near severed by a woman's teeth. Not wanting to get her involved any further he chose not to explain exactly why he attempted to ram his dick down Natalia's throat. In retrospect he realized his inane error. He had made himself vulnerable and for what, a little head? It wasn't until now that it hit him how his compulsion for oral sex had muddled his plan to the point of a disastrous failure.

"So some bitch bites your shit off and you come to me to put it back together again?" she asked, with folded arms.

"Wanda, this is a really fucked up time to start some shit with me. I'm begging you to just do what you can. Gimme something for the pain and I'll owe you big time."

"Man, I don't know what you got yourself into this time but why are you bringing this shit to me?"

"Because I need you, baby, you know how we do."

"No, you mean how we used to do and that shit is over and done with. I care about you but this shit right here is too much," she gestured for him to look at his crotch. His eyes followed her pointed finger. Blood seeped through his expensive name brand jeans. His eyes watered as he relived Natalia's cannibalistic attack. Wanda picked up on Manny's pain and became sympathetic.

"Alright, alright. Come in the bathroom."
Many followed her to the bright blue and white oasis of terry cloth and seashells.

As Manny watched her dress his injured cock with gauze and surgical tape he knew he'd have to give her a little more to go on than just saying he was attacked. She kept inquiring so he went for broke and fed her a line about a Rottweiler attacking him during a FED raid. She didn't exactly eat it up but it slowed down her inquisitiveness. After spouting lies he pleaded with her to keep her mouth shut about what she'd seen. She reluctantly agreed to clam up about what she had to do for him and not to give out any information to any detectives or anyone for that matter that just might come a knocking.

Wanda packed up her emergency kit, threw the wads of bloody ace bandages in a plastic bag and tied it closed. She moved about swiftly as if on a mission to erase any traces of his affliction. She looked up in time to catch his curious stare. Manny inched closer to her as she stood up from crouching. He pulled her into his arms and affectionately squeezed her.

"Thanks baby. I really appreciate what you did tonight."

She pulled away from him, "Your welcome Manny but I don't want to catch wreck behind this. So you have to go."

Manny looked at her in disbelief. She used to be his down ass bitch; the kind that would have your back when you went up North and needed dough for commissary. She was the kind of woman that would wake up at four in the morning so that she wouldn't miss the bus going upstate to make that obligatory prison visit. The kind of chick that would flash you with a peek at her breasts then steal seconds to discreetly jerk you off right in the visitor's room. He remembered those days of yesteryear when she sent him all kinds of goodies including pictures with close-ups of her *goodies*. He remembered the days of her fattening up his commissary and sending boxes of valuable canned goods, candy and books for him to barter with. When he was on lockdown she held him down.

"Babe, don't make me have to walk out of here with my dick all fucked up like this," he cupped his hand over his denim clad crotch.

"Hey, you caused this so deal with it," she spat regretting helping him now. When she was his woman he played her for a fool over and over and now here he was expecting her to play that part once again. This was a no win situation for Manny because Wanda's life had progressed to

84

the point where she found a good man. The kind of man who respected her, had a respectful job and helped her raise Manny's son since he didn't. He asked her to marry him and gave her a ring to prove it; unlike Manny's feeble attempt to string her along when he bought her a gold electroplated ring overwhelmed with a hulking Cubic Zirconia and tried passing it off as the real deal.

She walked away from him and pointed to the front door. Manny sucked his teeth and said, "You don't want me to leave. Don't do that. Don't be cold like that baby," he slipped an arm around her waist. He tried pulling her into him but she resisted.

"Stop playing, Manny. I patched you up now leave. We go way back so that's why I helped you but you ain't change. You are still out there doing dumb shit like back in the days as if you're still a teenager. I can't be bothered. And my fiancée's shift ends in another five minutes."

"Fiancée?" Manny chuckled then snidely remarked, "You on some shit. So you wanna throw that up in my face and kick me out? You is a cold bitch but, it's aiight. I should fuckin' stay and meet this lame ass dude you got around my son."

"Hmn. Your son? Nigga that boy wouldn't know you from a bum on the street!" she spat.

"Bitch don't disrespect me. And if he don't know me it's cuz I probably ain't his damn daddy."

"Oh, really? You really wanna go that route?"

Manny grew angrier by the minute and raised his hand to her. She flinched at first but quickly became brazen enough to stand up to him.

"You ain't stupid. Now get the hell out of my house."

Manny just stood there looking at her. This wasn't how it was supposed to be going down. He already had the shit planned out in his head. He was waiting for her to get emotional, start crying and then all he'd have to do is say that he was sorry and she'd forgive him. He expected her to choose him over her fiancée' and allow him to stay. But she didn't.

This was cutting to the core because he really did want to spend the night. One thing he had never found in any other female he'd dealt with was the sweetness she appeared to be made of. He always told her how she had picked the perfect profession because she was very caring.

She had always been domesticated and she used to take care of him the way most men wished for. She used to be obedient. He didn't like this newfound strength she displayed tonight. His brow furrowed and he contemplated saying something nasty and hurtful but decided against it.

"Aiight, Wa-Wa, I'ma leave," he said calling her bluff as he slowed down his walk as he passed her. This was her last chance, but she didn't make eye contact. He walked out into the hallway and heard the door slam behind him. He sighed as he flipped open his cell to call another woman he could sweet talk into allowing him to spend the night.

⊷❦⊶

Manny knew that with each hour that passed was more time for Shawn to either skip town or come gunning for him. He spent the night in constant pain. His penis was still sore and he couldn't clear his mind enough to catch a wink of sleep. He wondered whether he was a wanted man; wanted by the cops or worse, by his brother's murderer. He fished out the remote from under the covers and turned on the television surfing for a news broadcast. He expected to see Natalia recounting her ordeal to a reporter. He turned up the volume on the television, listening intently to each word the anchor man eloquently spoke. The woman who allowed him to share her bed was not about to lose the half hour of sleep that she had left before having to start her busy day. She grabbed the remote from his hand and turned off the T.V.

"What's wrong with you?" Manny asked, irritated.

"I need to sleep," she murmured, rolled over and snuggled up to the thick comforter balled up on her side of the bed. Manny sneered at her, snatched the covers from her and hopped out of the bed.

"Stop Manny!" she hollered.

"Shut up."

"You shut up! Better yet, get out!"

"I was leaving anyway you stupid bitch," he spat while getting dressed. He left with her on his heels cursing him out.

Manny stood outside a corner bodega smoking a cigarette and quizzing someone on the other end of his cell trying to find out if there was any word out on the streets about Shawn's whereabouts. He also needed to know if Natalia had made the morning news. This would determine how his day would play out. He told the person he needed a ride and he waited impatiently thinking of a new master plan. All of his original plans were dashed and he was determined now more than ever to fill Shawn with lead. Killing Natalia right in front of him first would be a much added bonus. After finishing his cigarette he made another phone call. During his call, a burgundy Suburban screeched to a halt right in front of the bus stop near the bodega. Manny's penis was irritated even more so as he waddled toward the enormous jeep. He tried not to let the irritation affect his stride but it was evident that he was suffering.

"Yea, that fuckin' bitch tried to bite my shit off!" he grumbled into the phone as he stepped up into the massive vehicle. As he adjusted himself in the seat he told the person on his cell phone to call him back when they had news. He turned to the driver and asked, "So did you find out where he's at?"

"Not yet. It's like everything is on lock right now. I tried to holla at this girl I know that works at his restaurant and she made it seem like he left NY already. But I sent Bain and em' to ask around too," the driver motioned toward the man sitting directly behind him. Manny was disturbed when he heard this. He turned around to address Bain and the other men in the backseat.

"None of y'all got real news?" The men shook their heads and shrugged.

"If that nigga is on the run that makes it that much harder for us to find his ass!" he yelled. The driver started to speak but Manny's cell rang and he flipped it open with an attitude.

"What?" He snarled as he listened patiently for a moment then calmly said, "I'ma get that to you aiight. Stop stressing me over some petty shit. I have bigger problems right now," he spat into the compact silver cell phone pressed against his ear. He slammed the cell shut then gave the driver his undivided attention again. "Now what were you saying?"

"Yo, P.B. must've left New York. That girl was talking like he did."

"Did she say that for sure?"

"She told me that he came in the restaurant yesterday and took all the money and had a long meeting with the manager but then she shut down on me."

"He ain't gonna go nowhere after what happened to his bitch."

"Well he just might, seein' as how they probably think she bit your dick off," he couldn't hold in his laughter. The men in the back joined in. Manny was heated and didn't find the humor in his misfortune.

"That shit ain't funny. Fuck y'all!" he sulked. There was more joking at his expense but he sucked it up knowing that if it happened to one of them he'd be the first to be laughing his ass off. He had to admit that his predicament was hilarious. His phone rang again,

"What's good?" he asked hopeful for good news. But it was more of the same. "Damn so nobody's talking? Well, Y'all niggaz better find him before he finds us," he mumbled then hung up, agitated.

The big burgundy truck turned down a desolate block laden with factories and boarded up condemned buildings. Manny looked over at the driver and asked, "Why you turn down here?"

"We'll get there quicker if we go down Cozine."

Manny shrugged it off and returned to gazing out the

window. Now the vehicle slowed down towards the middle of the block where a bunch of crack heads had assembled.

"Why you stopping?" Manny grumbled.

"Um, I gotta get this money right quick," the driver seemed skittish as he hopped out the S.U.V. then suspiciously ran down the block in the opposite direction of the crack heads. Now all the men left in the vehicle were confused. Three men who had been crouched down behind the crack heads stood up and walked out in front of them with automatic weapons aimed at the windows of the Suburban. The men in the back seat panicked and tried to exit the vehicle on the other side but to their dismay, two armed men awaited their egression. Before they could even make it out of the looming vehicle they were ambushed. Bain was the first to drop. Manny was forced to watch his friend's body being dragged on the gritty concrete like a rag doll. There was no gun shot so Manny couldn't figure out what happened to Bain. There was no blood either. Then he looked up from Bain's lifeless body to what appeared to be a body builder. The man who blocked his vision was massive. His shoulders seemingly spread from one end of eternity to the other. His neck was so thick Manny swore the man was a figment of his imagination. The gigantic building structured from cinnamon-colored flesh practically plucked him from the Suburban and threw him onto the floor next to Bain.

"Remember me?" He heard an angelic voice ask from behind as a sharp object was jabbed against the back of his head. The body builder ordered him to get on his feet. He struggled to raise himself from the floor so the monstrous stranger snatched him up from the floor in one effortless swoop. Manny was flustered as he apprehensively turned toward the direction of the voice.

There stood a honey glazed beauty that he recognized almost immediately. It was Natalia bearing a devilish smirk highlighted by glossy pink lips. Manny's trepidation drove him to gulp down his own saliva, his knees weakened as he perspired like a five hundred pound man in a sauna. Shawn emerged from the shadows as if out of a scene from a slasher movie. Manny could feel the penetrating beams of anger emitting from his icy stare.

"So, this is the nigga that disrespected my wife?"

Shawn, gently moved his wife aside and walked over to where Manny stood. "Let him go Stew. He ain't gonna do nothing stupid, right?" he addressed the question to Manny personally, still ice grilling him. He was now standing within striking distance of Shawn yet Manny felt paralyzed, frozen. Shawn swiftly bitch slapped Manny. The thunderous backhanded hit dazed Manny. Then Shawn asked his question once more.

"I said you ain't gonna do nothing stupid, right?"

Besides the humiliation, the slap hurt like hell. Manny instinctively rubbed his sore cheek and attempted to punch Shawn who blocked it, countering it with a powerful blow to Manny's left cheek. Manny stumbled back into Stew's awaiting arms. Stew put pressure on Manny's arms as he held them to his sides. Shawn smiled eerily and repeated his question,

"Let's try this again. You're not going to do anything stupid, right?"

Manny was almost out of breath, defeated and embarrassed.

"NO, MOTHERFUCKER!" he angrily shouted.

"Oh, you've got balls. I was starting to think you wouldn't give me a chance to have some real fun."

Manny understood now, he wasn't going to be killed tonight; he was going to be tortured. He fucked with the wrong one. Now payback was really a bitch, Natalia. Manny's eyes slowly searched the night for her.

He couldn't seem to focus long enough to make out most of the shadowy figures. He couldn't locate her silhouette so he turned his attention back to Shawn.

"I'm not gon' beg you for shit nigga, not for my life or for you to go easy on me. I'm not begging you for nothing. You killed my brother so you had to be dealt with."

Manny secretly hoped his reasoning would be

considered. He wished that Shawn would forego his anger about what happened to Natalia and feel as though they were now even. Manny wished for his life to end quickly right there on the desolate dead end block. He fretted the inevitable. It was clear that Shawn intended to punish him beyond the normal limits of human tolerance.

Bain awoke from the nap caused by Big Stew lulling him to the pavement with his bulging biceps. He sprang to his feet and sprinted down the block. Before anyone knew what was happening Shawn's M9 pistol complete with silencer was aimed at the fleeing man. A slight whir was all that was heard and Bain's head snapped forward then his whole body collapsed. Shawn grinned then looked down on the remaining last two of Manny's entourage and asked, "Anybody else have somewhere else they need to be?" The men remained silent before one shouted,

"Man I ain't got shit to do with this. Come on man, I got a brand new baby boy! Please just let me go I won't say shit." he groused.

Shawn directed his attention to Manny, "So should I set your boy free?"

"This is your show," Manny said through gritted teeth, indicating that he was in a world of pain. He was upset with his friend for being cowardly. But in the back of his mind he knew he'd probably do the same if the roles were reversed. Shawn looked down at the pleading man and said, "Well you're boy here ain't even vouching for you son. Damn, how you rocking with a nigga that don't give a fuck about your seed?"

The man was now in survivor mode so he slowly began to lift the top half of his body from the floor.

"I ain't say you could get up," Shawn reminded him, kicking him in the side of his head with his crocodile Maury loafers.

"Awww, shit!" he clutched at the lump forming at his temple, rubbing it he said, "I don't know what he did to you... but I ain't have nothing to do with it. I'm willing to help you man. Whatever you need but I gotta be around for my son. He

91

needs his father man, I'm begging you. Ain't no shame here man, I gotta live."

Shawn didn't appreciate this turncoat's pleading. The worst that one of his crew could ever do was to display disloyalty in this fashion. That irked his nerves. Manny's poor selection in friends prompted Shawn to shake his head and patronizingly say, "Tsk, tsk." He decided to grant the man a make believe reprieve.

"Aiight, I understand. Even though your man right here don't care about you or your kid, I'ma let you go. Just don't say shit to nobody you hear me?"

Stew and Shawn's other accomplices looked at him as if he had lost his mind. But Shawn maintained eye contact with the grateful man who hopped up from the floor and began thanking Shawn relentlessly. Manny was no fool. He knew better. As the man turned to run away he too was shot with Shawn's favorite handgun. The bullet went straight through the betrayer's left rib cage and shattered a window of a boarded up house. He yelped, stumbled and slowly attempted to drag himself away from Shawn.

Shawn was perturbed when he was forced to walk up on the traitor and plug him at point blank range in the top of his head. Shawn forcefully exhaled as if he had lifted a five hundred pound barbell.

"Man, y'all niggaz are stupid." He chuckled maniacally which quickly morphed into sinister laughter. The rest of his crew joined in. Unexpectedly, Big Stew pulled out his gun and released a bullet into the head of Manny's only remaining colleague. Manny cringed at the blood gushing out of his friend's head, his knees gave out and he dropped to ground, shaking his head.

With all the death happening around her, Natalia was the least bit turned off or afraid. Fervor led her adrenaline rush. She wanted a piece of the action. She went over to her husband and whispered, "Daddy give me your gun." He looked at his dainty wife, surprised by her insistence, "Are you serious?" he asked, his voice hushed. Mischief danced across her pouty lips as she purred, "As a heart attack."

Shawn took her small hand into his and led her further away from the others and said, "B.G., I have plans for this dude. I don't want him to die easy. So don't worry you'll get your chance to pay him back."

This was enough to keep her quiet as Shawn returned to his stance in front of Manny. Big Stew yanked Manny off the floor, forcing him to his feet. Manny stood tall, puffing out his chest like a peacock trying to impress female peacocks during mating season. Shawn was hardly convinced. "So you ain't gonna beg me for you life?"

"Naw, I'm a man about mine," Manny tried in vain to continue putting on a brave front. Shawn snuffed him—hard. He drew back his knuckle and saw the imprint of Manny's teeth. Manny's head was jerked to the side by the blow, his mouth leaked blood. The hit was so powerful that it forced two of his teeth to commit suicide by vacating their once permanent home inside his mouth. He spit out blood and teeth guts onto the hot pavement, glaring at his attacker.

"Yea, you keep up the tough guy act. I like that."

Shawn nodded slightly, running his left hand over the bright red skin covering the knuckles on his right hand. The story Natalia told him of the horror she endured at Manny's behest came to mind and Shawn clenched his jaw then asked, "So did you feel like a man when you pissed in that pretty woman's face?" he gestured toward his wife, his fist still balled up.

"I'ma fuckin' man so I'ma die like one!" Manny replied, exposing teeth pulp, roots and all, sputtering blood and saliva. From the minute the words left his lips, Manny felt like a ton of bricks were pulverizing his face and head. The night blurred into nothingness then finally consciousness eluded him.

Chapter VI
Death to Manny
❧

When Manny came to, his nose was swollen, stung like hell, even his head rang. His puffy eyes felt heavier than an elephant and were too blurry for him to make out any of his surroundings. His whole body ached and he was certain that his nose was broken since breathing had become a chore. He heard someone whimpering like a wounded animal. He couldn't make out what or who it was. His arms were tied in front of him so he brought his bound wrists up to his face and wiped away what he later realized was blood from his eyes. His vision was still blurred but now he was able to see two figures tied to a chair across from him. One was a woman in a blind fold that covered not just her eyes but her nose too and part of her mouth. The woman seemed so familiar. There was another familiar face. He figured out who it was instantly. It was the driver who betrayed him, brought him down the dilapidated block and abandoned him and the rest of his boys.

The driver wasn't blindfolded so he could clearly see Manny's piercing stare in his direction. His voice was filled with shame as he copped a plea, "I'm sorry man. I'm so fuckin' sorry." The tracks of ash decorating his face indicated he had been crying profusely.

"You fuckin' bitch ass nigga!" Manny spewed, angrily, "How the fuck you gon' do me like that Greg? We've been dogs from way back."

"I don't know man...I didn't want to die," Greg broke down, his eyes flooded with tears as he sobbed.

"You did that shit to save your own ass? Now look

where you at you dumb fuck!"

"I know, man, I know," Greg slobbered. Manny shook his head in disgust and turned his attention to the blindfolded woman. Her head was propped up somewhat by the bars on the back of the chair. She was tied to the chair right next to Greg. Her chest rose ever so slightly repeatedly so she appeared to be asleep.

"Who's that?" Manny gestured with his chin. Greg cried even harder.

"What the fuck is wrong with you man? Man up and stop crying like a bitch!" Manny chastised. Greg just couldn't stop, the tears kept coming and his chest heaved with each jerking sob. Manny watched and waited for the waterworks to subside. He was truly curious as to the identity of the mystery woman. Greg tried as best he could to compose himself then in a weakening voice he sobbed,

"I didn't know, man. Believe me I ain't know they was gonna get her."

"Get who?"

"Wanda," Greg sniffled. Manny's eyes widened. His heart practically stopped briefly as he affixed his gaze to the woman in the chair. He stared and stared until the uncertainty dissipated. He surveyed her posture in the chair, inspecting the visible parts of her face. Then he noticed something above where her nurse's uniform was torn from the seam around her arm. The one thing that proved this woman was his son's mother. It was a heart tattoo with the initials M.V. inside it on her right collar bone. The tattoo she bitched about having to remove as soon as she could afford to. The tattoo he paid for to brand her his woman and watched as it was expertly etched into her delicate pecan-colored flesh.

"Wanda?" he flung his head back in woe, contorting his face from the emotional pain wrenching within him. He realized that his stunt with Natalia would not only cost him his life but that of the mother of his only child. What had he started? He felt lower than scum at that moment. He looked up at Greg who only avoided his eyes, "Why man? How'd they even know about her? Why are they bringing her into this?" he shook his head solemnly.

"I don't know man. They ain't tell me nothing. They just tied me up next to her." Greg sniffled again but snot still escaped his snort and dribbled down to his top lip.

Manny attempted to stand up but quickly realized that his feet were wound tightly to the chair with electrical cords. He looked around trying to figure out where he was. The room was lit by a couple of portable lamps. He could see the black soot coating the walls. The place was rank with the smell of burnt ember. He saw puddles of dark grayish liquid. It was then that it dawned on him that he was in his own spot. The very place he himself dubbed the "clubhouse" and ordered it to be burned down to evade capture. Knowing all the rumors about Pretty Boy still hadn't prepared him for his cunning. He couldn't comprehend Shawn's capacity for revenge. Now the mother of his child would suffer for his limited range of preparation against an adversary out of his league. Guilt consumed him then spit him back out, back to reality to face...

"Hey, pussy cat, you up?" Shawn waltzed over to Manny then said, "See? I'm real considerate. I brought you company, our favorite dude and your girl."

"She ain't my girl. She ain't do nothing, man. Let her go!" Manny sounded like he was giving an order and this only angered Shawn.

"Let her go? You fuckin' pissed in my wife's face! She ain't do nothing to you, did she? No, she didn't, but you did that disrespectful shit to her anyway. Then you tried to make her suck your dick nigga?" Shawn asked rhetorically, disdain evident in his expression.

"Look man, this is between me and you. Don't do this. Do whatever to me but not her."

Shawn grew tired of listening to Manny rattle off commands as if he were running the show. Shawn grabbed a clump of Wanda's hair, yanking her head forward then he shook it. She came to and began screaming. Shawn snatched her head back on an angle then said, "You know, I just drank a lot of water. So you know what that means don't you?" he laughed while pulling out his mound of manhood. He proceeded to relieve himself all over her face. She began screaming and gurgling. He made a point to aim for her open mouth, jiggled his penis over her mouth while pulling her lips apart making sure it all dripped directly in. Wanda thrashed her head about, squirming, unavoidably swallowing while panicking, screaming and crying. Manny hung his head to fight back tears of anger. He didn't want Shawn to see how affected he was by it all. But Shawn knew that he was and decided to add insult to injury. "Now I'd do what you did and force feed her my dick but your ugly ass bitch don't do shit for me, man. My dick won't even get hard." Shawn slapped Wanda's face with his flaccid penis and his associates all laughed, then he yelled, "NEXT!"

One after the other Shawn's people came over and unloaded ounces of urine all over Wanda. With every unzipped zipper, Manny felt a part of him die. He was helpless. After the last man zipped up his pants Shawn demanded that Wanda be taken away. Manny didn't know her fate as he watched her thrashing about and screaming as she was being drug out of the half burned shack. The fear of the unknown injected him with a heaping dose of testosterone. He tried desperately to get out of the fetters securing him to the chair while shouting, "I'LL KILL ALL YOU MOTHERFUCKERS!"

Natalia slinked over and stopped his bantering with a flying kick to his face. He keeled over with the chair. She looked down on him, pressed the sole of her pointy shoe up against his neck and sweetly asked, "Do you feel helpless? Scared?" Manny kept squirming under the pressure of her foot, grunting and mumbling incoherently.

"Daddy, I think he's a star."

"Yea, B.G.? Well then let's put him in our movie." Shawn signaled to someone in the corner who walked over with a digital camcorder in hand. He had been filming all along.

"You're the star of my movie. Remember how you

97

made me a star in yours?" she asked Manny, pushing her foot down hard against his throat with each word. All of the taunting laughter she had endured at his hands rushed into her head, reminding her, disgusting her. She looked around the place where she'd been treated like shit. It was his turn. She knelt and grabbed at his belt buckle as she'd done before when he tried to force her to gag on pencil dick. Manny flopped about, raising his bound wrists trying to stop Natalia. Shawn realized what Natalia was up to and he ordered his men to lift Manny and the cheap metal folding chair and to put his hands behind his back. Natalia watched as they unwound Manny's hands, positioned them behind him and secured them once again. Now Manny was totally at her mercy.

Big Stew walked over to Natalia and opened his hand. She took the deluxe hunter's knife from his large palm and knelt in front of Manny. She placed the knife on the damp floor beside her and unzipped his pants. Natalia yanked the soft fleshy bulge from the opening in his boxers with one hand and picked up the knife with the other. He winced in horror as Natalia stretched his dick lengthwise then pressed the blade of the huge knife against its base. "NOOOO!!!" Manny yelled. Natalia began to easily slice into his shaft's flesh. The sight of his penis meat separating with blood drizzling onto the knife as it created a neat slit made Natalia queasy. She coughed then vomited all over Manny's trembling knees. She ran from the room, embarrassed. A tear escaped his eye as the crisp air hit his exposed wound inflicting searing pain. Although Shawn wanted to finish what his wife had started he wasn't about to touch another man's dick. He untied Greg and forced him at gun point to finish the job.

"If you want to live you better cut that shit off!" he demanded.

Greg's trembling hands kept dropping the knife as he tried not to look up into the face of his best friend. Manny pleaded with Greg over and over but Greg was too concerned with his own life. With one final grind of the knife Manny's penis came off and he howled. Manny's disturbing scream was too loud for his taste.

"Shove that shit down his throat!" Greg did as he was told then passed out along with Manny.

Shawn used smelling salt to wake Manny up who quickly realized that there was something in his mouth. Then he remembered what it was, his own penis! He instantly spit it out and looked down between his legs. There was an ice pack where his dick used to be. Manny growled from pain, frustration and overwhelming feeling of loss. He looked around and saw Greg strewn across the floor, bleeding from a gun shot wound in his chest. This did not offer any comfort. Now he felt woozy, tired and weak but he was still lucid enough to understand what Shawn was saying. He tried to focus on Shawn's face as he came closer.

"I was gonna be nice and take you out of your misery...I was. But I think that I'll be even nicer. I'm going to let you live. I mean it's the least I can do." Manny wasn't sure that he heard him right. Did he say he would leave him alive? Then Manny thought of what kind of life would he live without his penis. That would be more punishment than death. He'd not only be a eunuch but a walking billboard for Shawn's handy work and that was the last thing he'd want.

"Kill me..." Manny managed to mumble.

"What'd you say?"

"Kill me!" he replied even louder this time around.

Shawn intended on leaving him alive to advertise what could happen to anyone who messed with him. They wouldn't be killed. They would be left to live a miserable, painful, useless life. The only thing that made Shawn rethink his original plan was the fact that he wanted to stay in New York a while longer until his realty plans were completed in New Jersey. He couldn't chance the police investigating him now.

"Aw, come on man. You a man remember? Don't ask for the easy way out. Be strong brother," Shawn chuckled.

"I'm begging you," Manny finally relented. Shawn took one last disconcerting look at Manny before he gave him his wish. He doused Manny with lighter fluid and Stew lit a match and threw it at him laughing and saying, "Damn this is like déjà vu." Manny screamed while his flesh crackled practically melting right off his bones.

"Smells like a barbecue," Stew said, smacking his lips.

"Let's get some barbecued chicken?" Shawn grinned as they left Manny's heap of charred, melded flesh ablaze.

Chapter VII
Best Laid Plans
ॐॐ

Faye had spilled the beans and left Talea aghast. Natalia had ruined her life. In fact she actually thought how a death contract would've been better than her current circumstances. Talea was reminded constantly of how Natalia had wronged her. She couldn't leave the house without wearing a baseball cap, huge dark sunglasses and pounds of make-up to hide her hideousness; all because of Natalia, the woman who seemed to have it all. No matter what, Natalia would not go unscathed. She was lucky to have Shawn and her beauty. But Talea planned on lessening those odds. She packed a bag and headed for the bank. She relieved her account of 20 grand. Faye and Talea agreed that they would be avenged. Their revenge would be costly but well worth it. Faye's brother lived in New York and heard all about the fervor surrounding the infamous duo, Natalia and Shawn. Faye's brother convinced her that he could put a contract on Natalia for as little as twenty thousand dollars. Faye wanted to see Natalia get hers so she talked Talea into taking an impromptu vacation to the Big Apple.

Talea's nervousness wasn't because she sat on a plane but mostly from the fact that her traveling partner was missing. With each face peering through the first class curtains she stirred with hope. After a few people came aboard that weren't Faye, she accepted that she just might be flying solo.

"Miss?" she called out to a passing stewardess.

"Can you freshen this up?" she handed the young

woman her glass with a gulps worth of a Mimosa.

Moments later the plane began to jerk forward and Talea watched as the airport shrank with each mile as the plane approached the runway. As Talea checked her watch, a woman flanked with magazines and a shoulder bag whisked through the curtain, flouncing towards her.

"You were supposed to meet me at the departure gate inside the airport," Faye huffed as she flopped down beside Talea. "Girl, I waited for you and you ain't show up so I boarded the plane."

"I'm so fed up with always having to take all my shit off for those airport rent-a-cops. I practically had to strip for the mother fuckers!" Talea was embarrassed by Faye's foul mouth. She looked around them to see who was listening. A few wide eyed Caucasians signaled disapproval with their condescending stares before returning their focus to whatever they'd been doing before Faye's crass announcement.

"Faye, watch your mouth."

"What? Bitch, please," Faye playfully hissed. Talea gave her the kind of look that mother's give their children when they've been naughty.

"I'm just saying, we're in first class so you know how a lot of these people are," she spoke in a hushed tone.

"So? I don't give a fuck about any of them. Anyway girl, I spoke to my brother—"

"Which one, Jerome?" she asked, hopeful.

"No, Hayden. Why?"

"No reason, just wondering," she lied. From the day she met Faye's youngest brother, Jerome she was smitten. She attempted to make a move and he almost bit but because of his Army reserves status he traveled far too much for her to effectively stake her claim on him. Now that her face was like silly putty she was relieved that he was shipped off to Iraq to fight Bush's farce of a war. She definitely didn't want him seeing her at her worst. Fay glanced over at her and giggled, "You still want Joo-Joo, huh? Mmn, that boy got you open."

"Stop calling him that. He's a grown ass man!" she laughed then added, "And you know you're brother is fine!"

"Just like everyone in the family," Faye, twisted her mouth and jerked her neck then said, "But he's staying with Hayden when he gets back from Iraq tomorrow so you'll be able to see him."

Panic flashed across Talea's patched face. This would be a disaster.

"I can't see him, Faye, I just can't."

"Talea, trust me he won't care. I don't know why y'all never took it there because you were both crushing on each other," she smiled and finished with, "I never got the chance to tell you recently but you look so much more like yourself now. I know that's not what you want to hear but to me you're still very pretty," Faye spoke genuinely. Talea had been used to her beauty for so long that to her, any variation from what she'd grown accustomed to wasn't good enough. Although her scars weren't prominent they were very much visible and that detracted from her looks in her book.

"Thanks, Faye."

Her eyes glossed over so she turned to look out the window and watched as the plane glided over cottony clouds. Consciously she drifted off the airplane for a moment, idling above Earth's rich colors. Nature's beauty reminded her of her own lost beauty and she rued the day she met Natalia Foles.

⸙

The plane taxied the runway smoothly. A sleeping ex-beauty arose to her friend's light nudging.

"Huh?" she lifted her head from the window's glass pane.

"We're in New York, girl!" Faye screeched with enthusiasm then grabbed her bag from under her seat and searched for her cell phone. The plane door ascended and Talea and Faye were the first to leave. Faye called her brother as they walked toward baggage claim. A familiar voice answered on the other line.

"Joo-Joo?" she squealed with delight. After hearing that nick name, Talea sighed with regret. She truly was afraid to face him. Faye babbled on and on and Talea grew agitated with both Faye and awaiting her suitcase's debut on the luggage conveyor. Finally the red suitcase slid out from behind the rubber flaps and down the belt. Talea dragged it off and stood with folded arms as she asked, "So we have to take a cab, right?"

"Nope, they're here already," Faye grinned and continued speaking into her cell phone. Talea pulled up the telescopic handle on her suitcase and began walking with it in tow. As they left baggage claim a white Denali pulled up with a handsome man hanging halfway out the window grinning from ear to ear. Talea felt her heart jump and instinctively slid her hand up to partially cover her face.

"Joo-Joo!" Faye hollered and ran towards the vehicle. Jeremy jumped out the passenger's side. They embraced and Jeremy lifted his sister from the ground and whirled her around.

"Look at you!" she exclaimed, proudly.

"Damn, if you weren't my sister...," Jeremy laughed and turned just in time to catch a glimpse of Talea's face before she turned her back on him.

"Is that Talea?" Jerome asked in a hushed tone.

"Yes. I know that Hayden told you what happened already so don't stare and be real careful of what you say. She is fragile right now." More curious than anything Jerome inched over to Talea then gently touched her arm, "Talea?"

She was too anxious and afraid to turn around. Jeremy walked around to face her taking hold of her arms, he pulled her in for a hug. At first Talea resisted but gave in after feeling his powerful arms encircle her. His intoxicating cologne invaded her nostrils. She breathed him in, relishing his touch and the closeness. It was the first real taste of intimacy she'd received since her attack. He was the first man who wasn't a family member to pay her this much attention, come this close or tenderly embrace her with such care. The embrace lingered longer than either of them expected. It was more than a welcome back. It was the kind of hug that led to baby making. Jeremy slowly released her from his tight squeeze. He finally got the chance to gaze into her eyes again as he'd done so long ago. To him she was still attractive. Granted she had scars that took away from the face he once knew but she was still prettier than most. They never sealed the deal so to speak, so in his eyes, Talea was the one who got away.

"Hey girl, don't I get a kiss?" he leaned in before she could answer and pressed his lips onto hers. She obliged him, eagerly kissing back. Color bloomed in her cheeks as he pried his lips from hers.

"You still got nice lips," he complimented her with a glazed look on his face. He made her day regardless if it was piteous or not.

"You're still a sweet talker," she gushed. He tipped her chin with his forefinger and told her, "I heard what happened and we're gonna get that bitch back for what she did. And don't you worry because you're still beautiful to me." Talea's eyes watered and she smiled to let Jeremy know that they weren't sad tears. He'd done her justice with his words alone.

"Thanks," she said close to a whisper as their faces inched closer slowly, her lips slightly puckering to meet his.

"Come on lovebirds!" Faye shouted out the window. Talea snapped to attention, and she nervously pulled away from Jerome's arms and alluring stare. He grabbed her hand as she attempted to get into the S.U.V.

"Wait, we haven't finished conversing," Jerome informed her. She looked back at him and smiled briefly, then jumped down from the massive vehicle. He followed her.

"Listen, Talea, I know you know how much love I have

for you, right?"

He was embarrassing her now. She knew he had a crush on her but she thought he grew out of it. She was wrong.

"I have a lot of love for you too."

"Oooh, look at y'all," Faye intruded on their private moment and rested her head on her younger brother's shoulder, grabbing his biceps and squeezing,

"So it's back on?"

"Be quiet, Faye," Jerome shook his head, wiggling free from his sister's grip. Talea motioned for Faye to follow her.

"Faye, you gotta stop pushing us," Talea confided in her friend as they walked toward the curb.

"Hey, I call it like I see it. Y'all know damn well y'all wanna get it on and poppin' so stop frontin' and give my little brother some nookie!" she laughed boisterously, garnering stares from annoyed passersby.

Ghetto ass people, Talea shook her head embarrassed for her friend more so than herself. Jerome took hold of Talea's hand and led her away from his sister to finish their conversation. Faye got the message and went back to the Denali.

Chapter VIII
De Ja Vu
ॐ⌒ॐ

Shawn couldn't wait until his property in New Jersey was complete so that he could stop wasting money on expensive hotels and the rented duplex. He knew his wife's patience must've been wearing thin with not having a home and him having to stay in lower Manhattan away from her. That was his main motivation for pushing forward with the building plans in New Jersey. He didn't want to wait any longer but more delays were forced on him due to permit issues. Commuting from Manhattan to New Jersey for the monotony of the business side of being a developer was both tiresome and bothersome.

He entered the overpriced hotel he called home for the past two days while attending endless permit regulatory meetings with his business partners and lawyers. He passed by two bell boys as he walked across the foyer and boarded the awaiting elevator. He got off at the eleventh floor and pulled out his hotel room key card. Walking down the corridor towards his room, he paused for a moment as he could hear a slight commotion grower closer. Heavy footsteps, keys, metal clanging, static filled voices all at once. Appearing to be headed his way. He knew this noise was for him, he could feel it. His instincts told him to run. *Maybe I'm bugging.* Then again, he could make a run for it—just in case he wasn't.

"HEY! Don't you move! Keep your hands where I can

see em'!" an officer commanded. Shawn looked down at the hotel room key in his hand then up again in time to see four Caucasian officers barreling down the hall towards him.

"What is this about officers?" Shawn asked, innocently cursing himself for not following his instincts.

"Shawn Wilson?"

"Yes, but..."

"We just need you to go with us, Wilson."

Two of the officers were now in his face, one behind him and another was attempting to intimidate him further by unsnapping his gun's leather holster.

"You need me to go with you for what?" Shawn was quite aware of the officers' positioning. They swarmed him in a manner that was a dead give-away of their intentions. He dared not make a sudden move or he knew he'd be beaten like piñata.

"The D.A. just needs you to answer a few more questions concerning the Emanuel Vernon case."

"Well as I understand it I've already been more than cooperative with the police department, I answered all the questions asked. So I'm not obligated to be harassed. Is the NYPD stalking me?" Shawn knew his rights and declining to go back to the station with them was not a crime.

Once again, no matter how many precautions he took to distance himself from the illegal drama the police always found a link. It was just his luck that Greg lived long enough to utter his street moniker, Pretty Boy before croaking. The one thing Shawn had going for him was the fact that although Greg mentioned his nickname it meant absolutely nothing since it wasn't recorded and he supposedly said it to an emergency technician. Regardless to this fact the District Attorney's office continued to harass him.

Shawn respectfully eased past the two officers blocking his path and headed towards his hotel room. The officers were sent there to apprehend Shawn at the D.A.'s behest. They were basically given a free pass to whoop his ass so he was going down one way or another.

"Sir, we'd really appreciate you coming with us," the shortest of the officers lagged behind him. He couldn't match Shawn's long-legged stride so he demanded that Shawn stop walking. Shawn ignored him. Shawn's defiance lit a fuse under the officer's Napoleon complex, forcing him to grab a hold of Shawn's arm.

"Officer, why are you attacking me?" Shawn purposefully whined, to acquire attention from the oncoming hotel patrons. The German family of tourists seemed fascinated by the whole scene. The short officer was angered by Shawn's flippancy.

"You better stop playing that game, bro because you'll lose."

"Bro? Game? Owww, my arm!" Shawn performed for the people collecting in the corridor. The officer had had enough at this point and applied a massive amount of pressure to Shawn's arm. Shawn's hand instinctively went to aide his hurt arm. The officer saw his opportunity.

"He's reaching for something!" he called out to the other officers steadily approaching. They pounced on Shawn like a pack of lions on a gazelle in the sweltering jungles of Central Africa. Shawn didn't resist and could barely breathe with the weight from one burly officer who schlepped an extra one hundred pounds in his pot belly alone. The sweat from his porous hands smeared moisture all over Shawn's neck as his grubby sausage fingers tightened around it. Shawn continued on with his earlier act of the wrongly accused victim to the NYPD's infamous police brutality. He hollered and wailed in pain causing quite a commotion in the upscale hotel's hallway. Once he was handcuffed the officers attempted to clear the hallways of witnesses, ordering them back to their rooms. As they unnecessarily manhandled Shawn dragging him down the hall he made sure to scream out,

"Do you see how their treating me? I'm unarmed yet they're beating me and using excessive force!"

Now the officers were humiliated and angrier than

ever. They signaled each other with their eyes noting that Shawn was to get a serious beat down back at the station where there'd be no concerned, prying eyes. They eased up on him and allowed him to walk at a less rushed pace and restrained themselves from lacing him with baton blows. Shawn knew what would come later when they arrived at central booking. With all his protesting during his arrest he secured himself an excessive force complaint which would come in handy when he ended up before a judge.

Here he was in lock up and for the third time in his life. Granted the first two times were short lived but still grueling nonetheless. Shawn hated Central Booking but was grateful that in some weird turn of events he ended up in the pen all alone; a rarity for New York's penal system. As he sat on the bench with his back pressed up against the graffiti riddled wall he realized that he hadn't spoken to his wife all day. He had the misfortune of having to choose a man over his woman. In his quest for freedom he used his one phone call on his over priced retained attorney. But he knew this attorney was really worth his weight in gold especially when it came to property estate affairs. He made pigs fly when he worked the system to his advantage initiating building permits and licenses when other attorneys said it couldn't be done. But now it was time for his lawyer to show and prove. The way he finagled the City's building department to release holds on permits, Shawn was sure the same could be done for him since they didn't have any concrete evidence linking him directly to Manny's murder. He was praying that he could be released and soon.

"You've got some company tonight. You two lovebirds need some condoms?" A lanky officer snickered after thrusting a young boy in the cell. The boy could easily pass for fifteen, too young for lock up in Shawn's opinion. Shawn's cold stare could turn the corroded cell bars to ice. His pupils shifting to match the movements of the officer as he strode off pleased with himself. The young boy hunched his shoulders forward, twisted his mouth and grimaced as he stood in the corner opposite the bench. Shawn ignored him and his fake gangster stance. He knew the boy was putting on a show so that Shawn wouldn't punk him. This was all standard pen protocol. The boy's ability to distract Shawn was short-lived as his mind found its way back to the woman he loved. He hadn't seen her in two whole days, going on a third. He missed her, needed her. He wondered where she was and what she was up to. *Why didn't I ask that damn lawyer to call her for me?*

The kid interrupted Shawn's thoughts with, "What's good, son?"

Shawn sighed, knowing that the young boy must not have been privy to his status. So he let it slide and continued to fill his mind with thoughts of his plans once released.

"Oh, you ain't talkin'?"

Now this little runt was getting out of pocket and Shawn's tolerance for disrespect was non-existent.

"Do you know me?" Shawn asked, perturbed.

"Naw, but I was asking you something."

"And did I answer you?"

"Son, don't talk to me like I'm a child or some shit." Now that it was established that the young boy had heart, Shawn felt it his duty to school him.

"You must be, so take this lesson with you, *son,* I'm not in the mood to socialize. Period. Fuck you think this is?"

"Fuck you, niggah!" the young man balled his fists then began cracking his knuckles. He flexed his muscles as if he were in the animal kingdom making a stand for his territory. Shawn found it amusing yet chidingly remarked,

"You don't want none, *boy.*"

"Boy! Boy?" his voice rose.

Shawn just shook his head, ignoring the young punk's anger. The boy made the mistake of underestimating Shawn's calm demeanor and charged. His attack was wild and clumsy leaving his face at a disadvantage. Shawn brought his fist down hard onto the side of the teenager's face with a thunderous whack. The young man fell to the

111

floor dazed and confused. Shawn sighed as he idly awaited retaliation. He wasn't in the mood to beat the boy to a bloody pulp. But the anger ascending within him was sure to compel his fists of fury into raining lumps all over the youngin's peanut shaped head. The young boy groaned, sliding his hand up to the side of his head. Shawn watched and waited. If the boy tried attacking him again he already decided he'd put him in a sleeper hold and put him to bed— literally. The boy was so discombobulated he had to use the bench to pull himself up from the stained floor. He flounced onto the bench still palming the left side of his head.

꿍

Adonis's eyes were bloodshot and the puffy dark circles under them implicated sleep deprivation. He moved mechanically towards his convertible. The beautiful woman sitting in the passenger's side warranted stares from passersby. With the top down and her thick Chanel shades she could be mistaken for a celebrity and easily rouse paparazzi. She was the only reason Adonis emerged from his once happy dwelling which he shared with his seemingly comatose life partner. Days grew into nights painfully slow since Andre's attack. Without his man around, life became a chore and left him unattached to the world.

"Hi sweetie," Natalia chirped cheerfully.

"Hey," was all Adonis managed to utter. He looked around at the tall buildings and bustling New Yorkers as if he were a tourist seeing his block for the first time. Essentially he was a tourist. Staying holed up in his expensive digs with access to cable and food delivery ostensibly kept him from New York's flavorful ambiance. Natalia leaned over and gently kissed his scraggly 12 o'clock shadow as he got behind the wheel of his sports car.

"Sweetie, do I need to take you for a make over? You

112

can't see our Andy looking like a werewolf in drag!" It was then that Adonis' eyes lit up and he giggled ever so slightly. He turned around in the seat to face her, "I know. I must look a mess!"

"You said it, I didn't," she playfully nudged his arm then said with a countrified accent, "Gosh darn it, let's go n' get you done up all purty like."

They both laughed and Natalia was relieved to see Adonis' bright smile again. It had been missing far too long.

"So where do you want to do brunch?"

"I don't care," he said nonchalantly.

"Baby, I know you don't want to deal with the world yet, but you have to. And you know Andy isn't going to leave you alone out here for another man to snatch your sexy ass up. He's just resting, baby." Her smile made him smile. Her words were convincing too. And for the remainder of the ride all the way to the restaurant in SoHo, Adonis' mood shifted.

They ate and drank, shopped and she convinced him to see Andre regardless to him being unconscious. Adonis reluctantly agreed and insisted he go home to change because he came out the house dressed like a hobo. Natalia's ploy to get his spirits up was actually working.

They rushed into the building and headed back to Adonis and Andre's apartment.

"It's makeover time!" Natalia exclaimed as she clapped her hands frantically. Adonis searched out his shaving kit from the master bathroom. He shaved the sides of his perfectly structured face then applied a moisturizer. When he was done he and Natalia mulled over the clothing in his closet. She picked out a better suited outfit for the weather than the heavy denim buttoned shirt he wore earlier. Natalia laid out every piece of the outfit on the bed. "Well?" she asked, hoping he'd like what she selected. He was indifferent yet agreed to wear the outfit and soon after he got dressed she alerted him to his red puffy eyes.

Adonis ran to the mirror to see his bloodshot eyeballs staring back at him. Underneath were swollen lumps from lack of sleep. He sighed, defeated. Natalia didn't want him slinking back into depression so she retrieved some Visine from the bathroom cabinet and squeezed droplets into his eyes. To complete her treatment she cut up a cucumber and placed a slice over each of his eyes to reduce the puffiness. As he lay on the couch enjoying the way Natalia fussed over him, he thought of his life partner laying in intensive care. He started tearing up, "Oh, my baby, my baby... I can't take this anymore. I need him home," he lifted each cucumber from his eyes and used the back of his hand to wipe away the moisture.

"I know sweetie, I know." Natalia didn't know what to say to ease Adonis' pain. She herself was on the verge of breaking down not having her rock, Andre to support her.

"I pray, Adonis, I pray and pray," her eyes watered as she spoke, "Andy needs us to do that. We have to stay strong and let God work. Now stop you're whining and crying because you're defeating the purpose of these cucumbers!" she giggled and placed the cold cucumbers back onto his eyes.

"Now keep your eyes closed so this can work, sexylicious." She rubbed his arm down to his hand and held it. "I'm so angry! I want to kill those bastards!" Adonis grumbled out of nowhere after a few minutes of silence.

"I know, I know. But they got two of them already and I know they'll get the rest of them so don't you worry." She lifted the cucumbers from his eyes and examined each one. The puffiness under his eyes hadn't gone down totally but enough for her to notice a difference.

"Well?" Adonis asked.

"It went down some. You're still an Adonis, you friggin' Adonis," she giggled.

"But of course." He smiled then frowned, "I need to see Andy. Let's get out of here."

Natalia fiddled with the seatbelt as she secured herself in the passenger's seat of Adonis' car. Adonis glanced at himself in the vanity mirror and liked what he saw. He was human again as opposed to how he'd let himself go while in his recluse stage.

Driving through the sea of yellow cabs was beginning to annoy him. The annoyance grew to anger since he had not stopped thinking of the low-lives that took his man from him. He wanted revenge. He felt jail was too good for them. He had no faith in the U.S. justice system. He'd seen how inept a system it was and he didn't want them fouling this up. Andre was supposed to be on his honeymoon right now, not in the hospital. Natalia was fumbling through her purse when Adonis spoke.

"Where exactly did it happen?"

She looked over at him pulling lotion from her purse and lifting the cap, "What?"

"You and those fuckin' cops keep avoiding my questions about the location of where they attacked Andy. I need to know Nat, you have to tell me."

Natalia didn't tell Adonis where the whole incident took place for fear that he would stake out the restaurant's parking lot in hopes of catching the rest of the thugs responsible for Andre's attack. The cops didn't tell because the five star restaurant's lawyers immediately placed a gag order on them and the media from naming the restaurant or it's location in the incident.

Natalia didn't want Adonis to worsen his situation. But she understood his need to know. She understood the revenge boiling inside him. She'd been there done that. She remembered her release after she exacted her revenge on Manny. She remembered the satisfaction she felt as he screamed from the pain she inflicted. She knew this kind of release was probably what Adonis so greatly desired.

"NAT!" he shouted and startled her.

"Pull over Adonis," she relented.

He drove slower and slower until he could switch lanes and pulled over to a curb. He stared at her awaiting the information he hoped she'd divulge.

"I just don't want you trying to become a vigilante,

115

sweetie. But I understand what you need."

"You're flapping your gums but you're not saying anything I want to hear. Come on with it, girl!"

"Okay, okay...we were at Soule's, by one hundred and..."

"I know exactly where it is, thank you."

And with a determination she'd never witnessed before, Adonis shifted gears and zoomed out into oncoming traffic.

"Adonis! Slow down!" He ignored her cries and sped past the turn he was supposed to make that lead to the hospital.

"Where are you going?" Again he ignored her.

"Oh, no. Adonis please don't go over there!"

Adonis drove in a haze of anger. Natalia begged and pleaded with him, speaking as calmly as possible. But he ignored her pleas. She became worried, nervous and afraid for their lives. She knew if Adonis drove back to the scene where Andre was hurt not only did they risk seeing anyone from that night but the young men responsible were thugs and could have weapons. And this time she probably wouldn't escape unharmed.

"Adonis, listen to me this isn't going to help matters nor Andy! Please I'm begging you don't go over there. These boys could be killers! They don't care..."

"Neither do I!" he said, with a devious look that spooked her so much she almost peed on herself.

Chapter IX
Cat Fight
৵৽৾

Shawn's mini-bout was essentially over because the young boy had come to the realization that he was no match for his cell mate. The comedic officer from earlier opened the cell asking, "What'd you do?"

"I defended myself," Shawn replied.

"Oh? No, pal I believe you've just fucked yourself is what you've done." He remarked and tended to the knot on the boy's head then asked him, "Do you know you're name?"

"Yea, yea," the boy slurred.

"Mmn, man, you need to visit the infirmary. Can you stand up?" the officer asked then turned toward Shawn, "You think you're big shit don'tcha? Well try this shit with me punk," he threatened. Shawn just ignored the officer's threat knowing goading when he saw it. He had no intentions of fighting anyone but the boy agitated him. He was upset with himself for allowing his temper to get the best of him. There was a chance that this could slow his release process even more. Although, he realized that the D.A. was gunning for him or he wouldn't have sent all the manpower he did to apprehend him. This was where the mystery lay. Why would the D.A. give a fuck about him? He wasn't in the game anymore; he was a legitimate business man now. He covered his tracks after ridding the world of two menacing criminals. What could have the D.A.'s briefs in a bunch? So much so that he wanted Shawn's freedom this badly?

117

෫∞෨

Shawn dozed off awaiting his arraignment. Moments later he awoke to keys jingling.

"Ah, the illusive, Mr. Wilson." Shawn ignored the remark and watched the clean cut man's movements as an officer opened the cell door then held it open ,

"Come on, man. Let's go!"

The stranger threw in his two cents, "Yes, let's go, Mr. Wilson. Your fans await you."

Still, Shawn didn't respond to his sarcasm. In fact, Shawn was too busy trying to place the stranger's face. *Who is this cat?* The man was superbly tanned, as if he'd just come straight to the court house from the beach. His suit was sharp with a European cut.

"Are you court appointed? Because I already have a lawyer."

"You wish I was court appointed," the stranger chuckled, "Follow me," he gestured after the officer secured Shawn's wrists with handcuffs. Now Shawn was sure that something was truly off. Firstly, this wasn't standard procedure. They took him into an empty arbitration room. The officer guided him to a seat then left the room. Again, not standard procedure. Something was unnerving about this whole situation and Shawn wanted no part of it.

"What's going on here?" Shawn asked.

The stranger reached up to his tie, loosening the knot then said, "I'm District Attorney, Delucchio."

"Okay, Mr. Delucchio can you explain why I'm here?"

"Listen, you have a choice," the D.A. said snidely, pacing in front of the table. You either play ball, and I'll take it a little easy on you, or you can go against the grain...in which case I'll make your life, a living hell," he said coldly, making a point to lock eyes with Shawn.

"Get to the point already," Shawn, sneered.

"I want you to confess to the murders of Emanuel Vernon and Malcolm Mcbride. I'll offer you a deal, take the plea and enjoy your vacation."

Shawn laughed, and laughed, then laughed some more. His laughter trailed off when the D.A. slapped his manicured hand down on the table and leaned forward.

"This isn't a joke you asshole. I want a confession from you."

"You're kidding me, right? I mean you couldn't possibly think I'm that fuckin' stupid. You're not telling me to confess to a crime that I didn't commit are you, Mr. D.A.?" he started with the laughter again.

"SHADDUP!" the D.A. shouted, flustered.
The officer standing guard outside quickly snatched open the door, "You okay?"

"I'm fine, I'm fine," the D.A. blew hard, unbuttoning his suit jacket, "I'll call you when I need you," he said, dismissively. The officer rolled his eyes and slammed the door shut.

"I guess I need to let you know exactly what you're dealing with here," he said and took a seat across the table from Shawn, "I had to pick up the pieces you and that half breed whore left behind after you both ran off on your Bonnie and Clyde criminal spree. I was there for the anger, the tears, the break down," he clenched his jaw and removed his jacket, laying it in the chair next to him, "And in case you haven't noticed, were a tightly knit family so if he hurts, I hurt."

Now it was all starting to make sense. At first the name didn't ring any bells but now, *Delucchio* was chiming like a motherfucker. This bronzed stiff was related to Marco Delucchio, his wife's ex-husband. What a fuckin' small world, Shawn thought. He sat there dumbfounded, waiting for the other shoe to drop.

"I take it from your silence you either know exactly where this is going or you're too stupid to notice that your life is in my hands." Shawn remained silent but a bead of sweat formed at his temple. This was going to be a task for his lawyer. A District Attorney with a personal vendetta manifesting itself in an arrest would definitely be a legal challenge.

"You may have gotten away with murder, drug distribution, trafficking and God knows whatever else you've done in your poor excuse for a life with the previous D.A. but not on my watch, you fuck. I want you to suffer as Marco did. I'm going to take your freedom and piss all over it."

"Well now, are you threatening me with trumped up charges, Mr. Delucchio? Are you saying that you're abusing your position in order to avenge a family member? Is that what you're telling me?"

"Do you think this room is bugged or something?" he asked, looking around with his arms outspread, palms up.

"That's of no consequence to me, Mr. D.A., I have not consulted with my lawyer which I'm sure is an infringement of my civil liberties and I'm conferring with the D.A. prior to my arraignment as well as being threatened by the D.A. This is clearly unorthodox and inappropriate."

The D.A. laughed, "Don't tell me you got a high school diploma while you were locked up? Is that where you expanded your vocabulary? Reading dictionaries to pass the time?"

Shawn only smiled to himself, shook his head and demanded, "I want my attorney."

"Well you're in my world now. I can keep you tangled up in the system with red tape."

"Why do villains always insist on telling all about their plans?" Shawn chuckled.

"No one will believe you if you even repeat anything I say in here."

"That's what you think. My lawyer will be all over this."

"Not if I have a case that will stick. And if I can't get you on murder for now, I've got you on assault."

"Assault?"

"Yes, the young man whom you sent to the infirmary. I've convinced him to press charges."

Now that was a turn of events that Shawn could do without. That was valid and an officer witnessed him pulverizing the kid. An officer that could very well put his own spin on what went down to appease the D.A.

"So tell me what I want to hear, punk."

"I want my lawyer."

"Is that you're story and you're sticking to it?"

"I'm entitled to consult with my attorney."

"Going against the grain it is," D.A. Delucchio put on his jacket, grinned in Shawn's direction then left the room.

☙◆❧

Natalia's ride with Adonis was treacherous. She wished he'd slow down or just pull over and calm down.

She panicked as the sports car neared the restaurant parking lot in Harlem. She could clearly see a group of young men just like the one responsible for putting her best friend in a comatose state blocking the entrance. Adonis slowed down, then completely stopped a block away.

Natalia sighed with relief, "Thank God, you've come to you're senses. Get out, I'll drive." She began stepping out of the car and just as the platform sole of the shoe on her right foot hit the concrete, Adonis sped off down the road towards the crowd in the parking lot, thrusting Natalia to the pavement. Bruised and aching, she struggled to her feet in time for a big *BOOM!* She looked in the direction of the noise and screamed bloody murder at the sight. Bodies were mangled on the parking lot asphalt. Some were smashed into other parked cars, some lucky people were able to limp away from the furious driver who backed away from the damaged vehicles where he had two bodies pinned then spun 180

121

degrees to go after other people trying to get out of the lot. The bloody, broken bodies of the two men once pinned slumped to the ground.

Adonis hit another man who was trying to limp out of the lot then put the car in reverse and sped towards three teens running towards the restaurant's entrance. They didn't make it as their bones crunched under the pressure of the two thousand pound vehicle. Adonis' expression was maniacal as he revved the car's engine and growled out the window, vowing, "I'll smash every son of a bitch that put my man in the hospital!"

Natalia limped as fast as she could toward the gruesome scene hoping to talk sense into Adonis. She heard the sirens approaching once again, it was like déjà vu. This was the story of her life, filled to capacity with drama. A row of police cars screeched to a halt in front of the parking lot. The sea of blue and white moved in precision as they formed a barricade and aimed their weapons at Adonis' shiny MR2 Spyder.

"NO! STOP!" Natalia shouted at the top of her lungs running past the police to get to Adonis. An officer ran towards her and snatched her up in his arms to prevent her from entering the parking lot, "Ma'am you can't be here," he gently placed her down once behind the police barricade.

"That's my friend. You don't understand what's happening," she took a deep breath and began filling the officer in on the reason Adonis snapped. The officer relayed the information to his commander then escorted Natalia to one of the ambulances that arrived. It was just her luck that they insisted she ride back in the ambulance and be admitted for observation.

Upon arrival at the emergency center entrance, an EMT suggested to the emergency room staff to check Natalia for contusions from her fall. The amount of hands ripping at her clothing and tapping her arm for veins to plunge syringes into frightened her. She'd had enough of them invading her personal space so she sprang up on the gurney and said,

"Just stop! Please... I'm fine," she hopped off the table and tried to leave.

A woman in a lab coat grabbed her arm, "Miss you really need to let us check you out."

"No, I don't," she snatched her arm from the persistent intern. That was the last thing she needed. A bunch of needle happy interns fresh out of medical school using her as a class lesson or even worse, a guinea pig. The only good thing about the ambulance taking her to that particular emergency room was that it was in the hospital where Andre was hooked up to the tube of life.

She made her way to the main hospital lobby where she saw a woman dragging a toddler to the information desk. Everton! I'm the worst mother ever, she thought. She tried to call the apartment but wasn't getting a good enough signal so she rushed towards the glass doors leading outside to get a better signal and called the nanny.

"Gabriella, is Everton okay?"

"Yes, he's fine, Mrs. Wilson. Will you be home soon?"

"Actually no, I may be in very late tonight so don't be alarmed. What is my munchkin doing?"

"He's actually asleep for once," Gabriella giggled. Natalia did too then said, "Okay, kiss him for me I'll see you later."

"Okay."

Natalia called Shawn's cell phone but got his voicemail. She didn't want him to get crazy so she chose to leave him a mild message just urging him to call her instead of telling him what happened. After recording her message she ran back into the hospital and boarded an elevator up to find Andre's room. Andre's room was lit from the light from the monitors on the medical equipment. His eyes were still closed. He looked fake to her lying there like a mannequin. But he also seemed to be in a state of peaceful rest. She didn't want to deal with the nurse sitting at the nurse's station so she crept past her and into Andre's room. She began tearing up immediately at the sight of the once virile man now dependent upon the massive machines surrounding the hospital bed. She took his hand and kissed it, caressed it. Tears flowed, tears for her best friend and tears for the love of his life whose fate she knew included jail time—and a lot of it.

After watching her best friend's chest rise and fall for a few minutes she realized that she should hire a lawyer for Adonis. A good lawyer, one that could erase all the time he faced. Before leaving she whispered in her best friend's ear, "I love you so much and I really need you back here with me so the same way that you kept vigil by my hospital bed when I was comatose then catatonic is the same way I will be here every day if I can. I will not rest until I get you the best doctors that money can buy. You will not leave me, Andy. I won't let you," she sniffled then kissed his puffy cheek. She limped toward the door just as Andre's doctor glided in, his white lab coat flapping behind him as if he were Superman.

"Hello, how are you?" he asked glancing downward, noticing her limp.

"I could be a helluva lot better, doctor, I tell you that."

"I'm glad to see you because I wanted to give you an update."

"Really? Is he coming around?"

"Well, we had to perform a craniotomy to reduce the subdural hematomas on his brain. The good news is that we've noticed a slight decrease in the edema and there's plenty of brain activity so although he seems comatose, he's really just sleeping off all the meds in his system. I'm hopeful that by tomorrow he'll be completely lucid."

"Oh, doctor you have no idea how happy you've made me!"

"Well, I try, you know," the doctor chuckled. Natalia attempted to hug him, caught herself and opted to shake his hand instead. She ran back to Andre's bedside and said soothingly, holding his cold finger tips in her hand, "Get up lazy head, I know you can hear me." She watched hopeful as his lifeless heavily medicated body only heaved slightly with each assisted breath.

"I'll see you tomorrow, Andy. I know you'll be awake for me tomorrow," she kissed him again and left the hospital to place a very important call to find a competent lawyer.

As she dug her hand deep into her purse to retrieve her phone all while attempting to hail a yellow cab to the 32ⁿᵈ precinct her phone rang in her hands, "Hello?"

"Natalia?"

"Yes?"

"It's Big Stew, PB's friend. They got him on the island," Big Stew rattled off.

"What?" Natalia hadn't a clue what Big Stew was talking about.

"They arrested and booked him and the judge denied bail so he's going to Riker's tonight."

"Oh, my God! Why did they arrest him? Never mind, tell me what I have to do to get him out?"

"You need to find out exactly when he's being moved. It's too late to put a stop to that now but you need to call his lawyer and find out what can be done tomorrow morning."

"Okay, okay, thanks," she pressed the end button on her cell phone, her fingers trembling as she searched through her contacts for Shawn's business lawyer's name. Steinberg scrolled up on the screen and Natalia thumbed her screen and waited to hear the phone ring on the other end.

"Steinberg & Rillings," an airy voice answered.

"Ben, please."

"Who is calling?" the receptionist asked, winded.

"Natalia Wilson."

"One moment," the woman replied placing the line on hold..

When Ben Steinberg answered winded as well, Natalia envisioned him zipping his pants up and shooing his receptionist out of his office. For a brief second, she found humor in the image. Then another image of her husband behind bars pushed into her thoughts and returned the stoic expression she sported while trying to hail a cab.

"Shawn is at Riker's," she blurted, as a yellow cab rolled right up to the curb. She got in and pulled the phone from her ear and mouth as she informed the driver to take her to the central booking where the cops hauled Adonis off to. She placed the cellular phone back to her ear and heard, "Hello? Helllooo?"

"I'm sorry, Ben. I said Shawn is at Riker's Island!"

"Riker's? Well I knew that they had arrested him and when I spoke to him he wasn't even arraigned."

"Well why am I just finding this out?" she demanded.

"I've been putting together a motion to dismiss on his case. I thought there'd be no need to really worry, I planned on having him released by tomorrow morning but..."

"Really? Are you positive you can get him out?" A wave of relief washed over her, decreasing her panicked heart beat. Hearing what she wanted to hear, the word released was like a quick-acting valium.

"Well I'm not going to offer guarantees but from what I understand this is just another form of NYPD harassment. He's done nothing illegal to warrant an arrest. But if you're telling me he's at Riker's that means that he's been arraigned and apparently charged with something far more serious than I originally thought."

"What are you telling me? That he's going to jail?"

"No, not exactly...I need to find out what's going on with his case. It's just that he didn't get to call me until late. There was nothing more that could be done. Everything would have to wait until tomorrow morning. But I'll make some calls. I'll have definitive answers for you in the morning. Call me tomorrow around ten."

Now her heart kicked back into gear, pumping vigorously, raising her level of concern.

"Oh, God, what's next? Every time I think we're going to be okay, something else happens," her voice was saturated with sadness as it trailed off.

"Mrs. Wilson, I promise you, I'll get to the bottom of

this. Call me tomorrow and try not to worry yourself."

"Thank you, Ben." She caught a glimpse of a large white S.U.V. barreling towards the cab. The cab driver swerved out of its way.

"YOO FAWKING STOOPID!" the cab driver shouted, shaking his fist in the air as he pressed the button with his other hand for the passenger side window to descend.

"Sir, please calm down and just drive away. There's no need to argue, it's pointless," Natalia insisted. Then she heard a familiar voice screaming, "OH, SHIT! IT'S THAT BITCH, NATALIA, RIGHT THERE!"

Natalia looked in the direction of the large S.U.V. The female driving looked familiar but Natalia couldn't make out her features since the S.U.V. zoomed ahead of the cab then quickly maneuvered its way in front of it, blocking its path. The irate cab driver slammed on his brakes, put the vehicle in park and hopped out cursing and shouting at the driver of the white S.U.V. Traffic had come to a halt. The loudness, the stares from onlookers and the smell of burnt rubber was all too much for her. She had dealt with too much and wasn't about to wait around to explain to the cops what had happened. She retrieved her purse and phone from the seat and opened the car door. As she was stepping out of the cab, Talea hopped out of the S.U.V.

"Talea?" Natalia asked the air, incredulously.

Talea rushed the cab livid, cursing and threatening Natalia. She pounced on her like a crazed feline, putting the windmill fighting technique into effect.

Natalia shrieked, "Get off me!" By this time a muscular man came around to the driver's side where Faye and the cabbie were trading insults. His size alone intimidated the cab driver who feared for his life at this point. He ran back inside his car but now realized that Natalia was being attacked in his back seat. She was halfway in his cab so he couldn't drive off like he wanted to so he screamed at Natalia, "I DON'T WANT NO TWUBBLE PWEASE, GET OWT! JUSH GET OWT!"

127

Natalia pleaded with him to just drive. But he was trapped by the large jeep blocking their way and the stalled oncoming traffic surrounding them. Now Faye and her little sister joined Talea pulling Natalia all the way out from the taxi. They all began kicking, punching, slapping, even stomping her. Natalia threw random punches and kicked her feet in the air eventually connecting with Talea's wrist, causing a sprain that forced her to back off. Faye and her sister continued wailing on Natalia tirelessly almost as if their lives depended on her demise. Natalia's pinky bone cracked and tore through her flesh as she flung her hand upwards to protect herself. She was smart enough to protect her face and head and kept up the out stretched kicks to keep them at bay while she nursed her wounded hand. She lost a shoe as Faye's fist banged into her right foot.

A reluctant passerby with her own assembled crew recognized the poor defenseless woman and raced to her rescue. The burly woman flung Faye's little sister away from Natalia with nothing more than a slight tug. Faye now turned her fury onto the woman. The woman's friends grabbed Faye and pulled her away. The woman turned her wrath onto Faye. The muscle man, Faye's brother, came over and swung on the woman. Now the woman's crew descended on him like a swarm of bees. The melee went on for what seemed like forever to Natalia who was now safe from harm with everyone attacking each other. She watched as the woman who got Faye and her sister off of her held her own with the muscular man in a fair fight. It was as if the man's swollen body had slowed down his reflexes, limiting his ability to dodge the woman's fluid punches which connected again and again. She moved with such agility that he barely landed a punch. Natalia now got a better look at the woman's face as she dodged another swing from the muscular loser. It was a blast from her past that she would've liked to have forgotten. The cops grabbed the muscular man and led him to a police car.

The woman turned in time to lock eyes with Natalia who then mouthed the words, "Thank you, Frankie."

The one person inconceivable to help her, the one person who had taken her dignity when she was locked up; her rapist, Frankie, the boss lesbian on the island that had made her regret the day she'd met Shawn. Frankie just nodded with a knowing smile. She may have not been able to erase what she'd done to Natalia when they were in Riker's but she felt a sense of redemption now. Natalia picked up her cell phone, shoe and purse and limped toward the direction of the sirens. She dipped in between cars until she made it to the sidewalk. As if her life couldn't get any worse, an officer grabbed her. "Are you alright?" the female officer quizzed.

"My hand..."

The officer saw Natalia's protruding pinkie bone and yelled, "I need an E.M.T. over here!"

Natalia's finger throbbed as she sat in the crowded emergency room awaiting triage care. Even with the gauze wrapped around it, she could make out the protruding bone underneath the fibers. She closed her eyes tight trying to block out the image. The bloody gauze made her queasy as it is but to know that her actual bone was exposed was enough to make her want to pass out. She fought the urge to do just that by shifting her thoughts to poor, heartsick Adonis. *The hell he must be experiencing right now.* How could she be of help to him now that she herself was in need of help? Then there was Shawn. Everyone she depended on now needed her. She had to find a way to get Shawn and Adonis out of jail.

The triage nurse was busy running from exam room to the triage station then to the emergency room reception area. Natalia was exhausted just watching her. An older woman, the nurse managed to maintain her coffee stained smile amongst all the coughing, crying babies, belligerent patients and the dreaded smell of death lingering in the air. Natalia was impressed.

The nurse made her way over to Natalia and said, "Sweetie you should've come right into the triage

129

room, you're bleeding."

"Oh, I didn't know."

"Come with me." The nurse led her into the room. She doused her finger with disinfectant as well as the bruises on her forearm and leg. She removed her bandages and dressed her finger poorly with fresh gauze then made her wait outside again.

Finally she'd been examined by an orthopedic surgeon who put her finger in a special splint and wrote her a prescription for pain. Natalia was exhausted and wanted to do nothing more than lay down. She headed for the apartment where her nanny was probably wishing she hadn't taken the job. When she got there the faint smell of her husband's cologne reminded her of his handsome face. A tear formed in the corner of her eye. Even after defending her life against his ex-mistress she realized how badly she missed and loved him.

She tried not to make too much noise as she crept to the other wing where Gabriella's quarters were. She snuck into her room where she found both Gabriella and Everton fast asleep. She envied their peaceful slumber. She quietly shut the door behind her and limped to the bathroom to take a quick shower. The hot steam acted as a sleep aid and made her eyelids heavy. She was so tired that after she got out of the shower, she didn't make it to the bed. She eased her semi-wet towel clad body onto the sofa and nodded off.

Chapter X
Homecoming
ଈ∽૭

Shawn's stint would be tough seeing as how there were a lot of haters at Riker's. But the perks of being who he was certainly came in handy. He had the backing of all the correctional officers that were loyal to his brother and inmates that worshipped him and his brother. Today proved to be a good day. He was headed to court and heard good news from his lawyer. He was in a new suit purchased specifically for him by his lawyer and as he sat in the funky waiting area awaiting the van that would transport him from one end of the island to the next he read the newspaper.

"Whut up niggah?!?" a man in uniform called out as he walked into the room. "Oh, shit, Rico! You're a C.O.?" The two men pounded their fists in a friendly manner.

"Yea, man this is my first day back from leave though and they put me on court detail. Now a better question is what the hell are you doing up in here?"

"It's a long story," Shawn shook his head, "Let's just hope that after today I won't be here."

As he watched the D.A. give lip service to the judge, Shawn determined that the D.A. was way too invested in this case and his lawyer should be able to get his case dismissed due to the personal bias of the prosecution. He knew this simply because he was picked up for a minor infraction yet ended up on the island in a matter of hours. The D.A.'s crooked ways should be easy for the judge to spot. Franco

131

Delucchio conferred with the judge briefly, went back to his table and continued arguing that Shawn be remanded in custody. Ben Spiegelman arose from his chair and addressed the judge.

"Let's for argument's sake say that my client did resist arrest which we've clearly proven in court today that he hasn't, it is preposterous to think that a case of resisting arrest warranted an expedited arraignment, or the District Attorney's personal involvement let alone his actual presence in court. I find that this flimsy charge is a ploy on behalf of the D.A. to carry out a personal vendetta against my client, your honor."

"Approach, council," the judge tapped his chin with his forefinger as if he were in deep thought. As the lawyer approached the bench it was then that Shawn heard someone whisper from behind, "I'm going to fuck your wife every day while you're locked behind bars for the rest of your worthless life."

Shawn whipped his head around to see the smug look on Mark's face as he eased back into the wooden pew. Shawn was taken aback but quickly regained his composure and snapped.

"I see you're still salty that she chose me, huh?" he chuckled and turned back around in time to be asked by the Judge, "You do understand that you're in a court of law?"

"Yes, your honor." Shawn answered, respectfully.

"Well, then act like it."

"Yea, you animal act like a human for once," Mark whispered, following with a hushed tormenting laugh. Shawn rubbed his hand over his mouth as he fought every urge to tear Mark apart. Mark continued baiting Shawn throughout the proceedings but Shawn didn't bite. He could tell what Mark was up to. Thankfully his lawyer had earned every penny of the twenty thousand dollar retainer. He ran circles around Mark's cousin and made the judge see things for what they really were. The judge granted Shawn his freedom but reprimanded him, including an unofficial order that he make it a point to become a law abiding citizen. Mark moaned once the gavel hit the sound block. The D.A. grabbed his folders from the desk and stormed out the courtroom. This wasn't a smart move for Franco Delucchio who practically risked his career pulling this stunt all for his cousin's bruised ego. Shawn knew this wasn't their last attempt at getting him locked away in jail. Mark stood up, his nostrils flaring as Shawn's cuffs were removed. Shawn snickered as he left the court room. He looked back at Mark ominously.

Shawn was free and seeing his wife was all he could think about. While in his lawyer's expensive Jaguar he called his wife. She didn't answer and Shawn wasn't too worried since his lawyer filled him in on the conversation they had the night before. He just hoped she was home awaiting his return, butt naked. His lawyer dropped him off at the apartment and as Shawn waited for the elevator he sniffed himself, unhappy with the absence of odor from the city issued soap Riker's provided. He missed his expensive cologne's fragrance. The elevator doors opened and two old white biddies practically jumped out of their wrinkled skins at the sight of a black man loitering in their exclusive, upper East side building. Shawn was annoyed but he chose to be congenial despite their obvious bigotry.

"Good morning, ladies," he smiled and stepped onto the elevator. They barely acknowledged his greeting and scurried off the elevator. He ignored their crass behavior because nothing could damper his spirits this fine morning. He was a free man and there was a particularly sweet moistness awaiting his attention a mere fifteen flights up.

He opened the apartment door cautiously and as quietly as he could. He crept past the spacious living area and into the master bedroom where he thought his sleeping beauty lay. He found it empty. Baffled, he crept back out into the hallway to find her. He was going to creep to the kitchen but noticed a honey glazed lump on the large suede sectional strategically placed in the sitting room. Natalia was still knocked out, one leg hanging halfway off the sectional the other tucked under it, her breasts perked up on her chest like ripe melons. The towel she had used to dry herself off with the night before was partly trapped under her and the other part on the floor. Her naked body beckoned to his manhood.

"Thank you God," he whispered as he snuck over to her and knelt beside her. Tenderly running his hands past her calf and up to her thigh, he began undressing himself with his free hand. He gently parted her thighs, making sure not to awaken her. His moves were so precise that he managed to remove his pants and underwear all while enticing her clitoris with his slick tongue. He made sure to get it soaked with his saliva then sliding his tongue into her painstakingly slow.

She moved ever so slightly, adjusting herself as if to give him proper access to her juices. He began alternating between massaging her tits and softly kneading her nipples. She stirred under him as he slid his body onto hers. She automatically began writhing sensuously, he matched her rhythm. He marveled at how intuitive her body was. The way it moved to accommodate him as he rubbed his throbbing dick between her legs until her moistness tried engulfing his penis' massiveness. She moaned, awaking instantly.

"Aaaaaaagh!" she jumped.

"It's okay, baby, daddy got you," his sultry voice calmed her, excited her. Her man was home, figuratively and literally. He was at home inside her, moving so smoothly, so expertly. Only this man knew how to work her middle with such finesse. He made her body tremble each and every time he infiltrated it. Penetrated it. He. Was. The man. "Sss, aaah, oh, Daddy," she repeated every time he slowly pumped into her. He showered her with fluttering kisses, then devoured her mouth, slipping his tongue into it. She was on cloud nine through ninety-nine. It seemed like this was their first time together. Repetitiously, their bodies grinded in sync; their breathing and movements accelerated as they came simultaneously, drenching one another with orgasmic juices.

Shawn collapsed his weight onto her as he let out a loud sigh exclaiming, "Damn!"

She giggled and wiped her husband's sweat from her face while easing from under him.

"Where you going?" he slapped her ass as she stood up.

"I'm thirsty and sweaty thanks to you," she smiled and left for the kitchen.

"I'd like something to drink too." Shawn called out to her. He grabbed her towel and wiped himself off.

"B.G.?" he called out.

"I heard you, I heard you," she said loudly as she opened the fridge door. She turned with the orange juice container in her hand to see Gabriella bouncing into the kitchen.

"Oh, I'm sorry, ma'am," Gabriella, covered her eyes and abruptly left the kitchen, flustered. Natalia laughed to herself and continued to pour juice into a glass.

She entered the room with a bottle of water to her lips and a tall glass filled with ice and orange juice for Shawn. As he took the glass from her he said smirking, "You missed me?"

"Uh, duh!" she smiled, mischievously then whispered, "Gabriella just saw all my goodies."

Shawn laughed hard, "She probably went back in her room to play with herself."

"Oh, stop, she's not gay so stop insinuating that," she hit him playfully.

"Yea, okay, you sleep on that dyke if you want to," he laughed then became serious as he spoke again,

"You know, you're ex-man, aka THE WHITE BOY was the cause of me getting arrested, right?"

"WHAT?!?" she asked, stunned.

"Yea, his family has major pull with the NYPD."

"What do you mean?"

"His cousin is the Manhattan District Attorney."

Natalia seemed befuddled as Shawn continued.

"He practically told me how they have it in for me because of what you did to him. He had the nerve to be in court today saying slick shit to me the whole time. He was basically trying to get me to react in the courtroom so that they could keep me locked up."

"Oh my God, what in the world has gotten into that man?"

"You, of course," he said agitated. Natalia looked away from her husband's watchful eyes. He took her chin into his hand and forced her to look at him. "I know that all of this shit is really my fault. I know that. And you better believe that if you did to me what you did to ol' boy, I'd be going insane too," he laughed.

She laughed nervously then asked, "So this means he's going to be gunning for us then?"

"We're never going to be safe here. We'd have to leave the fuckin' country to find peace," he shook his head and released her chin. This was his argument before they took the apartment in Manhattan. He explained to his wife that they would need to watch their backs being back in New York, period. He also suggested they move to France where his older brother told him that he had set up a chateau for their family. Tymeek was now into bigger and better things as he put it but he still hadn't clarified exactly what these 'things' were. He still had the house in Holland but now claimed to own homes in Austria and the countryside in France.

He informed Shawn of how much money he was making in a legitimate manner now and wanted Shawn to come out and help him with his *new* business. Tymeek just wanted desperately to regain his brother's trust and respect. After all the drama they'd been through, the betrayal, coveting of each other's women, he knew it would be a hard road back to the way things were. Tymeek was willing to look past everything; forgive and forget and start over even if that

136

included extending an olive branch to his once despised sister-in-law.

"Oh, brother, here we go. Not this again."

"What? What's wrong with suggesting that we leave the country?"

"Because it's not that simple, we'd have to learn French and besides I'm not really a fan of French food. I have too much going on here. I can't just pick up and go like that to go live in some God forsaken place with your evil brother of all people!"

"Not with him, near him. We'd be moving to a beautiful romantic country to live happily ever after," he pulled her onto his lap, almost crushing his now flaccid penis. He began tickling her, trying to quell the anger he could tell she was about to unleash.

"Stop, daddy!" she unwillingly giggled and squirmed off his lap onto the couch,

"That's such a big decision. I don't know..."

"Just think about it. You were willing to leave America before. Look, I have to be honest with you, B.G., we're really not safe here. So from now on I need to be with you every time you go somewhere at least until we go to Jersey for good. But even in Jersey things aren't going to be so safe. I've pissed off a lot of people."

Natalia sighed, caressed his hand and said, "I know. We both have. There's something you should know," she fidgeted until she was flush up against his chest, safe in his bulging biceps, "I was attacked yesterday after Adonis...," she sighed and continued with, "Well he's probably going to prison for life." After saying that, her eyes watered and it hit her, all the hell she'd endured in such a short amount of time. She slid her damaged hand up his forearm and rested it there.

"What the fuck?" Shawn asked amazed, finally noticing his wife's bandaged finger.

"Yea, I know it's a lot. Can you believe it?"

"No B.G.," he sat up, took her bandaged hand into his

to inspect it, "I'm talking about this."

"Oh, that..." she sighed, hating to have to drudge up the memories, but she told him everything that went down from Adonis' revengeful mowing down of alleged homophobes to her smack down match with Talea, Faye and her family whom she lied about, omitting names of her attackers for fear that she'd have to explain why Faye and Talea would want to jump her. She even told him about Frankie saving her from the fictitiously named assailants.

Shawn couldn't believe all that he'd heard. He sat still for a moment after her update, taking it all in. Natalia just sank into his comforting chest, savoring the quiet.

Chapter XI
Snake Eyes
ई०ई

Everton's tiny scrotum looked abnormal. It was mashed and flat. His plump cheeks were rosy and he wailed like there was no tomorrow as his mommy changed his diaper. Natalia had given Gabriella the week off and was enjoying time with her son. He was a joy since he slept through the night and didn't complain or cry for no reason. He was a good baby but during the night he had given her a run for her money. Now this particular morning, he was screaming bloody murder! She wiped him clean then grabbed a diaper and tried to slide it between Everton's wiggling bottom and the changing table. He continued to scream at the top of his lungs while wiggling as if he were doing the twist.

"What's wrong with my munchkin?" she asked, and placed a tiny peck on his forehead. It felt warm, too warm. She put the back of her hand to his forehead and realized that Everton had a fever. Natalia was beside herself with worry. She switched into frantic mode and screamed for Shawn.

"What's wrong, baby girl?" he ran into the room.

"Everton is burning up!"

Shawn put the back of his hand onto Everton's forehead and pulled it back quickly, "Shit, he's hot as hell!

Hurry up and put some clothes on him and let's get him to the doctor."

❧

Dr. Frettini, what's wrong with him? Is it the flu?"

"No...well, we've brought down his fever but there's something more pressing that we've discovered."

"What is it?" Natalia asked, alarmed.

"Everton has Beta-Thalassemia Major."

"Beta-max Thalluh-what?" Shawn asked, upset.

"Sorry, I'm still paying back student loans for medical school so I like to use medical jargon whenever possible. Get my money's worth, ya know?" Dr. Frettini, awkwardly joked.

Realizing the inappropriateness of his misplaced humor he switched back to professional mode, "It's a severe hypo chromic anemia, in Laymen terms, Cooley's disease."

"Oh, God, is it bad?"

"Well, untreated this can result in death well before age twenty."

Natalia's eyes widened, she became light headed and stumbled. Thankfully Shawn caught her before she hit the ground.

"Natalia?" he asked, holding her up, fanning her with his free arm.

She straightened herself out, fixing her dress, "I'm okay."

The doctor motioned for an orderly passing by to come over, "Please take this woman to..."

"No, no, I don't need to go anywhere, I'm okay," she raked her fingers through her hair.

"Please, tell me, what do we have to do?"

"Firstly, I have to ask if either one of you have this disease because this is typically hereditary?"

"I don't have it," Natalia replied, nervously looking at

her husband's facial expression. Shawn didn't answer since he couldn't say that Everton was his son for sure. This was the moment that he dreaded; the embarrassment of being in the dark about Everton's paternity. The doctor looked to Shawn for his response so Shawn reluctantly said, "I don't either."

"So in order to cure him he's going to need an allograft which is a bone marrow transplant. He needs a donor. We'd just need to test the both of you to find out if either of you are a match. If not, we'd have to start treating him with transfusions immediately until we can find a donor that is a match."

Natalia looked at her husband who seemed troubled. She knew why. She suspected his thoughts were exactly like hers...who in the hell was Everton's father?

Natalia and Shawn were silent the entire ride to the apartment. They both took tests to determine if their blood was a match for Everton to receive their bone marrow. The results were just 48 hours away. This was perplexing on many levels for Natalia. Her son had a debilitating disease that derived from either her lineage or his father's. Everton's life depended on her being a match. In her heart of hearts she had always felt that Shawn wasn't the father. The timing was off and her gut kept warning her. Now she had no choice but to dredge up her past, make calls she'd rather not make to men she'd rather forget. Then it hit her, one of the potential fathers was dead. *What if Maleek is Everton's father? What in the world will I do then?* She thought to herself, stealing a glance at her husband as they walked down the hall to the apartment. He looked stoic and deep in concentration. It worried her. She'd have to tell him her secret. The one secret she didn't know if Shawn would be able to handle. It could mean the end for her marriage. Her nerves were rattled now and she couldn't help but tremble as she neared the apartment door. Shawn held the door open for her, avoiding her eyes as she entered the apartment. Shawn practically blew past her.

"Daddy..., I'm sorry about this."

She dropped her head. Shawn was upset but he knew that he was partly to blame for this situation. He knew that if Everton turned out to be his very dead ex-best friend's child, he'd be reminded daily of the gruesome act of murdering Maleek and the images of Natalia's betrayal. And if Everton wasn't Maleek's child but his brother's, he didn't think that he'd be able to stay with his wife. It would all be too much for him to deal with.

"Daddy?" Natalia interrupted his regrets.

"Yea?"

"Are you hating me right now?" she asked tearing up.

"No, B.G., I'm just...thinking." He sighed and rubbed his hand over his face and headed for the bedroom. Natalia followed him. He collapsed onto the bed and stared up at the ceiling. Natalia sat at the edge of the bed and stared at him. His eyes fell from the tiled pattern to her face.

"What do you want me to say?" he asked, agitated.

"I know you're upset because now we'll have to test ...everybody," she said, ashamed.

"You think? Of course, I'm upset. I mean, you really and truly violated," he rested his forearm over his forehead and shook his head as the memory of his dead best friend's brain matter splattering behind him played in his mind. He didn't want to remember but it wouldn't let him forget.

"I can't change what happened but all I can focus on right now is that little boy in the hospital. Our son, he needs us, daddy. You're the only father he knows and I understand it may be hard if it turns out that he's not yours, but, I'm hoping we can make this work somehow..." She was trying to delay the inevitable of the profession of her deep, dark secret. She was trying to find the words to put into a sentence that could ease him into the news without causing him to pop a blood vessel.

"Are you fuckin' serious?" he sprang up. His reaction made her nervous, very nervous. So nervous she thought it would be best not to tell him.

142

"You fucked my brother of all people, Natalia. You fucked my—" Shawn stopped short realizing that he was about to reveal his deep dark secret. But he also realized that Natalia still hadn't confessed to her affair with Maleek and with the need for paternity tests he knew she'd have to come clean. This pissed him off even more, the fact that she didn't even have the decency to tell him. *She must feel like she's gotten away with it. Maybe she thinks that her affair died with Maleek. Hmn, I wonder how she's going to explain asking Faye to dig up Maleek's body for a paternity test.*

The disgust showed in his face as he spoke, "You're gonna hafta do a lot of testing, I suppose." He looked away, disappointed as images of her honey-glazed body being pounded by his best friend kept popping into his head at that precise moment. He wanted them to disappear but with each thought of Everton's predicament came the disturbing sex scenes. He wanted none of this to matter. He loved her and Everton, but if the boy wasn't his how could he go on living this charade of a life with a woman who'd taken revenge too far? He marveled at how easy it was before this situation arose to foresee a future with his family. Now all he could see was a disaster approaching. He didn't want to keep being so hard on her so he pulled her to him and said, "I'm trying not to let this get to me. I'm really trying," he gently nudged her head into his chest. She wiped a lone tear from her cheek and in a trembling, weak voice said, "I don't want you to hate me or Everton... please don't let this ruin us. It was all a mistake. I wasn't thinking..." she sniffled. It was now or never. The truth had to come out and she was in his arms, the safest place she felt she could ever be. He might release her after her confession but she believed in their love. She believed, wholeheartedly.

"I-I have to tell you something..."

Shawn gently pushed her away to look in her face.

"What?" he asked, hoping that she was finally going to be honest about what she had done.

"I don't know how to tell you this," tears began

143

streaming down her face. Shawn wiped them away with his thumbs and encouraged her to continue, "Whatever it is, just say it. It's okay."

He was so understanding, she wondered how she became so lucky? She sat up straight and grabbed a hold of his powerful arms, bracing herself, "Promise me that no matter what I say, you won't leave us."

"I promise," he awaited her words with bated breath, hoping, preparing for a confession.

"I found out about you and Talea...I was so angry with you. I was hurt, and very, very angry. I couldn't, I didn't think straight and that's partially how I ended up doing most of the dumb things that I've done. But there's no excuse for my idiotic decisions and I'm not asking you to give me a pass."

"Okay, okay," Shawn responded, wishing she'd shut up with the disclaimer bullshit and get to the important part.

"I cheated on you with Maleek, I'm so sorry," she broke down, laid her head on his chest and prayed he didn't explode.

Yes, finally! After unloading the guilt along with her confession, her body felt ten pounds lighter. Shawn was glad that the cat was out of the bag and he readied himself to release his own tiger into the wild. Her confession gave him the courage to tell her what he did.

"We've been through so much B.G., but we're both still here so that should tell you something," he started, he nudged her head from his chest so that she could look him in the eyes when he dropped his bomb.

"It's all for a reason. See, I knew about your affair with Big Mal. In fact, you're the reason he's dead."

"What are you talking about?"

"I killed him."

"Oh, my God, daddy, no!"

"Yes, I did," Shawn answered, bluntly.

Natalia grabbed at the sides of her head, clumps of her tresses were trapped in between her delicate fingers. She

144

was in a state of flux. What in the hell was happening? How could the man she loved be this callous human being looking at her right now?

"You killed Maleek? But...why?"

"What the fuck do you mean why?!?" Shawn, stood up abruptly and began pacing as the memories of his dying friend forced their way into his conscience.

"Shawn, I don't understand why you had to kill him? Because I had sex with him you felt he had to die? Then... then you were going to kill me too?"

"No, I wasn't...I wouldn't have killed him if I felt that his betrayal wasn't as severe..."

"Sex, Shawn? Sex is severe enough to warrant death?"

"Are you fucking kidding me right now? You fuck my best friend, my brother and God knows who else out there stuck their dick up in you, and you wanna get upset with me now because you caused this crazy shit to go down?"

"I didn't put the gun in your hand and tell you to kill him!" she shook her head in disbelief then said, "I can't believe you took that man from his children. Shawn he had children...Oh, my God," she began sniffling, holding back tears. Tears for a father, a husband, a man that despite all of the wrongs he'd done, had done so much right in regards to his family. She mourned his fatherhood. It was now that she began to feel for Faye. *Poor Faye.*

"You think I don't think of that man all the time, what I did, to him, his family, to Faye? I do, alright! I wish I never did that shit. But the alcohol and the anger..."

Natalia saw it in his eyes. He was a manly man but if he kept on reminiscing about Maleek, she was certain he'd start bawling. She was to blame. If she had curbed her ridiculous need for revenge they wouldn't have to relive anything. They wouldn't be in this predicament, not knowing the paternity of her child, having set horrible events into motion with her naiveté or her mini sexual revolution. She stood up and went to him, held him, squeezed him, pleaded with him, "Daddy, please don't give up on us. We're going to

145

get our happily ever after if it kills me!"

Shawn looked down at his wife, shook his head and smiled halfway, "You're crazy, you know that?"

"Crazy for you," she looked up at him, innocently, lovingly, "I know we've got a battle ahead of us but I'm just asking you to bear with me. I'm going to make things right one way or another."

"How, B.G.? I mean, if this baby is Maleek's do you think I'll be able to stick around?"

"But we love each other and it can be..."

"Get the fuck outta here with that love bullshit. Love ain't gonna make me forget that I killed that kid's father."

"We have to make this work, daddy. We have to." Natalia was readying to release the waterworks. Shawn didn't care to console her. Not now, there was too much drama transpiring. His mind was spiraling out of control with detrimental thoughts. What would he do if the baby wasn't his period? Part of him actually wished Everton didn't exist right now. Natalia backed away from him, sat at the edge of the bed, folding one leg under the other and nervously raking her fingers through her hair.

"If Everton's Ty's son, do you really see me playing the happy uncle daddy?" he asked rhetorically so as soon as she began to respond he cut her off, "I mean none of this can be fixed. My brother is practically unreachable. I mean I risk his freedom any time I try to get word back to him. And how are you gonna get Faye to give up Maleek's body for testing? She fuckin' hates us! That woman has dealt with so much already because of both of us, Natalia. I fucked up and you fucked up. There's no putting Humpty back together, yo. There's no amount of Krazy glue that can stick all this shit back into place. How do you propose we make this work after all of this?"

Natalia dropped her head defeated. She really didn't have an answer. But right now her focus was on Everton. He needed bone marrow and if she or Shawn weren't compatible to be his donor, she'd move heaven and earth to find one. So if it depended on Faye or whomever, she was willing to swallow her pride, beg, steal or borrow to save his life. He was priority numero uno.

"I don't have the magical answer. All I know is that I have to do what I have to do. If you're around then that's great. If you're not, then...," she just sighed.

Shawn could see that she was hurting too. He watched as she grabbed her purse and indolently left the room. He wanted to go after her but his disappointment in her was too fresh to allow him to give a damn.

∂∾❦

Andre was finally out of the hospital and his face was back to normal except for a few scars left to tell the tale of his near death experience. Andre's heart was more scarred than anything. The man of his dreams faced life imprisonment. There was nothing to be done for Adonis except pray that the temporary insanity defense held up at his trial. Andre didn't want to live in the city after his ordeal so he sold his condo and moved into his beach house in New Jersey. He loved being right by the water and not having to deal with the city's congestion. When he was there it was just him the ocean and seagulls.

Natalia had come out to New Jersey to chauffer Andre so that he could do his shopping and stock the beach house with all the essentials. Andre met her outside in the winding driveway.

"There's my Natty!" he couldn't move as fast as he used to so his excitement was dulled by his slow movement to get to her as she escaped the confines of her compact Lexus.

"How's my honey bunny?" Natalia got on her tippy toes to peck Andre's cheek.

"I'm hanging in there, babe." Andre smiled, showing

147

his pearly whites. She cautiously wrapped her arms around him for the first time since his attack. He returned the hug and they rocked silently until Adonis' plight reared its ugly head in hers.

"When is Adonis' trial?" She wanted desperately to unload all of the events of her life that unfolded while he was sleeping. But she wanted to ease him into it. The last thing he needed was to add her drama to his own.

"Next week, it starts on Tuesday. Girl, I just pray for him every day. His lawyer told me that if the temporary insanity plea is accepted that my baby will only have to do 18 months in a sanitarium, get another evaluation and if he passed he'd be free! I can't wait for him to get out of that friggin' hell hole they got him in now."

"Is he holding up okay?"

"As well as he can, I suppose," Andre schlepped over to the car and eased into the passenger seat.

"I know how it is in there. It's a horrible experience. Trust me."

"Oh, I do, convict, I do. Speaking of convicts, where's yours?"

"Leave my daddy alone," she giggled.

"Mmn, you still calling him that? Y'all make me sick, you know that?"

"Yup, that's why you call Adonis daddy too don'tcha?" Andre cackled and coughed, "You know when he be tearing it up I do!"

"Thanks for the visuals, Andy, geesh," she chuckled.

"Bitch, you know how many visuals you gave me over the years?"

"A lot."

"Exactly, make this left right here," he said, pointing to the windshield, "So how's my God baby?"

"Not so good. He's still in the hospital." Natalia's eyes saddened.

"Baby, you know if I could I'd donate my marrow in a heartbeat."

"I know, Andy, but you're still too weak even if you were a match. So don't worry about it."

"I have to. That's my baby. This is awful. He shouldn't have to go through all of this in the first year of his life. Let me shut up before I start crying," Andre's eyes glossed over.

"Me too," Natalia took a deep breath to head her tears off at the pass then told Andre the biggest news ever. She told him about Everton's paternity issues. She told him how she would have to call Faye and beg for permission to get Maleek's body and how she probably lost Shawn for good this time. It felt good to have Andre back even if not in full capacity. Just being able to talk to him was enough. She could tell that Adonis' situation was weighing heavy on his mind even though he acted otherwise.

"Do you think the lawyer I got him is any good?" she switched the conversation back to him.

"I can't tell, really. I just want Adonis home again, Nat."

"I know. We have to keep praying on it." Natalia took his hand into hers brought it to her cheek, "I missed you so much. I'm so glad that you're okay. I love you so much Andy," she began sniffling. Andre reached over and hugged his best friend in the whole wide world.

149

Chapter XII
Character Flaw
ം

Natalia dreaded making this call. As she sat watching her cell phone's backlight flicker with each screen transition, her knees broke into nervous knocking. Then her feet wouldn't stop tapping. She took several deep breaths to force herself to release the calm. It didn't help. She wasn't ready to hear Faye's voice. She wasn't ready to tell her that her dead husband just might be her baby's daddy. The words seemed unreal even as she thought them. Neither she nor Shawn were matches for Everton. The doctor assured them that just because Shawn wasn't a match didn't mean that he wasn't Everton's biological father. But after the news Shawn moved out of the apartment claiming he needed to be in Jersey to oversee the ground breaking and foundation installments. And since his departure from New York his calls became fewer and fewer. She could tell that Everton's paternity was too much for him to deal with. She felt that she'd already lost her husband. She cried regularly the first two weeks that he left for New Jersey. But then she became determined, focused on getting Everton a donor. He was back in the hospital now and new complications had set in rendering the transplant imminent. She didn't tell Shawn and planned on fixing everything including her marriage.

Now the diligent search for Everton's father began. Shawn wanted to handle notifying his brother. He promised to find a way to get word to him abroad because he knew what was at stake. But she was on her own with the other two on her list of potentials. She exhaled loudly, shook her hands out and picked up the sleek piece of technology she bought just days earlier and began tapping its screen. As she waited for Faye to answer her cell phone, the hairs on the back of her neck stood up.

"Hello?" Faye's chipper voice threw Natalia for a loop.

"Please don't hang up…"

"Who is this?"

"It's, Natalia." Natalia thought Faye hung up since there was nothing but dead silence, a long pause but then she heard whispering in the back ground.

"Faye, I know that I'm the last person you'd want to speak to but there's something extremely important that you need to know."

Still silence.

"Faye, are you there?"

"Hold on," Faye said abruptly then seconds later she was back on the phone asking, "What important thing do you have to tell me?"

"I guess I should just come out with it…my son, Everton, may be Maleek's son."

"Oh, HELL NO!"

"Faye, I'm so sorry…please listen, there's more."

"More? Natalia, why did you do this to me and my babies? Why? How do you live with yourself?"

Natalia thought about the question, really thought about it. How in the hell could she live with herself knowing that she was the catalyst for all Faye's pain? Then the answer just came to her like a whisper traveling on the wind. Everton was her fuel. His existence made her life bearable. She had to fight for his life.

"I promise you that I never, ever intended to hurt you. Ordinarily, this is not me, it's not in my nature to do what I've done. I'm not at all the way I was when I did what I did. But I have no excuse. I let my emotions get the best of me and I made the most ridiculous choices possible back then. I don't expect forgiveness. If I knew...if you told me what to do to make it up to you I would, I will, but I know there's nothing that can be done to bring him back and for that, Faye I swear to you, I'm truly sorry," Natalia spoke through sobs. In between sniffling and sobbing she could hear Faye, sobbing too.

"I loved you like a sister, Natalia, I really did," Faye was outright crying now.

"I know. I loved you right back. You were so good to me, I don't know what came over me...I just can't say sorry enough." Natalia was now bawling too. The women cried together over the phone.

"You said there was more?" as Faye pulled it together.

"Yes, it's my son. He has Cooley's Disease. He needs a bone marrow transplant but the donor must be a match," Natalia fidgeted as she prepared to ask Faye the ultimate question but Faye beat her to the punch,

"You need Maleek's bone marrow?"

"Well...we'd need to exhume his body to test for Everton's paternity first and then deal with the bone marrow to find out if he'll be a match.

"So, basically, I hold the key to your son living or dying?"

"Yes," Natalia said, weakly, hoping Faye would be compassionate. She heard more whispering in the background. Then Faye said, "So you thought that you'd call, say you're sorry then beg me to help save your little bastard child's life because you wish my husband was his father?"

"Faye, I told you I don't expect anything. It's up to you what you decide, but the truth of the matter is Maleek could be his father."

"He's not the father. You better go test the other hundreds of niggaz you were fucking. You ain't getting shit from me!"

"Faye, this is not about us, it's about a child. A child that may very well be your children's brother! Please don't be this way..."

152

"Don't be this way? Bitch did you think about my kids when you decided to ruin their lives? Well what's good for the goose is good for the gander! You should've thought about karma coming back to bite you in the ass when you fucked my husband!"

Natalia could hear another female's voice in the background snickering then the voice became louder and louder.

"I hope you're fuckin' baby drops DEAD! Choke on that bitch!"

Natalia recognized Talea's hateful voice then the phone line went dead. Natalia dropped the phone and began crying violently, unable to catch her breath. She ran to the bathroom and splashed her face with cold water. She looked up into the vanity mirror and saw her red puffy eyes and knew that she got what she deserved.

She now had to prepare herself for the next telephone call she had to make. She had to call Seth, the third man on her list and the only man she personally knew wanted a child more than anything in the world. She knew that if he was Everton's dad, he would want to spend every waking moment with Everton, making life very difficult for her.

At this point, she'd heard the worst as far as she was concerned so she wasn't jittery for this call. She simply dialed and impatiently waited to blurt out the news to Seth. He answered enamored, as if she were the love of his life.

"Hey, Sexy lady, I knew you'd come to your senses. I missed you."

She stumbled across her words, "Um, I called to, well, I, er... this is Seth, right?"

"Yes? What's wrong, sweetness?"

"Well, do you even know who this is?"

"Of course, Natalia your name came up on my cell's screen."

"Oh, well, I just thought..."

"What? That I'd bark at you because of that time you let that man answer your phone?" he chuckled, full of himself.

"Oh, you mean my husband?"

"Uh, yea, whatever, okay so what's up?"

"I've got something to tell you. There's no easy way to say this so...I have a son and he may be yours. He has Cooley's disease and needs a bone marrow transplant right away."

"Whoa! Whoa! Gimme a minute!"

Natalia imagined Seth taking a knee or sitting down with his hands at the sides of his head trying to soak up all the information she had so anxiously dispensed. She only hoped that he would be understanding and work with her through this nightmare.

"So let me get this straight, you had my, my son? How old is he?"

"No, maybe, I don't know, yet. You have to take a paternity test so that we can find out if you're the father or not."

"How old is he?" he spoke emphatically.

"He's 10 months old."

"10 MONTHS?!? Damn it, Natalia, you stole those 10 months from me!"

Oh, boy here we go.

"No it's not like that, Seth. Listen it's very intricate but we're kind of under time restraints so..."

"Speak to me in person. Meet me somewhere, anywhere, your choice," he sounded desperate and Natalia knew this was going to be the tone of their dealings. He'd be over enthused about becoming a father. She'd have to play nice if he ended up being Everton's father. He held the power and she had to concede.

"Let's meet at JahMecca, Downtown," she suggested.

"I know the place. I'll be there in twenty minutes."

"Wow, you must be close by."

"I'm staying in Manhattan right now. But we can catch up when we get there. How long will it take you?"

"Well, about a half hour."

"That's women's code for an hour isn't it?"

154

"Uh, not really but you may want to add ten minutes to that projected time," she giggled. He sighed, her voice still excited him. For him time stood still and picking up where they left off especially if they had a child together would be no problem.

~∞~

Shawn was looking at the blueprints for the South West section of his property in New Jersey when his lawyer called.

"I've got word that Delucchio is on a fishing expedition so I just want to give you a heads up. Be careful and law abiding because all eyes are on you."

"Thanks, Ben. I'm being a good boy," Shawn chuckled.

"Okay, so how's the building coming along?"

"It's starting to resemble a mall, lo and behold. I just can't wait for this to be finished."

"Well, all good things take time. So how's the family?"

That was the wrong question to ask a man who recently had to get word to a brother on the lam that he might have fathered his wife's child. Shawn didn't want to think about his wife or *her* son right now so he decided it was time to end the conversation.

"Uh, they're good. So, I'll be on my best behavior, Ben. Just keep me updated," Shawn rushed off the phone without saying goodbye or giving Ben a chance to say it. He rolled up the blueprints and jumped in the golf cart and drove to the opposite end of the property where the foreman was drinking bottled water.

"Phil, give me a time frame on the South West section."

"I told your partner it's going to be another eight months."

Shawn sighed, disappointed. He wanted desperately to be done with this project and see it in all its glory. And having a permanent place to live would only be icing on his cake. He smiled to himself imagining his mall then his cell phone rang interrupting his vision, "Yea?"

"Hey, you pretty motherfucker!"

"Ty, what up, man?"

"Ain't nothing, just caking over here. A birdie told me you need me."

"Yea," Shawn tried to gather his thoughts in order to relay them coherently to his brother. This was humiliating to say the least especially since he neglected to tell his brother about Everton at all. But he knew that Everton's life depended on him managing to swallow his pride.

"I have to ask you a favor."

"Anything, baby boy. Speak."

"Natalia had a baby..."

"Congratulations, son, so does he have a big head like you?"

"Well that's the thing, Ty, you might be the father."

"What the fuck are you talking about?" Tymeek asked, indignant. He had pushed what he and Natalia had done so far back in the recesses of his mind that it was almost blasphemous hearing Shawn even suggest anything of the sort. It was also a reminder of him neglecting to wear a rubber. Having to recall the events was tearing him up inside. He never wanted to hurt his brother the way he had hurt him then.

"Man, this is hard enough. Don't make me have to recount shit in order for you to get what I'm saying. You might be the father of her son, okay? I just need a blood sample from you to get it tested because the baby has Cooley's Disease and needs a transplant."

"Wow, man you said a mouthful. I don't even know what to say to you right now."

"Just say you'll get that blood sample to me ASAP. The boy is gonna die if we don't move fast."

"Damn... uh, yea. I'll make it happen. I'll get to looking over here for answers too. You know I'ma do whatever it takes, right?"

"I know. So what else is going on over there?" Shawn wanted to eliminate the awkwardness of the discussion.

"Like I said, I'm just over here making money. But let me go work on that situation for you. I'll get back to you soon."

They were both relieved to end the conversation. Shawn slipped his cell back into its case, rubbed his hand over his chin and sighed. Why in the hell did his life with the woman he loved have to be so hard? Why couldn't they just be happy once and for all? It was then that his heart ached for his wife. He missed her in more ways than one. She didn't deserve to be abandoned especially now when she needed him the most. She needed him to be her rock and he left her to fend for herself. Right then and there he resigned himself to at least being by her side until Everton's paternity results came in. He'd deal with the aftermath when the time came.

He headed back to New York, back to his wife with a new sense of excitement. As he pulled up to the building he noticed unmarked detective cars were parked in front.

"Oh, you've got to be fuckin' kidding me!" Shawn sucked his teeth, slapping his hand against the steering wheel. He decided to drive past his building and sneak a look inside the lobby. Just as he was about to pull off, a well dressed white man stepped in front of his vehicle.

"Get out," D.A. Franco Delucchio ordered.

Shawn stuck his head half way out the driver's side window and asked, "I'm starting to think this is sexual harassment," he joked.

"I don't think you'll be in such a joking mood when you find out why I'm here."

"What do you want from me, man?"

"Please step out of the vehicle sir."

An undercover detective appeared out of nowhere at the driver's door attempting to open it. Shawn sucked his teeth as he complied. He made certain not to give them any reasons to use brute force. He knew that would just make the D.A.'s day. The detective read Shawn his rights, glossing over the specific charge so Shawn asked him to repeat it but he ignored him. Shawn looked up and saw the doorman then said, "Remember all that you're seeing and hearing right now!"

The doorman just looked on with fear. He'd never seen an arrest up close in all his fifty-three years of life. Franco ordered the detective to place Shawn in the car he rode in.

"Gimme a minute with the perp," Franco commanded. The detective sitting in the driver's seat got the message and got out. When the car door slammed shut, D.A. Delucchio turned in his seat to face Shawn.

"You're going away you pale piece of shit."

"Mr. D.A., such language. Is that a racist joke because I'm light-skinned?" Shawn chuckled, trying to quell the anger building within.

"You think you're so fucking cool, huh? Well you'll be crying like a baby when I'm done with you."

"What fake charges are you trying this time?"

"Oh, just murder in the first!" he laughed
heartily, enjoying every minute of his momentary victory. The more confused Shawn looked, Franco became increasingly smug.

"What the fuck are you talking about you lying motherfucker?"

"Watch the language Mr. Wilson. Well, let me count the ways...oh, I mean list the counts, let's see, there's murder 1, kidnapping, obstruction of justice, um, illegal arms...woo, I can go on but I'm sure by now you get the gist."

"Are you fuckin' insane? I did not kill anyone."

"Well, I've got a 93% fingerprint match that says otherwise."

He grinned and whipped back around to face the front of the squad car. He signaled to the detective through the window, who jumped in and sped off.

Shawn wracked his brains going over every diminutive detail of his retaliations. Malcolm's death and cover-up was flawless. He personally watched Big Stew take care of it all. He burned everything as usual. They did the same for Manny He knew that it wasn't Manny's bitch either because she was kept blindfolded the entire time. She hadn't seen anyone's face. Besides the fact that she was warned not to mention what she'd gone through to anyone if she wanted her son to live, a threat against her own life was more than enough incentive for her to keep her mouth shut. Shawn couldn't figure out which murder was Franco referring to. He couldn't believe that he was bested by Franco and Mark. He knew that Mark had a hand in it. One way or another, they would both be dealt with.

ॐ

Natalia pulled into JahMecca's parking lot. She was more than ten minutes late. She wondered if Seth would even still be there. He hadn't answered his phone the last time she called to update him while she was in traffic. She rushed into the restaurant hoping he'd be there.

"Yes? How many are in your party?" The hostess quickly asked as soon as Natalia entered the restaurant.

"I'm meeting someone," she replied while scoping out the dining area. A warm hand slid up her back to her shoulder, turning her body around. She was now face to face with...

"Seth, hi," she said, trying to graciously wiggle out of his embrace.

"You're still as beautiful as ever," he beamed. He was still his sexy bald self. His skin still impeccable, his goatee trimmed and shaped to perfection.

"Ditto," she smiled nervously. He led her to the table where he had emptied two glasses of alcohol waiting for her. He held out her chair and as she sat down she said sincerely, "I'm so sorry for running so late. The traffic was

159

horrible from the upper east side."

"I guess it's my fault for not deciphering that time code," he smirked.

"No code, it was really bad traffic."

"It's okay. I've already ordered my meal. What will you have?"

"Oh, I love their Jerk shrimp sushi roll."

"Jerk shrimp roll it is," he looked around for the waitress, signaling her to come to the table.

"Ready to order?" she flipped open her order pad, prepared to write.

"Jerk shrimp roll, please," Seth replied then gave Natalia his undivided attention, then asked, "So we're parents, huh?"

"No, actually, you're not the only possible father."

"Oh, right, right, I forgot about your *husband*. Why don't you forget about him too?" he smiled slyly, making her uncomfortable.

"Seth, Everton hasn't got the luxury of time so we have to get on this right away," she reached into her purse and pulled out a card attached to a document.

"Everton?"

"Yes."

"I like it," he responded, pensive. She slid the documents across the table to him and said, "This is the hospital and doctor that you'll need to see to get tested for both the paternity test and to see if you're a match to be a donor. I'm begging you to get the testing taken care of as soon as you possibly can. I mean if you can do it tomorrow that would b..."

"I understand, I understand," he cut her off as he glanced over the paper and card then folded it into a neat square and stuffed it into his wallet then said, "But you need to understand that you can't just drop this sort of thing on someone and expect them to just roll with it. If he is mine then what? What will that mean for me? I don't expect your husband to roll out the red carpet for me and welcome me

160

into you're life. Will I even be able to be a father to my son?"

"Of course, I would never keep you from him. My husband isn't the issue here. We have to save Everton first and foremost. I'm willing to share custody with you. But he needs bone marrow pronto. I'm not a match, so you need to get tested right away."

"I said I understand," he emphasized each word, displaying his annoyance with her insistence. He moved his two empty glasses to the side as the waiter placed a plate of jerk shrimp rolls in front of him.

"If you don't mind, I'm gonna eat. Ordinarily I'd be a gentleman and wait for your food to arrive but I'm starved."

Moments later Natalia's food came and she daintily picked at it. In between bites and sips of water, then wine, they discussed more of the same. Never coming to the ultimate resolution Seth desired which would be Natalia giving up Shawn to be a family with him and his *newfound* son. He looked across the table and in one last plea said, "I have something you need, right? You have something I want. I can't really make it any clearer."

Now she understood what he was getting at. He was blackmailing her. He was using her child's illness to get her to come back into his life. It made her sick to her stomach and she wanted no part of this shake down.

"Are you trying to tell me that you're willing to bargain my son's life to satisfy some adolescent unrequited fixation?"

"Don't look at it like that. I want what's best for this child if he's mine. He deserves to have both his parents."

"And he will. I promise you that."

"You can promise me that it will rain money tomorrow but that doesn't mean it will happen. I need you to understand what this would mean to me if he is mine. You know how badly I want children."

"Oh, yea, I remember. But do you want one so badly that you're willing to barter my child's life just to force me into a relationship? If I wanted to be a bitch I could just deny you any contact."

161

"But I doubt you want to go that route seeing as how you need me more than ever right now. I want to be there for the boy but...well, I need assurances."

Her nose flared as she became agitated by his smugness, "You son of a bitch! I can't believe you'd stoop this low. Are you really sitting there blackmailing me?"

"I'm not blackmailing you. That's absurd. I'm just letting you know that I need to be absolutely positive that I'll be able to be in my son's life, all the way. I think you should really think about that before you make any rash decisions, ya know? Think of how much the kid can benefit from having mommy and daddy together," he smirked.

She was fuming now and if there weren't so many witnesses, she'd stab him with the fork she'd been flicking food around in her plate with.

"Well? Maybe you need more time to mull it over. Why don't you come home with me?" his stern voice transformed to a sultry, charming one and he wormed his hand over to hers, caressing it.

"Are you fucking serious?!?" she snatched her tiny hand from his massive manly ones.

"Very."

"I'd rather eat shit and die!"

Seth sucked his teeth, dug into his pocket retrieving his wallet. He fished through it for cash then threw a few dollars on the table. He rose and said snidely, "That's the tip for our waitress. Now here's a tip for you, if that kid is mine you'd better get a damn good lawyer! You know how to reach me if you smarten up."

Natalia was so angry that she snatched up the money, crumpled it and threw it at him. He picked the money off the floor all the while laughing at her. Then he left her embarrassed and with the check.

Her phone vibrated as she fished out her keys from her purse. It wasn't a number she recognized so she answered cautiously, "Yes?"

"B.G., I'm in central booking again. I need you to call

Ben and tell him D.A. Delucchio is trying to indict me for murder."

"What?"

"Just tell Ben that for me and tell him to get bail. If they allow bail I need you to get me out, okay?"

"Yes, daddy." Natalia wanted to cry but didn't. She was all cried out.

"I love you baby girl, don't worry, we're gonna get through this. I love you."

"I love you t—".

Click.

The sound of the phone hanging up lit a fire under her. She called Ben and told him exactly what her husband instructed her to. Ben hurried off the phone to find ways to free his A-list client. Natalia got in her car and headed to the one person she thought could help her.

Chapter XIII
The Way We Were
৵৽৶

As she mulled over how she'd save her husband from the D.A.'s clutches, her phone rang. The number was blocked and the only reason she answered was because she thought it could be Shawn again.

"Hello?"

"Hi, stranger."

"Mark?"

"Nice to know I haven't been forgotten."

"That's so strange."

"What?"

"I was going to come to your office."

"Well, great minds think alike. So are you coming?"

"Yes, I'm on my way, meet me downstairs in fifteen minutes.

"For you? Of course."

Natalia hadn't a clue what to expect from Mark but she knew that only desperation could make her gravel to her ex-husband whose life she single-handedly devastated. When she pulled up in front of his office building she thought that he looked extra handsome for some reason. It was as if he managed to make himself even sexier. *Ah, you sexy white boy.* She smiled to herself. He walked over and opened the car door for her, watching her every move as she stepped out.

"You look gorgeous!" he exclaimed, failing to hide his excitement.

"Ditto." She blushed.

"I'm a man, I can't look gorgeous," he laughed, she joined in.

"Well your car can't stay here like this so why don't we park it in the garage? It's free for my company, so don't worry about it."

"Okay."

After walking into his office she noticed that things were very different. His office was bigger, better.

"Promotion?" she asked, admiring his extravagant taste in office furniture.

"Aw, you noticed," he chuckled, "Yes, I'm a partner now."

"Congrats, Mark. I knew you were boss material."

"Did you now? Seeing as how it all seemed to happen right after our break up, I should thank you."

"For what?" she asked, incredulously.

"Our breakup made me focus on my work. I put extra effort in and this is what it got me." He smiled. She smiled; unaware that Mark wasn't smiling because he was happy for the promotion. His smile was to hide the anger he still harbored because of the shambles she left his life in.

He managed to charm her into dropping her guard and talk about their past. He reminded her of the good times only. Then he tricked her into talking about her marriage.

"So, I see he's been taking pretty good care of you."

"Yes, he does, actually," Natalia lied. He'd caused her so much stress in the last year alone that she was sure he knocked off ten years of her life. But it was an adventure. Then she remembered her mission. She had to convince Mark to call off his bulldog cousin. Shawn had to be freed.

"Mark, honestly, I'm here to ask a favor of you." She sat in a lounger and crossed her legs.

Mark knew what was coming. He orchestrated too much to not know that Shawn was once again behind bars.

"A favor, huh? What is it?"

"I know you're well aware of your cousin, Franco

165

harassing my husband. I'm asking, no, I'm begging you, please call him off."

"Call him off? You think I've *unleashed* him on your husband?" Mark asked, hiding his guilt quite well.

"Well he practically admitted that to Shawn."

"I don't know why. I have nothing to do with whatever it is your husband is involved with, nor my cousin's involvement. So you came here intent upon getting my help for what's his name?"

Natalia sighed, annoyed, "Yes, Mark. I need Shawn freed. Your cousin just arrested him, again. This harrassment has got to stop."

"Look if you're husband's criminal activity has gotten him arrested why is that any of my concern. It sounds to me like Franco is just doing his job."

"Doing his job? He is obsessed with paying me back for what happened between us," she pointed to him and back to herself, "So trust me, he's not doing his job. My husband is not a criminal! He is a prominent businessman, okay? So stop trying to degrade him."

"I only know from what the news reports state and it's in black and white that he's a suspected murderer, drug peddler and kidnapper." he spoke condescendingly, hoping the latter of his sentence would jog a few memories. Hurtful memories that would remind her just how much of a criminal Shawn truly was. Natalia's patience wore thin and rather than blow up on Mark in his office she decided to get as far away from him as she could before she caused a scene and was arrested too.

"Thanks for nothing," she spat, jumped out of the chair and began storming out.

He grabbed her and asked, "What's happened to you? You're not even the same person I knew. Is this boy really worth the idiocy?"

Without hesitation Natalia defended her husband, "Of course he is," she sneered then finished his ego off with, "He is the man I love come hell or high water. He is everything to me. Everything, do you get it?"

"No, I don't get it. That piece of shit is NOTHING! He's going to get you killed with that crazy lifestyle. You should've stayed with me. We're perfect together, Nat. I'll never stop loving you."

This was news to her. She didn't expect Mark to have any romantic feelings toward her whatsoever. Not after the way she left his heart torn to shreds. Even still she didn't want him getting any misguided signals about him and her. His hopes would be dashed if he remotely made a play for her now. She rested her hip and her purse down on his desk and said,

"Mark, I could never be with you. That would be going backwards. I can only go forward... with *him*. So I'm asking you to help me because essentially your cousin is operating on your behalf. So please, Mark make him leave us alone. Please... help me."

"You mean help *him*," Mark blew hard and raked his fingers through his shiny, loopy curls.

"Yes."

Natalia couldn't hide her eagerness while anticipating his answer. His expression bore disgust as he spoke, "The hell I will. He stole my wife, my child, my life! There's no way I can help him to run off into the fucking sunset with the woman I'm in love with."

"What the hell are you talking about, Mark?"

"Nat, I never stopped loving you and that's what cost me, Caroline."

Natalia's jaw dropped.

"That's right, I'm divorced. Caroline left me."

"Mark, I'm so sorry to hear that," she consoled him by gently rubbing his arm. Mark looked down at her fingers as they slid down his arm. Her cumbersome seven carat saber tooth diamond engagement ring tauntingly winked at him under the florescent lights.

"Nat, we were so good together. That thug can't be good for you."

"Mark, don't start that. I came here for your help and you're either going to give it to me or not."

"Then, NOT." He walked away from her and sat in his plush, smoky-grey, leather, executive recliner.

"You are a real asshole!" She grabbed her purse from the modern glass and chrome desk and stormed out. She was so irate that she slammed her palm onto the elevator button causing a rush of agonizing electrical currents throughout the nerve endings in her hand.

"Ouch!" She looked at her red palm regretting the hasty move.

The elevator doors opened and the empty elevator car was a welcomed sight. She stepped in and sighed, a lone tear formed at the corner of her left eye and began to trickle. Just as she attempted to press the L button on the elevator console Mark's face peered in, he forced open the elevator doors and got in. He grabbed her hand and apologized.

"Nat, I'm sorry if I upset you. It's just that I know what a prize you are and I would never endanger you or do anything to cause you any problems like I've had to watch you go through since you've been with him."

Natalia's mind was made up about her husband. But even though her love was loyal she had to admit that Mark's words rang true. She looked up into his once olive face, its newly bronzed hue made his blue eyes brighter.

"I love him and I won't apologize for that. I understand you're hesitation, I do. But I really need your help, Mark not a lecture," she huffed, nervously.

Mark hovered over her as she watched the lights on the console, ignoring his intense stare. She really didn't want to piss him off because she believed that without his help Shawn would be up shit's creek. She hoped he'd come around to feeling sorry enough for her that he'd help based on their history together. Okay so she cheated on him, humiliated him and in his own words cost him his son. As she rehashed their tumultuous relationship she realized there wasn't a snowball's chance in hell that Mark was going to actually bail out his nemesis.

"What is it you need?" he surprised her as the elevator doors opened and they stepped out into the lobby. As they left his office building she found it hard to organize her thoughts. His question threw her off track and now his once hardened expression dissipated, a softened stare replaced it. He rested his hand on her tense shoulder and repeated his question, "What is it that you need, Nat?"

"You mean it?" she asked.

"Yes. So what has your pimp gotten himself into now?" he chortled.

Natalia's glare was enough to send the message of her disapproval of his tactless wit.

"I didn't mean anything by it. Don't take offense, Nat," he spoke ruefully.

She bowed her head, not in shame but to hide her annoyance. She didn't want him to feel awkward, so awkward that he'd decide against pulling the strings necessary for Shawn's release.

"I need you to call a cease fire. Tell Franco it's over. He's insistent upon holding Shawn on trumped up charges. He seems to be holding a vendetta against me," she began tearing up as she spoke. "Tell him to release Shawn on his own recognizance and drop whatever convoluted charges he has against him."

Mark's cousin had only recently been appointed New York's district attorney. He was the best man at their wedding so of course Shawn's name making its way across his desk was a gift from God. He would make both Natalia, whom he considered an ingrate half-breed and Shawn a miserable miscreant get their just desserts. He'd kill two birds with one stone by nabbing a former F.B.I. fugitive, garnering a pat on the back for a job well done while exacting revenge on the mutt his cousin married, disgracing their Italian heritage.

"Are you kidding me?" Mark seemed appalled and insulted. Was this woman really asking him to appeal on her behalf to the relative whose shoulder he cried on over her; the man who had witnessed his blatant humiliation by both her and Shawn? Was he to make a complete ass of himself by asking such a favor of him that would benefit the man who robbed him of his happiness?

"I know that it's a bit much to ask of you but I'm desperate."

She fidgeted inside her purse to retrieve the card for Shawn's lawyer then handed it to him.

"You see, the lawyer says that they're trying to tack on extra charges based on false pretenses. They're trying to send him away for murder! But none of it is true. Franco is just angry that he can't pin those murders on him so he's trying to be vindictive. He's doing this as payback, I just know it."

Mark seemed agitated at this point. She was serious. So serious, enthralled in her plea that she followed him all the way into the parking garage to his car and didn't even notice. He had long tuned out her nattering. His attention had since moved elsewhere. He was amazed at how she still looked radiant and beautiful in the midst of all the drama surrounding her. His mind harping on how much he missed that radiance, her melodic voice, titillating kisses, and the alluring scent which crept into his nostrils at that very moment. She stood there right before his eyes vulnerable. Devious scenarios plagued him and he saw a way to profit from this newfound vulnerability.

"Have dinner with me."

"No thanks, I'm not hungry," she sighed then asked, "So, will you please talk to Franco?"

"Only if you have dinner with me," he grinned mischievously. Her eyes were doubtful as she turned to face him, raising a disapproving brow.

"What?" he asked, maintaining his mischievous grin.

"This is not a game, Mark. I really need your help here. Can you help me?"

"Like I said, have dinner with me and I'll consider it."

170

"Mark, please. I know you want to take this opportunity to torture me but can you please just..."

"Okay, okay. I will help you. But only if you allow me to feed you, my lady."

He smiled a friendly smile, reeling her in.

"Um, okay," she answered apprehensive then said, "But my car's on the upper level."

"I'll drive you in my car for now and later I'll bring you back to your car."

"I need to find out what time the garage closes."

"They're open 24 hours, so you don't have to worry."

"Alright, Mark but if I can't come back and get my car tonight, that's your ass!" she giggled as her words echoed in her head. She was sounding more and more ghetto.

Mark took her giggle as a sign of her loosening up. This was all he needed to give credence to his plan's success. What made it sweeter was that she didn't suspect the malice he intended. He had the upper hand and he loved it. He held the door of his car open for her, licking his lips as her dress rose ever so slightly revealing her honey-laden thighs. He slid into the driver's seat of his convertible ready for action.

Immobilized by New York City rush hour traffic, Mark took the opportunity of having her ear captive to lull Natalia with empty promises of helping her beloved husband. The more bull he shoveled in her lap, the easier it became for him to bait then hook her. He parked in front of a modernized brownstone in the West Village. Natalia stretched out her arms, restless from the long spell in Manhattan's treacherous traffic. She looked past Mark towards the well lit building asking, "What kind of restaurant is this?"

"Chez Marco," he laughed. "You do remember that I know my way around a kitchen don't you?"

"What are you up to?" she watched as he pressed a button and the convertible top of his car enclosed them. Mark got out the car while asking, "Can't a man offer to cook his ex-wife a meal?"

"Not if said man has a vendetta against said ex-wife!"

171

she replied as she got out, shutting the car door behind her.

"A vendetta?!?" he chortled, "Are you kidding me? I don't have a vendetta. You insult me. Don't confuse me with Franco, Nat. I'm fine with helping you out but not if you're just trying to use me for the moment then discard me. We have history...granted most of it is bad but we don't have to keep it that way. We can start fresh, be friends again."

Natalia folded her arms, pressing the side of her curved hip against his car watching him suspiciously.

"Come on. Let me cook for you. I promise not to poison you," he joked. Natalia laughed, "Hmmm...I do remember you're ziti. It's been a long time."

"That it has," he smiled.

Once inside, Mark gave Natalia a quick tour of his brownstone. She recognized a constant in the color scheme which included muddled hues of burgundy, green and brown. It was all so dark, befitting his tortured soul. The furniture didn't echo the exterior's futuristic sentiment. It was all old fashioned immersed in blah tones and evoked depression. For a moment she could swear that she'd seen one of his rooms in a haunted house flick. She wanted to giggle out loud at the thought but dared not bring attention to her aversion of his decorative taste.

"Well, what do you think?" he asked, sure that he'd done a great job with the interior of his bachelor pad.

"Well, it's...wow. It's....really, really grown up."

"I see," his eyes formed suspicious slits, "Is that you're way of saying you hate it?"

"No, not at all I like it...for *you*."

They both laughed nervously. It was the icebreaker of the evening and Mark found comfort in the return of her sarcasm.

Natalia helped out in the kitchen as Mark sliced and diced up a storm. It was as if he were trying to impress her with his culinary skills. She had to admit that watching him maneuver the knife was sexy. He sautéed, whisked, boiled and stewed all without breaking a sweat, literally. The ziti brimmed with Italian sausage and gooey fresh mozzarella cheese. Natalia gobbled up a serving, reminiscing when Mark treated her to his gourmet style cooking on a regular basis. As she finished off a piece of soggy garlic bread, she dunked in marinara sauce she gazed over at him, thinking, How is it this man is still single? He was single because he had made the mistake of pitting his soon to be ex-wife with his already ex-wife. Every argument with Caroline he'd throw Natalia into the mix. Natalia never did that, or Nat was better at this, or yea, I do miss Natalia! These were all major marriage violations. That and the fact that Mark shoved her on one occasion after she threw something at him. That was the last straw and the prenuptial agreement she reluctantly signed awarded her a nice bag of change. Caroline was no fool, so taking the money and run so to speak was as good a decision as any.

"This is nice, huh?" he asked in between bites.

"Mmm, hmn." She nodded, enjoying her garlic bread a bit too much.

"I meant us sitting here eating together, like old times."

"Oh," she murmured, keeping her eyes on her food to avoid his eyes.

"I remember how much you loved my cooking, always asking me to put sugar in my sauces. You and your sweet tooth," he chuckled then said, "You love desserts so much that you'd even eat dessert for dinner," he laughed, she did too and added, "Yea. But I'm so full, no dessert for me."

"Aw, come on, live a little. I have some leftover tiramisu from that bakery you love," Mark pushed himself away from the table and stood up. He patted his flat torso and picked up his near empty plate. Natalia watched him maneuver around the kitchen then asked,

"Really? Hmmm, I just might have a smidgeon of room left," she giggled then said, "Here let me do that. It's the least I can do after that great tasting meal."

Natalia got up and began tidying up. Mark helped her

and they joked the entire time. Mark took the last plate that she was washing from her hands and placed it on the dish rack. He pulled her into him and attempted to kiss her.

"What the hell are you doing?" she jerked her head back, and backed away from him.

He grabbed her hand, pulled her into him and attempted to kiss her again.

"Stop that," she seemed baffled and swatted at him.

"Stop what?"

"Stop trying to get fresh with me, Mark."

"Heh, heh, forgive me. It's just that the moment...well it was just like old times, you know?"

"Yea, like old times," she snidely remarked, "It's time that I go."

"Don't leave." Mark grabbed at her hand, still hopeful. Natalia snatched her hand away.

"Nat, please don't."

"Don't what? Feel offended? Was this your plan? Get me here under false pretenses then pounce? Look, Mark, I just need to know one thing and then I'll go." She found her purse, grabbed it then spun around to face him, "Will you help me, yes or no?"

"Well, now, that depends. What's in it for me?"

"A halo? A spot in heaven? The satisfaction of knowing that you did a good deed?" she rolled her eyes.

"None of that is useful to me," he said, inching closer to her. He grabbed her shoulders and yanked her closer to him. He forcibly pressed his thin lips against her supple ones. His tongue tried to pry her lips apart but she refused to part them. He squeezed her with so much force that she thought she'd pass out.

"Mark please, I can't breathe," Mark ignored her plea. His hands explored her softness, her rotund rear end, the slopes of her hips, even the curve in her back.

"Why don't you love me, Nat?" he breathed heavily in her ear.

"Let me go," she was drained and disappointed with

his behavior. He quickly devoured her lips once more catching her off guard; this time his tongue made its way into her unsuspecting mouth. She fought his advances, eventually straining to pull her head way back to rid her mouth of his furtive tongue. Mark wasn't ready for the kiss to end and forced himself upon her again. She kneed him in the groin and ran for the front door. He ran after her only to spew taunting obscenities and damaging threats.

"You stupid, fucking, bitch! That bastard is gonna rot in jail and if I can work it out with Franco maybe your frigid ass can do a little time with your beloved jail bird!"

"You're a sick, pathetic man, Mark," she snarled as she fumbled with the door knob.

Mark was behind her now, the heat from his breath and heated words wafted across the back of her neck warming it.

"Would you like that you drug-dealer loving bitch?!? Bet you'd do anything for that bum, huh? You'd suck on a crack pipe too wouldn't you?"

She finally got the door unlocked, he grabbed her arm again, "I'm sick of you treating me like shit and getting away with it!"

"If the shoe fits, then stick it in your ass! Now get your perverted hands off of me!"

"I guess you only want murderers touching you now, huh? Guess if I went out and shot people that'd turn you on. You're the sick one, Natalia. You're the sick, demented stupid bitch that doesn't know what's good for her."

"Get off of me!" she finally snatched her arm free and ran down the steps.

"I'm going to personally see to it that you both suffer. I'm going to make sure he gets sent to prison for a long time! And if I have to pay inmates to fuck him up the ass daily I will!"

"FUCK YOU!" Natalia screamed at the top of her lungs as she walked hastily towards the middle of the street, "You fuckin' pathetic rapist! MARCO DELUCCHIO IS A RAPIST!!!"

she shouted for all his neighbors to hear. He quickly ran back in his house and slammed the door.

She had become ruminative with thoughts of how idiotic it was for her to trust Mark. She ran to Avenue of the Americas and tried to hail a cab. She promised herself to fix Shawn's legal woes and a promise is a promise. This was not the kind of promise she wanted to break. Anger grabbed a hold of her and as she stuck out her arm to hail a cab her eyes welled up with hot tears, the kind that burn when they fill your eyes. The kind that indicate there would be hell to pay.

⪻⪼

Thankfully, Ben was able to work magic as usual. Shawn was free on 50 gees, a modest bail by any standard let alone for a murder charge on a man with the means to jump bail. It was a bargain in his eyes. He knew that he had one way out of this mess and that was to squash the bug that kept buzzing in his ear. Franco Delucchio didn't know it but he was now Shawn's obsession. Shawn enlisted Big Stew as his accomplice. Big Stew staked out Franco's office, home even his girlfriend's house. Today was the big day. The day that Franco realized why Shawn had so many get out of jail free cards.

Big Stew knew that he and his consort didn't have much time to abduct the district attorney. There was a very small window in which Franco Delucchio would be without probing eyes. This short window happened to be at this precise moment when he headed from his fiancé's home in the wee hours of the morning supposedly off to his house which would enable him to get to his office faster but instead he was headed to an off beat hotel in Suffolk County to meet up with the sexy barely legal intern he fucked on the side.

176

Shawn loved Big Stew's style. He didn't need any henchmen to help with this plan. He knew Big Stew was all the muscle he needed. His loyalty was unsurpassed and his capability to put the fear of God in someone was invaluable. At first Shawn believed that fear alone would stop Franco from continuous frivolous prosecution but when they surprised him while getting head from the sweet-faced brunette, he became enraged, indignant.

"What the fuck is this?!?" Franco spat, pushing the brunette's head away from between his legs. She collapsed beside him on the bed then sprang up,

"Frankie what's going on?!?" she asked, frightened.

"Yea, Frankie, what's going on?" Big Stew mimicked and grinned, watching the woman's naked body as she scrounged for her clothes.

"Nice piece of ass you got there, Frankie, baby." Big Stew walked over to her and slapped her ass while she palmed under the bed still searching for her clothes.

"Is this supposed to scare me? I'm the D.A. You'd never get away with killing me. They'll be all over you for this one. You're my biggest case! The F.B.I. will find you for sure. You'd go down hard!" he seemed to be trying to convince himself more than anything.

"You think that the F.B.I. cares about you? They don't give a flying fuck if you die. All they care about is getting their man. Me. I'm the fuckin' superstar. You? You're just a pain in the ass looking to ride on my coattails. So I've decided to make you famous." Shawn walked up to the brunette and told her, "Lay face down on the floor."

"I d-didn't see your face, please, don't kill me! I didn't see your face!"

Shawn knew that just because he and Stew wore oversized black shades, leather gloves and caps didn't mean that she wouldn't be able to testify to the fact that Franco mentioned his biggest case or i.d. them if not by voice alone. She had to be erased from the crime scene too.

"Oh, come on. She doesn't know anything. Don't do

this, let her go." Franco jumped up.

"Shut the fuck up!" Big Stew, back handed Franco, knocking him back to the bed.

"PLEASE OH, PLEASSSE! DON'T KILL ME!" the woman shouted. Shawn felt sorry for her but it was out of his hands. Franco had sealed her fate with his grandstanding. The woman relentlessly screamed more pleas for her life, making it harder for Shawn to concentrate. Big Stew simply grabbed a pillow from the bed, walked past Shawn, threw the pillow up against her and popped her in the left side of her back. He was tired of hearing the noise.

"Oh, My God! Why'd you do that? You didn't have to kill her!" Franco panicked now. Big Stew approached him as he slid from the bed to the floor beside the woman's limp body.

"Oh, God, I'm sorry, Eileen, I'm so sorry," he began blubbering.

"Touching," Big Stew joked then said, "Yo, let's get this shit over with."

"What's the real deal with you obsessing over me?" Shawn was standing over Franco now. Franco ignored his question and kept crying. Big Stew kicked him in his side and warned, "Answer him!"

Franco nursed his ribs and took short breaths to curtail the pain flaring through out his torso. Big Stew readied his foot to strike again.

"OKAY! OKAY! Gimme a minute...," he sniffled then spilled his guts. The F.B.I. was still on the prowl for Shawn to his dismay. He had become an unofficial pet project of agent Strect. A nemesis he long forgot about. Agent Strect had assembled a select few to help him find a way to finally take down the only criminal who slipped through his fingers.

"What are you gonna do to me? I was only doing my job!" he copped.

"You did your job well. So well you're going to get a promotion." Shawn inched closer to Franco.

"I promise you, you won't get away with this. They're

onto you and if you kill me you're putting a big fat target on your head!"

"The target's on your head," Shawn cocked the piston on his gun."

"Don't do this! Please, please...," Franco released a wallop of farts, sounding like a symphony of tubas.

"Click!" Shawn imitated the sound of a light switch, laughing hard. Big Stew joined in.

"YOU FUCKIN' BASTARDS! YOU SCUM OF THE EARTH MOTHERFUCKERS!" Franco shouted at the top of his lungs. The laughter stopped and Shawn reached behind him and slid a long thick metal pipe out of his back pocket.

"What'd you call us?" Shawn twirled the pipe as he spoke.

"You really are a thug aren't you? So now you're going to beat me with a pipe?"

"Nope," Shawn grinned.

THWACK!

Without so much as a word, Shawn had cracked Franco over the head with the pipe with such brute force, blood, remnants of his skull and brain tissue flew all over the place, including in Shawn's face. He wiped away Franco's brain matter and blood from his face with the back of his sleeve and said, "I didn't beat you. I killed you with a pipe." Big Stew laughed at Shawn's dark humor.

The back of Franco's head was split wide open. The white, pinkish meat was there for all to see and the skin from his scalp dangled as blood trickled down his cranium and onto his shirt collar. His body keeled over. They looked all around the hotel room at the blood splattered all across the furniture, sheets, walls and carpet.

"We've got to get rid of everything that will connect us, Stew. You know what I'm thinking?"

"Lemme guess. Uh, we torch the place? Damn, that shit must run in the family. You and your brother love burning and blowing shit up," Big Stew laughed, "I miss that sick motherfucker," he cackled then asked, "Aiight, how we gon' do this?" Big Stew yanked the woman's body from the floor and put her on the bed. He did the same with Franco's body.

"Shit!" Shawn mumbled.

"What happened?"

"The problem is the fire department would get here too quick for everything to burn. The only thing I can think to do is acid down these walls and everything else." Shawn thought long and hard then remembered he knew someone with an auto junk yard in the vicinity. He needed gallons of battery acid.

"Where the fuck we gonna get acid at this time of night? And how the fuck we gonna do all that and manage not to draw attention to ourselves, two black men buying acid? Them motherfuckers gonna know we ain't scientists," he chuckled.

Shawn shook his head as he laughed, "I was thinking of using battery acid. But that's gonna be annoying opening up mad car batteries and shit," he stuffed his gloved hand into Franco's pants pocket until he felt cold metal. He pulled out car keys then said, " So the next best thing because we're running out of options is to pop off those smoke detectors and break the automatic sprinkler valves," he gestured, looking up at the ceiling.

"That'll work," Big Stew commenced to snatching the smoke detectors from the ceiling leaving their exposed wires dangling. He took the pipe from Shawn's hand and went to work on the sprinkler valves. Shawn ran out to Franco's car and was relieved when he popped the trunk and found an emergency can of gasoline. He rushed back into the house and doused the furniture, the carpet and the blood spattered walls, neglecting the bed and bodies.

"Put their bodies in his car. You take the junk car and I'll drive his. We're gonna take them out to the woods in River Head and burn em'."

Big Stew rolled the woman's body in the flatted sheet from the bed and wrapped Franco's with the bedspread. He grabbed both bodies but even with all his might he couldn't carry them at the same time. So he left Franco's carcass and easily flung the mummified woman over his shoulder, casually sprinting to the car and rolling her from his arms into the open trunk. He rushed back and scooped up Franco's heavier body and chucked it in the trunk as well. Shawn emptied the last bit of gas from the can, splashing it all over the bed. He carefully flicked his Bick and threw it inside the hotel room while he watched from the hall as it ignited quickly. Fire blazed trails throughout all the gas soaked spots, eventually consuming most of the cramped room within seconds. He slowly closed the door then ran to the car.

❧

The incubator seemed to swallow Everton. He looked so frail behind the dull glass. Natalia slid her hands into the special latex gloved tubes on each side of the incubator. She touched her sleeping son whose plump cheeks seemed deflated now. Everton seemed to get sicker with each passing day. It was breaking her heart to not be able to place her child against her bosom, feel his soft baby skin against hers. It was at that moment that she got bitter sweet news. "Ms. Wilson, may I speak with you?" the doctor led her out of the room, stopping in the hallway.

"Well, Everton is doing better than expected. He's responded to the meds without any drawbacks and we're hopeful that he can leave in a couple of days."

"But?" Natalia interjected.

"But...without the donor, he's going to require extensive, consistent care. And like I told you before, considering complications throughout this illness, he may not make it to puberty."

Natalia remembered that she still hadn't received the

results for Everton's paternity from the lab. Tymeek submitted his blood via overnight delivery thanks to an international laboratory he found online; Seth went in to get tested. Faye was still ignoring her phone calls so now she was willing to get Maleek's decomposed body one way or another even if it entailed grave robbing. But, for now she was surprisingly hopeful that she would end up finding a match without having to go that route. All she wanted was good news to secure her baby's future.

"We may have some donors. I just need to make a call," she excused herself. Stepping off the elevator was like falling from the Empire Sate Bilding to her. As she walked outside into the blinding sun's glare she knew that this was a make it or break it moment. If the lab didn't have any good news she'd be forced to get drastic.

The woman on the other end of the phone might as well had been speaking another language after she revealed the paternity and donor match results because Natalia had stopped paying her any mind. She couldn't respond to the woman's question, she was too busy feeling numb as if she were in a galactic vacuum. So the woman repeated her question but then the mother of all irony happened. The bane of her existence was on the other line, beeping in. Something compelled her to answer.

"Hello," she answered mechanically.

"Hey, mommy. So it's official. I'm a dad! You've made me the happiest man on Earth!" Seth gleefully proclaimed.

ᔰᓭ

The miracles of all miracles occurred when Shawn found out that Everton's father was actually Seth Williamson. He was of all things, relieved; not just because he didn't have to face the fact of raising the son of a man he killed, but mostly because raising his own nephew was not something he could do. Finding out that Seth was not a match, but Tymeek was a match, was the shocker of all shockers. It was all good news to Shawn. His wife on the other hand had real issues with the idea that her son would have to leave the country to get the transplant performed. But, it was something she was willing to accept since Tymeek was saving Everton's life.

Tymeek claimed to find the perfect medical institute to perform the transplant surgery and care for Everton's condition. He insisted that he would continuously check in on him and make sure they took excellent care of his nephew.

Then came the bad news, Seth was pulling an evil stunt. Not even a full two days after finding out he was the father, Natalia was served with a subpoena. Seth wanted full custody.

Watching his wife suffer through hospital visits then hiring pediatric nurses to keep watch over Everton until he could leave for his transplant was disheartening. Shawn confided in Tymeek about Seth hiring a high profile celebrity lawyer to acquire full custody of Everton. Shawn knew that he had to do something. Tymeek offered his services to eliminate the custody threat along with helping Shawn devise a scheme to get out of the country under the radar of 'Big Brother'. Once Everton was safely on his way, Shawn was to hitch a ride with one of Tymeek's friends who specialized in boat exporting. Shawn knew the perfect spot to meet up with the boat. Andre's beach house was above the sea and not too far from the ports. Everything was coming together nicely.

Shawn took the opportunity to run his plan to leave America by Natalia again even though whether she knew it or not, they were leaving regardless if she protested.

"Alex and Brimney set up that off shore account for me and transferred the funds. Tymeek verified it all," Shawn stuffed bottles into a bag and continued, "I'm officially no longer apart of the Mallplex."

"Daddy, I'm so sorry. I know how proud you were to be apart of building the largest mall on the East Coast. So did you make out good on your end after selling your stake?"

"Don't be sorry. I made out like a bandit. Plus, I've been wanting out of this country for so long now, now's the time to get out. Especially after... well, the less you know the better."

Natalia sighed. She had an inclining of what Shawn was referring to. His case was mysteriously stalled indefinitely due to the D.A.'s mysterious disappearance and missing case files. She knew that Franco Delucchio's unknown whereabouts and Seth missing his court date in Family Court couldn't have both been a coincidence. She constantly wondered what actually happened but was afraid to ask her husband. Part of her felt bad for both men but then another part of her was grateful she didn't have to deal with either of the assholes anymore.

"So, is this your lame attempt to sell me on leaving New York again? Are you still trying to convince me to move to Holland?"

"Actually, I'm thinking more like the Caribbean."

"Really?"

"Yea, Mon!" Shawn laughed hard, grabbed his wife and caressed the side of her face, peering into her doe-like eyes.

She reached up on her tip toes to plant a kiss on his lips.

"You've sold me," she simpered.

"Seriously?"

"Yup."

"So you're okay with leaving next week? "Next week?"

"The sooner the better, okay?"

"I guess," she sighed.

"And B.G., I don't want you being worried about handing Everton over to Tymeek's people. Trust me, if he says that Lil' E will be safe then he will be, alright?"

Natalia went back to packing her baby's clothes,

184

neglecting to respond. That was the one part she was not okay with. Her son had to stay in the medical facility for a month. This didn't sit too well with her. But knowing he'd be in the care of top pediatric hematologists was enough to ease her fears for now.

Shawn sensed her fear and hugged her from behind, rocking her gently, "Baby, think of the bigger picture. E will be all fixed up, we'll get our living situation handled then we'll go get him and we'll all be happy together. No lame dude trying to take him from us or nothing, just us."

"I know, daddy, I know."

Then the million dollar question popped into her head and she just had to ask it, "Is Seth dead?"

"No, I just made him an offer he couldn't refuse."

"What kind of offer?"

"Like I said, the kind he couldn't refuse. Just know that your boy was a real bitch in every sense of the word. But he knows that Lil' E belongs with his mother and that's why he chose not to show in court that's all."

"I probably shouldn't ask but I'm really curious because Mark's ranting on CNN about you being involved with Franco's disappearance, it has me wondering...is it true?"

Shawn just looked at his wife as if she had three heads. She realized at that moment this was about the time for her to play her position and shut the fuck up.

"So, I know you want to see Andre before we go don't you?" he asked matter-of-factly.

"Of course," she put her hand to her heart and said, "Oh, no, Andy will be so far out of reach. Whatever will I do?"

"Keep all his numbers. We'll find ways to contact him. In fact we're going to visit him on our last day here. Spend the whole day with him, okay?"

"We are?"

"Yes, we are."

Natalia was pleasantly surprised. It was the first time Shawn actually showed interest and concern for her and

Andre's relationship. *More reasons for why I love you.*

≈≈≈

Andre was in his sweat pants working out on his elliptical machine when Natalia and Shawn peered through his glass terrace doors. She could hear the waves crashing against the rocks at the bottom of the bluff near his beach house on the Jersey Shore.

Their presence outside the doors startled him at first then he hurried off the machine to open the terrace doors.

"Get in here you stalkers!" Andre joked and hugged Natalia tightly.

"Wassup?" Shawn awkwardly gave him a manly pound followed by the obligatory back pat.

"Wow! To what do I owe this honor?"

"Besides me missing you, I come bearing bittersweet news."

"Oh, lawd, what is it now dynamic duo?" Shawn and Natalia couldn't help but laugh.

"Sit, sit," Andre insisted.

"We're leaving," Natalia said sadly, as she lowered her buttocks on a stylish, wheat-colored, pinstriped, tufted sofa.

"I know, as soon as his mall thingy is done. But you'll be here in my part of town, so that's no biggie."

"Um, no, we're leaving America."

Andre put the back of his hand to his forehead and feigned a faint spell then sprung back up,

"Why?"

"We have to get away from the craziness," Shawn replied.

"Mmn, hmn, craziness, please, the craziness is right there," Andre said, frantically pointing at Shawn and Natalia.

They all laughed.

"True, true," Shawn finished off his laughter, "But we had a lot of help," he smiled then said, "I'm gonna take good care of her. And we'll find ways for y'all to meet up, vacations, all of that," Shawn offered hope with a huge grin.

"Well as long as she's safe, that's all that matters to me."

Andre hugged Natalia.

∾

Shawn was subjected to a lot of reminiscing and cackling by way of Andre. It was becoming unbearable and he was happy to see that it was very close to the time for him and Natalia to meet with Tymeek's guy at the boardwalk. Natalia was in the bathroom, her ass hovering over the toilet when she heard the sounds of a police radio through the window. She pulled her pants back up, choosing to snoop rather than empty her bladder. She stepped into Andre's sunken tub to get to the huge bay windows. She slid the curtain over just a bit to sneak a peek and saw two men whispering. She recognized their official federal gear. She covered her mouth to stop herself from screaming. She made sure not to make too much noise as she tip-toed to warn Shawn. Andre was showing Shawn video footage of his and Natalia's 1995 Brazilian vacation. Shawn was enjoying the bikini shots when Natalia crept into the room and put her fingers to her lips.

"What is it?" Andre whispered.

"There are agents here, daddy. What do we do?"

Shawn sighed; they were too close to freedom to get caught now. Just then the doorbell rang accompanied by loud knocking, practically causing Andre and Natalia to jump out of their skin. Shawn remained calm as he took his wife's arm to lead her to a safe hiding place and he instructed Andre to answer the door, but deny their presence.

༺·༻

Shawn stuck the tip of his gun under the pantry door and let off a few rounds right into the federal agent's feet.

"Aaarrggh! Strecht! I'm hit!" the agent yowled in pain.

He fell to the ground, reaching for his bloody foot, attempting to get his scuffed up Doc Martins' off. It was then that he stared right in the direction of where the shots came from. First a flash of light, then an unimaginable surge of pain ripped into his top lip and darkness swallowed him as the bullet from Shawn's gun made its way through his mouth finally nestling in his cerebellum. Shawn was grateful his aim was dead on and he quickly got up from the floor and cautiously opened the pantry door. The creaking noise angered him; he prayed the other agent hadn't found Natalia. He left the safety of the pantry to check on the agent lying on the floor. One would assume that all the blood trickling from the back of his head would suffice as indication of death but Shawn was extremely cautious now. He checked for breathing, a heartbeat but found neither.

Then he saw the communicative device dangling from the agent's right ear. Shawn yanked it off, searched the agent's pockets, taking all of its contents and stuffing them into his own. He snatched up the bloodied gun. He ran to find his hiding wife.

He had thrown her into Andre's closet before the first agent spotted them after bum rushing the front door causing Andre to run out of his own house screaming like a banshee. One of the agents threw open the guest room's closet door to find Shawn and Natalia huddled under the racks of clothing. They bolted, knocking him over but he yelled freeze and Natalia actually froze. By abiding by the agent's command she nearly cost them their freedom. Shawn knew the F.B.I.

would rather catch them alive then dead so he had no problem not complying. He only froze just enough for the agent to feel confident enough to approach them. Then he elbowed the agent in his nose sending him to the floor, grabbed Natalia who was stiff like a deer caught in headlights.

Shawn opened the closet door slowly to find Natalia curled up in the fetal position on the floor in the corner of the closet. He snatched her up from the floor and they fled the house like track stars leaving trails of sand-filled dust as they made their way to the hooptie Shawn got from a hookup. Shawn put pedal to metal and gassed past the approaching Fed cars. He zigged when they zagged. He made a right, a left, zoomed over sidewalks foreboding all traffic rules just to get to the boardwalk. He was not going to miss the boat.

He drove halfway onto the boardwalk then dashed out of the vehicle with Natalia in tow. He slung a knapsack around his shoulder and grabbed his wife's hand as they ran down the boardwalk. Natalia slipped and fell to the ground. Right when Shawn was about to go to her aide an agent appeared at the end of the boardwalk, blocking their path.

"B.G. you can't be all scary. You gotta be 'bout your shit right now. I need you to remember all that I taught you with the guns. You gotta get gully right now and handle yourself cuz we at war," Shawn yelled at his wife as he ducked behind a load of imported containers. "HIDE!" he shouted at her. She dashed behind a dock trolley filled with large crates as her eyes welled up. She began sniffling, trying to hold back tears. She wanted to be strong and fearless having had dealt with all the chaos in her life ever since becoming entangled with him, but her conscience was preventing her from crossing over to the dark side. But she knew that it was all or nothing now. If they were caught, life as she knew it would be over. Everton would be parentless or worse, dead. She knew that the only thing stopping her from getting to her son and a new and improved life was the federal agent.

She peeked past the agent to see the boat swaying on the tranquil waters and the slight sea breeze whipped strands of her silky straight hair into her face as it seemed to whisper, *freedom!* The agent was so young, baby-faced; she didn't think she could do it. She heard her husband's voice in her head egging her on, encouraging her to do what was necessary. She popped out from behind the loading dock trolley and did as she was taught to do. The agent was too quick for any of her shots to hit and he dove down, rolled toward the protection of an anchor and began letting off rounds in Natalia's direction.

Thankfully, Shawn came running down the boardwalk blazing a path with bullets, shooting up the agent who groaned and pleaded for mercy. Shawn was merciless. He finished off the agent with a couple more rounds. He ran back to where his wife was sprawled out on the wooden planks. Her eyes were tightly closed and her teeth clenched as if she were in pain. It was then that he noticed the blood stain on the side of her shirt.

"FUCK!" Shawn yelled. Natalia attempted to get up from the floor.

"No, baby girl don't try to move," he tried to soothe her with a calming tone to keep her from panicking. He quickly pulled off his shirt, then his wife beater. He balled up the wife beater, pressed it up against her gunshot wound then tied his shirt as tightly as he could around her midsection.

He looked around erratically wondering how he'd get past the other agents carrying his injured wife. He had no choice and the boat was off in the distance diminishing in the grey mist taking his new found life with it if he didn't get into the dingy perched at the edge of the boardwalk. It seemed so far away...unreachable. But determination and ascending anger over his wife's predicament empowered him.

He cautiously loaded his wife into one of the empty crates on a huge trolley and began pushing while using the tower of crates on it as a shield. As he neared the edge of the boardwalk he could hear the agents shouting their usual corny threats.

Shawn pressed on regardless to not having an escape plan. All he knew was that the ship was almost out of view. He stopped midway and looked into the crate at his wife. Her eyes were glazed, almost lifeless. The sight tore through his heart. His choices were more than limited now. He could go out in a blaze of glory or give himself up but lose not only his life but his wife's as well. Just as the three agents closed in on him a litter of shots rang out like firecrackers on the Fourth of July.

They seemed to come from all sides and Shawn stood still at first from shock but then he realized the bullets weren't meant for him since the agents were laid out on the boardwalk like exterminated roaches. A powerful hand palmed his shoulder and he turned to lock eyes with a sight for his sore eyes.

"Ty?" he asked in amazement. His outlaw brother was back in the states and just in t ime to save his ass. He couldn't believe his own eyes.

"To the rescue," Tymeek smirked as Shawn threw his arms around his brother, overcome with emotion.

"Thank you, man." Shawn's voice trembled with gratitude.

"Hey, I am my brother's keeper," he chuckled and they released each other. A stranger came running up with a gun in his hand. Shawn reacted but Tymeek stopped him, "They're with me," he motioned as two other men came out from the misty shadows as night fell upon them.

Tymeek looked into the crate at his wounded sister-in-law and asked, "Is she...?"

"No!" Shawn interjected protectively, refusing to here Tymeek proclaim Natalia's death. He filled Tymeek in, "It went straight through but she's losing a lot of blood. We've got to get her some help."

"Well, I've got a boat on the other side waiting for us but there's no doctor onboard."

191

"There's got to be something we can do," Shawn reached down to check his wife's makeshift bandage.

"Baby girl, you still with me?" he asked, hopeful.

"Yes, daddy," she managed to whisper after wheezing as she withstood the pain to talk. She took his hand and squeezed lightly. Just then one of the men accompanying Tymeek spoke as if he were a living and breathing Wikipedia page.

"I saw it somewhere that you can disinfect gunshot wounds with vodka. We got some Grey Goose onboard."

Then Tymeek's eyes brightened as he remembered pertinent information.

"The captain told me there's a cruise ship out there headed to St. Kitts and we should board it because he called ahead. The co-captain will be expecting us. Cruise ships have doctors so let's get her on that ship," Tymeek hustled toward the yacht bobbing gently on the water. Shawn sighed with relief and gently retrieved his wife from the crate and followed the other men as they trailed behind Tymeek.

Aboard Tymeek's borrowed Ferretti yacht Shawn marveled at its pristine décor. His brother was definitely living in the lap of luxury in order to be so close with anyone who could afford such a thing of beauty let alone allow him to use it. Tymeek's client had the elite 881 custom built with extra powerful motors to enable an expedient getaway if necessary; which would definitely come in handy for the business he conducted with Tymeek.

Tymeek was into a lucrative, yet extremely risky business nowadays as an up and coming select arms dealer operating out of Austria and occasionally exporting to Paris.

"You doin' big things out this muhfuckah!" Shawn, chuckled.

"You like?" Tymeek grinned then braggingly said, "When you grow up you can be like me."

Shawn shot Tymeek a dirty look and laughed at his brother's bravado.

"I'll be back. I'm gonna go talk to the driver of this fine

vessel and see if he can get us to that cruise ship ASAP," Tymeek announced and did his thug bop toward the control room.

Shawn went back to the lounge where his wife was laid out on a circular mole hair bench. He checked her wound and gathered piles of paper towel to re-dress it. She was losing a lot of blood and it scared him. "Talk to me baby girl... you still with me?"

"D-daddy, I'm so tired, cold...and it burns."

"I know, I know. We're gonna get you help real soon."

Tymeek rushed in with good news, "Just spoke with the captain aboard Regal Cruise Line and he said he'll have things situated by the time we get to the boat. We'll be close enough to climb aboard in another ten minutes or so."

"Thank God," Natalia murmured before passing out.

The humongous boat looked like a mini city with a phalanx of bright lights. The yacht captain was at the side of the yacht holding a metal ladder attached to wires hanging from the cruise boat. He beckoned for them to come forth. Tymeek and two of his armed men climbed the ladder first and aided Shawn as he carried his wife on his back up the ladder onto the huge boat. The co-captain proceeded to lead them all toward the medical center.

The doctor apparently had no qualms with taking dirty money to not only treat Natalia discreetly and efficiently, but he vowed not to alert authorities and gave them all the information they needed to find a doctor in St. Kitts so when the boat docked, Natalia's wound could be thoroughly tended to.

He disinfected it and told Shawn how lucky she was that the bullet had passed straight through. He patched it up to prevent further blood loss but insisted she'd need a blood transfusion. Upon hearing this, Natalia adamantly refused the suggestion citing unclean blood donation practices in other countries and the possibility of her contracting defective blood or even AIDS. The ship doctor assured her that all blood was tested prior to transfusions. He gave her a mild sedative to calm her nerves and help with the pain.

As she slowly nodded off she could hear Shawn and Tymeek off in the distance discussing their next move.

"When we get to St. Kitts we'll have her taken care of then we can board a charter plane. And don't worry about living arrangements. I started setting shit up for you from that day you called."

"Man, I can't believe all this shit. I'm just thankful you came when you did."

"You know I'll always be there for you lil' bro. No question," Tymeek's sun-toasted skin made his pearly whites dazzle under the overhead track lighting. Shawn smiled back and realized how things had gone back to how they once were. His brother was taking care of him again back on top in his element. Tymeek patted his younger sibling's back, gave him a knowing look and left the medical center. The doctor came back into the examining room and said, "She'll probably be out for a short while. My nurse is right outside so if you need a little fresh air or so, go ahead, she'll be alright here."

"Thanks," Shawn replied and with that went out on deck to see the beauty of the ocean and enjoy the cooling sensation of the dense sea mist. He looked forward to getting away from his past. There were too many negatives embedded in it.

As his eyes scoured the moonlit waves he sighed with relief. He was tired literally and figuratively of running, fighting, killing and wasting valuable time on escaping his past life. And as he reflected, intuitively he began to feel as though he were being watched. He turned around in time to find a man decked out in all black creeping up on him. Shawn reacted quickly enough to crack the man in his jaw with his balled up fist, full force. The man stumbled back slipped on the wet deck and fell backwards, his gun sliding away from him thanks to the gentle sway of the cruise ship.

Now it was clear to Shawn who his attacker was. The cheesy black garb along with the government issued firearm were tell-tale signs that the man was an FBI agent. The agent had witnessed the shootings of his fellow brethren and cleverly snuck onto Tymeek's yacht before any of them could board. He stowed away without Tymeek's captain ever suspecting a thing. He waited patiently for them to near the cruise ship and after they boarded it the captain was about to detach the ladder but the agent knocked him out with the butt of his gun and boarded the cruise ship too.

"You motherfuckers don't give up, huh? Damn!" Shawn grumbled and reached for his gun forgetting that he left it at his wife's bedside. Realizing that Shawn was unarmed, the agent attempted to reach the gun on the deck. Shawn pounced on him, snuffing him repeatedly then managed to grab the gun.

The agent wasn't going out without a fight. He used all his might to keep Shawn's powerful blows from forcing him to take a nap. He kneed Shawn in his gut, foiling his aim. While Shawn was incapacitated the agent clumsily reached for his secretly hidden .22 caliber securely fastened in an ankle holster. Using only one hand he quickly unsnapped it and snatched it from the stiff leather pouch then swiftly aimed it at Shawn. Now both men had weapons pointed at each other in an unexpected standoff.

The scream from a woman who'd wandered out on deck with her two children startled the agent allowing Shawn to take off running back inside the main hall of the cruise ship with the agent following suit. Shawn knocked over patrons as he tried to make the split decision on which direction to run in. All of the dazed people brushing themselves off as they collected themselves from the floor were now in the agent's way blocking his view and aggravating the hell out of him.

Shawn rounded the corridor and saw the dark unoccupied banquet hall which was a beacon of solace. He ran to it and ducked inside through the open doors straining to see in the darkness. He closed the door behind him and used his fingers to feel his way around to locate any locks.

195

He couldn't find any and angrily continued to search within the darkness with his hands for a sign of a light switch. He tripped over a porcelain flower stand. He righted himself and continued his search for a port window to climb out of or somewhere to hide. Shawn could hear heavy footsteps off in the distance becoming louder. He turned toward the noise with his gun raised. The lights came on and the agent stood in the archway and pointed his gun at Shawn's chest and angrily spat, "Drop the gun!"

Shawn wrestled with the pros and cons of him not dropping his gun. If he did he was caught and compromised his brother's freedom as well as his wife who lay on a gurney because of another ass-wipe who worked for the government just like the prick standing before him. If he didn't he stood a chance, however slight, to make it off the boat and secure his brother and wife's escape.

"I said drop it, NOW!" the agent shouted, he put his other hand at the end of the butt of his gun. Shawn continued his standoff. He refused to go out like a sucker. He didn't fear death, only life without parole made him wince and that is why he was going out like a soldier because he'd rather be killed than captured.

"You know I oughtta just shoot you dead. No one will miss another worthless thug anyway," the agent snarled with disdain.

"So do it," Shawn taunted, fearlessly. The agent cocked his head like a confused puppy and realized his threat was just that, a threat. He knew that he wouldn't kill Shawn unless absolutely necessary since not only was Shawn and Tymeek on the top 25 wanted list, but there was a big pool back at the office over the capture of the Wilson brothers being brought in alive. If he could bring in even one of the infamous duo, he knew that he'd garner kudos and respect amongst his colleagues. This alone was worth sweet talking Shawn into turning himself in to prevent further incident.

"Look, I don't want to bring you back in a body bag. I

want you to get your day in court. You'll probably get off scott-free again anyway. My concern is your wife. You don't want her locked away do you? I mean once your dead that will happen unless..."

"Unless what? You're gonna promise me that she'll be taken care of right?"

"What I will do is go one step further and *guarantee* you that she'll never see inside a cell because I'll personally see to it that she is exonerated, especially since one of our boys shot her."

Shawn laughed, "Do I look like stupid or something? You think I believe anything that comes out of your mouth? I know exactly what will happen. So go ahead and fuckin' shoot me, but be prepared to catch a bullet in return."

"So, that's how you want to play it, huh?" the agent asked, shifting his eyes to Shawn's knee caps. Shawn stood firm, holding his gun raised midway pointing in the direction of the agent's chest. He anticipated the destination of the agent's gaze and was prepared to counter his shot. It was a standoff and the agent knew this was life or death so he very well wouldn't be able to collect his 'prize' because Shawn meant business and his business involved killing him.

Many scenarios took center stage in Shawn's mind as he stood there ready to die. His wife would be left alone on the lam with fragile Everton. All they had worked for was falling apart before his eyes. If he killed the agent he stood a chance to have the life he and Natalia so badly attempted on many occasions but just couldn't accomplish. Shawn's arms grew tired and he could tell that the agent's arms were too. It was now or never.

Both men's eyes were affixed on the other's eyes. Shawn's trigger finger itched and was about to press down when there was an echoing loud popping noise like that of a champagne cork propelling through the air full throttle. Instantly, the agent's eyes rolled up in his head. He fell flat on his face with a thud revealing Natalia literally holding a smoking gun in one hand and her side with the other. Her wrist had taken the brunt of the force from the gun rendering it limp and the gun slipped out of her hand.

"Daddy..." she gasped, staggering towards him.

"That's what the fuck I'm talking about!" Shawn shouted, practically boasting as he ran over to his wife and caressed her lovingly, looking into her face he said sweetly, "You got this nigga on lock for life."

Natalia tried desperately to return his enthusiasm but pain shot through her and she nursed her side with her trembling fingers.

"Aight love birds we gotta move," Tymeek ordered as he ran into the cavernous banquet hall with his lackeys not too far behind. Then Natalia collapsed to the floor.

 බංග

Tymeek took the medication from the doctor's hand and stuffed it in a bag.

"Make sure that she continues to receive prenatal care. She needs to be monitored."

Shawn was too busy showering his wife with affection to realize it was time to go. A nurse grabbed the handles on the wheelchair and in her strong Caribbean accent warned Shawn that he'd get rolled over if he didn't move out of the way. Shawn ignored her rudeness since he was elated from the news the doctor gave him and his wife moments earlier. Not only was his wife going to be fine from her gunshot wound, despite the substantial blood loss which prompted a much contested transfusion, but she was also pregnant.

Shawn had accomplished his ulterior purpose. He was definitely going to be a father unlike the other two times that his wife was pregnant. The joy he felt was unsurpassable and he had never known such bliss.

As they boarded Tymeek's sporty yacht headed to the other side of the island so they could board a plane next, the tropical scenery made it hard for them to leave. Tymeek looked back, regretfully and admitted to himself that he would definitely go back to St. Kitts but the next time would be a much needed and well earned vacation.

Natalia glowed as she watched the waves flounce against the yacht. Her life was headed in the right direction now. She would miss America but Europe offered great promise to her growing family. They were going to live with Tymeek in Versailles outside of Paris for a short period of time until they found a mansion of their own. Between Tymeek's newfound fortune, Natalia's liquidated assets, overseas accounts, the money Shawn made from selling his stakes in the Mallplex and money he managed to salvage from his thwarted businesses, they were set for life.

Shawn eased up behind her, slipped his hands around her waist then rested his palms on her stomach and rubbed it while delicately kissing her neck.

"I feel like I'm in a fairytale," her eyes twinkled as she leaned her head back into his chest. She looked up to catch a glimpse of the clef in her husband's chin. He turned her to face him, she puckered up and they smooched.

"You are. I'm the King, you're my queen and Everton's the little prince and..." he palmed her still flat stomach with both his hands and finished his sentence, "And this youngin' will be the princess."

"How do you know it's a girl?"

"I just know."

He kissed the top of her head, resting his chin at her temple.

"I love you daddy."

"I love you a helluva lot more that's for damn sure," he declared.

They both looked at each other and just smirked knowingly. She held onto the brass rail and smiled a bright-toothed smile as the shore shrank and Shawn squeezed her sweetly in his taut arms.

Amongst the tropical bird calls came an annoying

squawking. They both cracked up as their ears were assaulted by Tymeek singing out of tune with the song playing on the humongous CD boom box he brought out on deck. Tymeek looked over at the photogenic couple and realized that their love for each other was nothing like anything he'd ever seen or known in his entire life. It was a love that ran the gamut from tragedy to full on triumph. Although laden with sins it prevailed above all else and had come full circle.

৵৽

COMING SOON
A NEW YORK'S FINEST

October 30, 2008
9:00 P.M.

"Don't move! Don't you fucking move! Get out of the car now!"

The driver of the burgundy MPV looked at the passenger. Everything had happened too fast for his mind to react. One minute ago, they had been driving along Vernon Boulevard, the sounds of Biggie providing the rhythm as the rode. Next thing they were being cut off by a blue Crown Victoria with blue lights flashing in their grill, forcing them to skid across the street nose first into the entrance of a chemical plant parking lot.

"What the fuck is going on?" asked the passenger already knowing what he and his partner were holding inside the car. He gripped his gun in his right hand, tipped off the safety with his thumb, ready to blast. And as soon as he was about to he realized that they weren't being robbed, but worse... *It's a fucking detective's car?* he cursed to himself and lowered the gun back down to his lap.

"Fuck we gonna do?!" he hissed to the driver, as the detectives jumped out of the car.

"Just chill," the driver said, gripping the steering wheel. His first thought was to hit reverse and make a break for it, but the way the female detective had her gun trained on him, he knew the attempt would be futile. This was the NYPD, he already knew they shoot to kill and he wasn't

1

about to take the chance.

The other detective, a tall lanky Black dude, had his gun aimed over the roof of the Crown Vic and had steady eye contact with the passenger of the MPV, his eyes mockingly daring him to move. He slowly came around the trunk of the car, gun held with both hands, his left cupping his right, as he slowly approached the driver's side.

The female was a lot more gung-ho. She was half way out the car before it skipped to a complete stop. She had the complete uniform including police cap and knee high black shiny riding boots. Her long mane of autumn brown hair was pulled in a pony tail, but still flowed down her back, bouncing with the fluidity of her movements as she eased up on the passenger side of the vehicle, her gun aimed at the passenger's head.

"Turn off the car and toss the keys out the window!" her partner ordered.

A few cars drove by, but seeing the guns aimed and ready, made them only drive by faster.

"Is there a problem, officer?" the driver asked calmly and simply asked as he carefully complied with the demand, reaching slowly toward the gear shit as he looked at the cop pointing the gun for his head.

"Just do it!" the male detective barked.

The keys hit the ground with a jingle.

"Now reach out and open the door from the outside...slowly," the male detective instructed.

"Passenger, you too!" the female detective added, angling herself for a clean sight line.

Both driver and passenger did as they were told. The passenger kicked the gun as far as he could under the seat as he got out, hands raised.

"Yo, man, what y'all stop...."

That was the last word the passenger got out, before the female detective fired three quick shots. The first hit him

2

in the throat and went straight through the back of his neck, coating the inside of the MPV with warm blood and tissue. The second and third shots hit him execution style in the head and his heart. His body slumped over the open door then gravity pulled him to the pavement.

"What the fuck?! You-you killed my man!" the driver screamed in anguish and confusion. As it hit him in the face like a ton of bricks. *They're not even cops.* Then, the whole picture opened up to him, it was a set up.

"Y'all ain't no fuckin' police!"

"We never said we were," she giggled, rounding the car as her accomplice put two in the driver's face. The impact blew him back into the driver's seat, bent double in a grotesque position of death, just as a dark brown Buick hooptie pulled up. Inside the hooptie were three men, all jumped out the Buick, one carrying a duffle bag, and quickly got in the MPV, throwing the deceased driver to the pavement. The driver of the Crown Vic, got in the car with them. The other female officer, got in the Buick, skidded off in one direction as the MPV headed in another, leaving two helpless bodies leaking blood into the concrete.

~~~~~~~

Several minutes later, the MPV pulled up into the parking lot of the Jade East motel on North Conduit Avenue. It was a seedy motel that catered to prostitutes, tricks and dope fiends. There were only a few cars in the parking lot of the open faced motel. An old rusty Nissan on one end, a grey Bronco with Jersey plates a few spaces down and a yellow '92 Mazda RX7 parked in front of the office. The MPV pulled up beside the RX7 and killed the engine.

The four men in the MPV checked and double-checked their weapons. No one spoke and no music played as they mentally prepared them selves for the task at hand. Bop, Face, Mellow and Tank were no strangers to the stickup game. Coming up in Brownsville, they had mastered the trade early in life, so there was never any amateurish mistakes. In this case, all were well aware of what was about to go down. But they were also aware that this wasn't just a robbery. This would be an all out massacre. Usually in a stickup, if a robbery became a homicide, it's a problem, something went wrong. But this would not be that and this time it was different. Everybody in the room had to die, that was their instructions. But it was worth a bunch of dead bodies. Seven hundred and Fifty stacks was worth a lot of dead bodies. On top of the seven fifty, there were six kilos of pure heroin somewhere in the MPV. It was in a hydraulic stash somewhere hid. They didn't know how to get it, but they knew a nigga who did. It was for that person they had agreed to do this hit for the seven fifty.

"Ya'll niggas ready?" Face asked from the front passenger seat. At nineteen, he was next to the youngest in the crew. But he was its de facto leader. His wiry build and average height weren't impressive. However, it masked a temperament that was pure dynamite. Face was by far the wildest. But he was also a planner which made him doubly dangerous and effective.

Tank cocked back the Mac-10 and sneered, "Naw, is them niggas ready?"

"Yo Tank, I'm dead ass," Face turned around, looked at Tank in the seat behind him, "These niggas ain't playin' no games. They smell a cross and shit gon' get ugly real fast. And if one of 'em live and find out it was us...." Face shook his head. "You gonna see what real beef is."

"That's why we ain't gonna give 'em a chance to smell nothin' but gun smoke," Mellow confirmed, in his laid back style.

Face nodded, then added, "Exactly, so everybody stick to the plan. They bust the door, we start blazin'. And remember..."

"Nobody lives," Tank finished for him in an aggravated

tone. "Nig-ga, I got it! Now, are we gon' talk about it or be about it?!"

Face knew that Tank's adrenalin was intoxicating his blood stream, so he let his tone slide. Instead, he answered by holding up the twin Glock-45 he was gripping. He looked at Bop in the driver's seat. Bop was the wheel man of the crew and had also been the driver of the Crown Victoria.

"Bop, be on point," said Face knowing his team put in work.

"Always, my nigga," Bop smiled, giving Face a dap.

Face, Mellow and Tank got out, tucking their weapons. Tank grabbed the duffle bag he had brought as a decoy, because the occupants of the motel room they were visiting were expecting a delivery.

As they slowly entered the motel's small office, they heard the sounds of a television coming from the back room. The door behind the counter opened as Antoinette peeked around it before stepping to the counter.

"Took you long enough," she quipped with a smirk.

Face hit her with the dimples that made her pussy twitch. "Did you handle your business?"

"Room 232, at the top of the stairs."

"How many?"

"Three niggas, two bitches"

Face nodded letting her know she did good, then he and his crew walked out. As soon as they did, Antoinette left out behind them, taking one last look at the blood that was beginning to seep from under the back door.

Face and his crew headed for the stairs while Antoinette headed for the RX7 in the parking lot. As she was about to get in, a bone skinny, light skin chick in a halter and mini skirt came out of a motel room.

"You straight?" she asked, scratching her neck and licking her ashy lips.

Antoinette eyed her with disgust. Dope fiend hoe was

written all over her.

"Naw, yo," Antoinette replied, opening the RX7's door. "Can I get a ride to Farmers?"

Bitch you can't get nothing, Antoinette sucked her teeth and answered her question by slamming the door in the dope fiend's face. She pulled off just as she heard the first shots ring out from inside the motel and break the stillness of the night. She floored the RX7 and disappeared on North Conduit.

Face and his crew had climbed the single flight to the second floor cautiously. The cold October air swirled around them. In the distance, they heard glass breaking and car alarms wailing. Face smiled to himself, remembering that it was Mystery Night, the night before Halloween, that in every hood, the devious used it as an excuse to be at their devilish best. Face remembered his childhood antics when he was younger. As he knocked on the door, ready to do his own devilments, Mellow kept going walking to the end of the breezeway and positioned himself. His job was to make sure no one came out of any room and pinned Face and Tank inside.

An Asian chick peeked out the curtain, then disappeared. A second later, a fat brown dude peeked out. Face nodded subtly and so did the dude. When Face saw the Dude's eyes fall on the duffle bag Tank was carrying, he knew they were in. Tank had the Mac-10 concealed behind the duffle bag. As soon as the door opened, they went into action. Tank slung the duffle bag in the fat dude's face, catching him off guard as Face quickly fired three shots into is chest. Boom! Boom! Boom!

Before the fat dude hit the floor, Face put the gun in his right hand to the Asian chick's screaming head and the gun in his left to some Spanish chick's sobbing temple, and splattered them simultaneously.

"Where's the money?!" Tank barked at another dude,

6

holding his gun to his head. The dude was a short, muscular bull of a man, almost as bullish as Tank.

Seeing that the gunmen didn't wear masks and had killed his man from jump, the dude knew he was about to die.

"Nigga, suck my dick," he hissed, eying Tank hard.

"I got it," Face exclaimed, snatching a bulky duffle bag from under the bed.

Tank put his gun under the dude's chin and blew his brains all over the wall and the ceiling.

"That's four," said Tank

"It's supposed to be five," Face remarked, looking around frantically.

"What?!" Tank replied. He was so amped up he had forgotten all about Antoinette's info. They didn't have long to wait. They had to get what they came for and get the hell out of there.

"Down," Face yelled, snatching Tank to the floor right before automatic gunfire erupted and whizzed over their heads.

Face saw the gun nozzle sticking out the bathroom door a split second before it spit with murderous intent. He and Tank, half covered by the bed, returned fire, trying to shoot through the wall into the bathroom.

"Aaaaargggghh!" Tank bellowed, spraying round after round until the wall and the door of the bathroom looked like Swiss cheese. Then the gun went silent when it clicked on empty.

"Let's go," Face ordered.

Mentally, he was shaking his head at Tank. You never empty your clip in a shoot out if you can help it. Face had emptied one Glock but he knew he still had a few rounds left in the other. Always save something for the get away.

Tank and Face scrambled for the door, as another

burst of automatic gunfire blazed the room, blowing chunks out of the wall and door frame. Face, with the duffle bag in one hand and the gun in the other, took the stairs three at a time, with Tank right on his heels. They would've been dead if it wasn't for Mellow. The stairs went right under the trajectory of the room, so all the gunman had to do was stand in the door and pick them off. Thanks to Mellow, that didn't happen. He opened fire on the front plate glass window of the room, effectively cutting the gunman off from the door and allowing Tank and Face to make it to the MPV.

Mellow jumped the second floor railing and landed squarely on his feet, then scampered to the MPV. The gunman, an authentically built Dred, came out reloading his Callico then blazed the MPV as it skidded out of the parking lot. The Dred hopped the railing like Mellow and took off on foot behind the MPV, the Callico spitting shells like sunflower seeds. He managed to blow out the back window and the rear left tire, but to no avail. The MPV screeched on to North Conduit, cutting off a taxi and a station wagon, and made its getaway.

Just as the MPV was heading southbound, a police cruiser was headed northbound. They saw the flame of the Callico muzzle and the crackle of gunfire in the air. They skidded hard into the parking lot.

"Shit!" Dred cursed, then turned to run.

The passenger cop jumped out.

"Freeze!"

Dred ignored the command. All he heard was boom! Then his left leg went out from under him, and blood gushed from his calf. He fell face first to the pavement.

"Bumm-bah-clod!" Dred yelled in anguish as the cop put his knee in his back and his gun to his head.

"Don't fucking move," the cop hissed, cuffing Dred high and tight.

October 30, 2008
10:00 P.M.

"You sure you ain't hungry? Mystery night's always a busy night," Detective Rahjohn Griffin asked, offering his partner Natasha Bagley a free meal.

She sucked her teeth and looked away.

"Okay, don't say I didn't warn you," he replied with a shrug, as he · turned to the McDonald's drive through receiver. "Let me get the number two and two large Pepsis."

"Diet Pepsi."

"Huh?"

"Diet Pepsi," Natasha repeated with an attitude.

Rahjohn smiled to himself.

"Make that one Pepsi and one Diet Pepsi."

"That'll be $6.78, sir. Please drive thru," a woman's voice could be heard through the large menu display board box.

"Yeah, sure thing," Rahjohn said as he sat back and waited in the drive-thru line. The police radio periodically sounded off in the background. Natasha silently studied his profile out of the corner of her eye.

I hate you Rahjohn Griffin. You make me sick and how dare you have nothing more to offer me than McDonalds. I really can't stand this man. He really makes me sick, she sat thinking to herself. She was a woman that was used to being in control, but somehow this weasel named Rahjohn Griffin had a magical power that took over her and always made her lose her own self-control, not to mention lose the lock she had on her feelings. Only he had the power to make her stomach quiver or her blood boil with a simple gesture. He had the power to drive her crazy.

"So you just gonna sit there?" she huffed. "Act like shit is all good?"

Rahjohn glanced over at her.

It ain't? he asked himself looking at her wondering what was the problem.

"Is it?" she shot back asking the question again already knowing it wasn't.

Rahjohn sighed. He knew sexing his partner would be a mistake. *Why did I fuck with my partner? Why?* His best friend Gee had told him not to, but of course, Rahjohn Wilson Griffin better known as John John, sometimes simply called John, simply wouldn't listen. How could he listen to any voice of reason?

Detective Natasha Bagley was the baddest lady officer in the 17th Homicide Division, hell, maybe even the NYPD period. If Lil' Wayne wasn't talking about her, then who was he talking about? She was 5'9" and a succulent golden Crown that reminded him of Egyptian gold. Her chunky light brown eyes and small upturned nose gave her a smoky, sexy cover girl look. She wasn't ghetto thick, but her body was toned like a track star.

"Come on Tash, don't act like that. You're the one who said that it's not. Not me, I never said that," he added.

Natasha eyed him for a minute, then folded her arms across her chest.

"Where is this going, Rahjohn?" she asked calling him by his government. And don't you dare say, 'what do you mean by this' because you know damn well what I'm talking

10

about.

The line moved up a car length.

I wish we could just listen to the radio. She wouldn't like it if I suggested that right now at all.

"I mean, what's wrong with the way it is now?" John hedged.

"You mean, just fucking, right? Casual sex and no commitment," she probed as if he must be retarded.

"Friends with benefits," he smiled coyly.

"Friends with benefits," she repeated, testing the words on her lips, then added, "So it's cool, if I see other people?"

She was trying to arouse his jealousy, but it backfired when he answered, "Sure, no problem. Why not?"

"Damn, just put me on the corner," she huffed, turning away from the conversation.

Rahjohn was use to this scenario with women. He was 32 years old, no kids and he was what all women in the world would describe as sinfully fine. He had brown cocoa skin, curly black hair that made people think he was Dominican and greenish hazel eyes that could melt the heart of the coldest women when he used them to seduce.

He was dedicated to his daily work out sessions that kept him in the shape of a boxer, weighing in at one hundred and eighty pounds and standing six feet even. Rahjohn was the consummate ladies man. Born and raised in Harlem, he was undeniably Mr. Swag, and obviously he was far from a thug, even though he was born and bred in the hood. Being a cop was his life's dream. He grew up hating the way white cops came into Harlem and treated Black people like animals and illiterates. At the same time, he despised the way the neighborhood thugs blatantly disrespected the elders and terrorized the community. He made it his business to take it to the racist cops and the street's corrupt with equal force.

Rahjohn was a solid Black man, but when it came to

women, he was a floater, a rolling stone and he was extremely allergic to any commitment that lasted longer than the morning after. Natasha cursed herself for even getting involved with the notorious precinct playboy. He had already run through most of the attractive women at the precinct, and she knew it. But she too couldn't resist. At first, it was mutually understood that it was just a fling between two mutually, consenting, adults. And somewhere along the way, her feelings got involved and now more was at stake than just her feelings.

She started to tell him what she really needed to get off her chest, but before she could, the dispatcher came over the radio.

"Ten-ten, Dispatch to Charlie Six."

Rahjohn picked up the handheld and answered, "Charlie Six, go ahead."

"I've got a report of shots fired at 1637 North Conduit Avenue..." He cut her off.

The Jade East Motel?"

"Affirmative. Several victims, all likely." The Dispatcher squawked, using the term 'likely' which meant likely deceased.

"Copy that. Charlie Six en route," Rahjohn confirmed.

He inched back, blowing the horn for the car behind him to let him out then pulled out, commenting wistfully, "Damn, I'm starving."

A few traffic lights and several minutes later, he pulled into the Jade East parking lot. The flashing blue and red lights of the several police cruisers and the ambulance always reminded him of some kind of macabre carnival. The crime scene investigators, EMT and the press scurried back and forth, while beyond the yellow tape, onlookers gawked at the spectacle of death.

Rahjohn and Natasha approached the sergeant who was in charge of the crime scene. He was a heavyset guy with a bald head and thick mustache.

"Well, I guess spending my day tomorrow trick or treating is out, huh Frank?' Rahjohn cracked, shaking the sergeant's hand.

"Well, you can still go through the house of horrors," the sergeant replied, referring to the open motel door. "Four victims, two male, two female, and real messy. We've got one, Lambardi took him down. He ain't sayin' shit though."

"One of the shooters?" Rahjohn quizzed, expectantly.

"I wish... looks more like an intended victim."

Rahjohn nodded, then all three headed upstairs to the room. Inside, the crime scene investigators busied themselves taking pictures, dusting for prints and searching for slugs and spent cartridges. The broken glass crunched under their shoes as they entered.

Natasha had seen scenes like this a thousand times, but death was something she'd never get used to. It always reminded her of her own mortality and disgusted her with the evil that men do.

The two females both laid on their sides, the Asian girl's eyes still open in an expression of the final horror. The fat dude, slumped between them, his brains soaking into the carper and the bedspread. The other male on the bed, leaned against the raggedy head board, half his head exploded and his thoughts still dripping off the ceiling in crimson streaks.

"From what we can tell, looks like an ambush," the sergeant explained, pointing to the doorway. "No signs of forced entry and neither guy had a chance to pull their weapons, even though they were both armed."

Rahjohn could see the pistol stuck in the waist of the dead man's jeans. Rahjohn ruled out robbery as a motive, seeing that both men had on diamond encrusted watches and platinum jewelry. In his mind, this was definitely a hit.

The sergeant began to move around the room,

recreating the crime.

"I'd say it was at least two of them, too much damage for one guy unless we're lookin' for Rambo," the sergeant chuckled. "So they come in blasting, hit whoever answers the door then drops the other two closest to the door. One of 'em runs up on victim number four on the bed and whacks him point blank."

Rahjohn pointed to the wall that fronted the bathroom. It was so full of holes, you could see light seeping through from the bathroom, and the shadow of someone moving around in there.

"If everything was so clean, why all the fire power?" he asked.

"I was getting to that," the sergeant answered. "There was a third man, probably the guy we collared, in the bathroom when the shooters came in."

"Lucky guy," Natasha quipped.

"Depends on what side of the fence you're standing on. So they pin the guy in the bathroom once he made his presence known, then made their getaway."

"There was another shooter outside the room," Natasha remarked, gesturing to the glass on the floor. "Someone had to be shooting from the outside in or the glass would be on the outside of the room. So the other shooter waited outside, kept the ones inside covered as they got away."

The sergeant nodded.

"How'd I miss that? I must really be getting old."

"Where's the perp now?" Rahjohn asked.

"St. Luke's," the sergeant answered.

"He gonna make it?" Rahjohn inquired knowing how his people went in.

"No reason why he shouldn't, he was hit in the leg."

Rahjohn scanned the room once more.

"Any witnesses? This place have a surveillance

system?"

"Yes and yes," was the sergeant's reply. "Some female says she saw a woman leaving the office right when the shooting began."

"Leaving the office? What's that have to do with this?" Rahjohn asked.

"You haven't seen the office yet."

Her face looked angelic, almost like she was sleeping. Cinnabrown with long luscious eyelashes, full pouty lips and a slit throat, through which her life seeped out on to the dirty tile floor. Rahjohn kneeled down beside her, examining her throat.

"This cut looks almost surgical. Pretty girl, who is she?"

"Renee Owens. She was the manager on duty, " the sergeant informed him, shaking his head. "She wasn't even twenty yet."

· Rahjohn could hear the anguish in˒ the sergeant's voice. He knew the sergeant had a daughter about the same age. Rahjohn stood up.

"Where's the witness?" he asked.

"Took her down to the precinct to take her statement."

"What about the tape?"

The sergeant beckoned for them to follow him deeper into the back room. "At first we thought the perps had taken the tape because we found the recorder empty, but....," the sergeant explained as he moved several books aside that sat on a lone shelf. Behind it was a compartment that housed a VCR. "The owner told us that he'd been robbed so much, and every time, the perp would take the tape. So he decided to setup a backup."

"Smart man," Natasha remarked.

"And lucky for us," Rahjohn added.

The sergeant pressed play then rewound the tape. They watched as everything played backward in blurry super speed. The sergeant didn't stop until the night manager pulled up in the grey Bronco.

"This was about five o'clock when she arrived," said the sergeant.

Rahjohn and Natasha watched Antoinette pull up in the RX7, look around, then head inside the office, where she disappeared from view.

"Too bad the guy didn't have a camera in his office too," Natasha said.

They fast forwarded the tape watching the sun set in seconds. Then after several minutes of accelerated nothingness, an MPV pulled in the lot and parked.

"This is when it gets interesting," the sergeant commented.

As they watched Face, Tank and Mellow go in and out the office then head for the stairs, a uniformed officer rushed into the room.

"Detective Griffin."

Rahjohn turned his attention to the officer.

"Yeah?"

"The captain's over on Vernon Boulevard. He wants you over there, pronto!"

Circle of Sins by Nurit Folkes

ORDER FORM

TERI WOODS PUBLISHING
P.O. BOX 20069
NEW YORK, NY 10001
(201) 840-8660
WWW.TERIWOODSPUBLISHING.COM

PURCHASER INFORMATION:

NAME _____

ADDRESS_____

_____

CITY_____ STATE____ ZIP_____

PURCHASING INFORMATION:
(Please mark the books you are ordering)

TRUE TO THE GAME I   _____
TRUE TO THE GAME II   _____
TRUE TO THE GAME III   _____
B-MORE CAREFUL   _____
THE ADVENTURES GHETTO SAM   _____
DUTCH I   _____
DUTCH II   _____
TELL ME YOUR NAME   _____
TRIANGLE OF SINS   _____
RECTANGLE OF SINS   _____
DEADLY REIGNS I   _____
DEADLY REIGNS II   _____
DEADLY REIGNS III   _____
ANGEL   _____
DOUBLE DOSE   _____
PREDATORS   _____
ALIBI   _____
BEAT THE CROSS   _____

PRICING INFORMATION:
Book Cost $14.95
Shipping/Handling $ 4.05
Total $19.00

INMATE PRICING INFORMATION
(For Order being shipped to inmates only)
Book Cost $11.21
Shipping/Handling $ 4.05
Total $15.26

MANUSCRIPT SUBMISSION GUIDELINES

TERI WOODS PUBLISHING
P.O. BOX 20069
NEW YORK, NY 10001
(201) 840-8660
WWW.TERIWOODSPUBLISHING.COM

Teri Woods Publishing accepts solicited and unsolicited manuscripts. We do not, however, accept short stories, poetry or screenplays. We ask that manuscripts be forwarded in their entirety along with a brief synopsis and a cover letter. Your manuscript must be a minimum of 70,000 words, typed, double-spaced, on regular 8½" by 11" paper. You must send in a self addressed stamped envelope at the time of your submission should your manuscript be rejected and you wish for it to be sent back to you. All manuscripts received will be *discarded* once they are rejected if they are not sent in with a self-addressed, stamped envelope.

Once your manuscript is received, it will be cataloged by the postmark date and you will receive a letter of acknowledgement. Please note, it generally takes three to six months for a manuscript to be reviewed, however it can take longer. Please do not call inquiring about your manuscript status. When the review process is completed you will be notified.

Thank you for inquiring with Teri Woods Publishing, the largest independent publisher in the country.